ChangelingPress.com

Tex/Zipper Duet

Harley Wylde

Tex/Zipper Duet
Harley Wylde

All rights reserved.
Copyright ©2019 Harley Wylde

ISBN: 9781092514835

Publisher:
Changeling Press LLC
315 N. Centre St.
Martinsburg, WV 25404
ChangelingPress.com

Printed in the U.S.A.

Editor: Crystal Esau
Cover Artist: Bryan Keller

The individual stories in this anthology have been previously released in E-Book format.

No part of this publication may be reproduced or shared by any electronic or mechanical means, including but not limited to reprinting, photocopying, or digital reproduction, without prior written permission from Changeling Press LLC.

This book contains sexually explicit scenes and adult language which some may find offensive and which is not appropriate for a young audience. Changeling Press books are for sale to adults, only, as defined by the laws of the country in which you made your purchase.

Table of Contents

Tex (Dixie Reapers MC 6) 4
  Chapter One 5
  Chapter Two 17
  Chapter Three 30
  Chapter Four 41
  Chapter Five 56
  Chapter Six 67
  Chapter Seven 80
  Chapter Eight 91
  Chapter Nine 104
  Chapter Ten 118
  Epilogue 133
Zipper (Dixie Reapers MC 7) 140
  Chapter One 141
  Chapter Two 155
  Chapter Three 169
  Chapter Four 187
  Chapter Five 200
  Chapter Six 214
  Chapter Seven 226
  Chapter Eight 238
  Chapter Nine 250
  Epilogue 262
Harley Wylde 267
Changeling Press E-Books 268

Tex (Dixie Reapers MC 6)
Harley Wylde

Tex: I made a mistake fifteen years ago, one that could have landed my ass in jail. Instead, I made a deal. I signed away the rights to a child I'd never see, and then I joined the Army, putting the Dixie Reapers and my life in Alabama firmly in my rearview. But now I'm back, and I can't help but wonder what happened to my son or daughter. What I discover makes my blood run cold, and I vow to do anything in my power to save the daughter I've never met. I just didn't count on rescuing two damsels, or that the second one would look at me with haunted eyes that would make me do something stupid. I'd vowed to never let another woman fuck me over. I just hope I don't regret letting Kalani into my home and into my life. She has trouble written all over her.

Kalani: Hillview Asylum looks presentable enough, but I know firsthand about the horrors inside those walls. I'd always expected I'd die there, until *he* came. Not that he was coming for me. I've sheltered his daughter, Janessa, as much as possible, and in return I gained her trust and loyalty. I'd have never guessed those two things would save me. Or maybe they didn't, because now I'm faced with a man who makes me want things I shouldn't. His club suggested a marriage of convenience, to keep me out of Hillview, but I want more than just his name. I have no doubt this is going to end with my heart shattered at my feet, but he keeps the nightmares away. For the first time in my entire life, I feel safe. Protected. But now I want more... I want to be loved.

Chapter One

Tex

I stood outside the gates of the Dixie Reapers' compound, my bag slung over my shoulder, and the weight of the world pressing down on me. I felt like the fucking prodigal son returning home, and maybe that's exactly how it was. Fifteen years ago, I'd walked away from this club, from my life, and I'd joined the Army. I'd been on a downward spiral and knew something had to give if I'd wanted to survive. The Army was the best thing for me at the time.

My Dixie Reapers cut was clutched in my hand, and I knew it would magically open the gates in front of me. I hadn't been able to put the damn thing on because of how much I'd bulked up while I was serving my country. There was a glow from a cigarette just inside the gates, and I knew a Prospect was there, watching and waiting. If I got any closer, he'd be on alert until he figured out if I was friend or foe. Just as it should be. Hell, that had been my job once upon a time.

At the clubhouse across the lot, I could see a line of bikes. I wondered if mine was still stored here, or if Torch had given up on me returning and sold the damn thing. I hadn't exactly kept in touch over the years. At first, I'd reached out when I was able, even stopped by during my leave the first few years, but as more years passed, the calls became fewer and fewer, the visits non-existent, until I stopped communicating with the club all together. And now here I stood, wondering if I would even be welcomed back by men I'd once considered family.

"You coming in or are you gonna stare all night?" the Prospect asked, tossing the cigarette away.

I approached the gate and held up my cut when I got there. His eyebrows lifted as he looked at the Dixie Reapers patch on the black leather, then his gaze took in my Army-issued duffle and the dog tags hanging around my neck. Something entered his eyes, like understanding, then he slid the gate open and let me inside.

"My name's Johnny. Welcome home, soldier."

I smiled a little. "Thanks. Torch inside?"

"Nah. He's at home with his wife and kid. Same for the VP."

Torch and Venom were married with kids? Hell, I'd never seen that one coming. It made me wonder what else had changed around here. I guess I hadn't given it much thought, almost like my past had just stayed frozen in time while I'd been off being a soldier. My thoughts must have been showing on my face. The Prospect smirked and shook his head.

"If you can't believe that, then you definitely won't believe that Bull and Preacher have old ladies now too. And Ryker Storme claimed Flicker's sister. Even though his daddy is the Pres of Hades Abyss, he's stuck around so Laken can be near Flicker."

"I don't know what the fuck is in the water around here, but I think I'll stick with beer. No way I'm letting some woman into my life like that," I said, shifting the weight of my bag.

"Now that you've said that, you've just doomed yourself." Johnny smiled. "I bet you're leg-shackled before the end of the month."

I snorted. Yeah, not fucking likely. With a salute, I headed toward the clubhouse. Better to get this shit out of the way. I had no idea who was inside, or if I'd know anyone in there at all. As far as I knew, all my old club was still active, but I had no doubt a lot of new faces had joined over the last fifteen years. The kid at the gate couldn't have been more than twenty. The club needed some young blood. The rest of us were getting too fucking old.

I pushed open the door and stepped inside. A mug was slammed down on the bar top, and a moment later, I was engulfed in a hug from a man nearly twice my size.

"Jesus, Tank," I wheezed. "Can't fucking breathe, man."

He slapped my back and pulled away, smiling broadly. "It's fucking good to see you, Tex. Thought you'd never make it back."

"Guess I got tired of following the rules."

"Torch know you're here?" he asked.

"Nope. Thought I'd surprise everyone."

He motioned to the cut clutched in my hand. "Why aren't you wearing that? You're still one of us."

"Doesn't fit anymore."

He took it from me and tossed it to the Prospect behind the bar. "See that a new one is ordered for Tex." His gaze scanned over me again. "Better ask for an XXL. Fuck, man, you're almost as big as me."

"Yeah, right. No one's as big as you, Tank."

He grinned and slapped my back again, nearly knocking me off my feet. I didn't know if I even still had a room here at the clubhouse, and I wasn't sure how to go about asking. Yeah, these guys were considered my family, but I'd pretty much abandoned them fifteen years ago. It was a little presumptuous of me to just appear and expect everything to go back to normal. I'd hoped Torch would be around so we could talk.

"Why don't we grab a beer and catch up?" Tank asked. "A lot of changes around here since you've been gone."

"I heard Torch and Venom both have old ladies. And Bull? Shit. After what happened with his baby momma, I thought for sure he'd steer clear of relationships. That bitch was something else."

Tank smirked. "It gets better. His new woman is younger than his daughter. Ridley gave him grief. And he now has a son, Foster. His kid is younger than his grandkids."

"Shit, Ridley is married?" I asked.

"Uh, yeah. She's with Venom."

I spit out the swallow of beer I'd just taken. "Are you fucking kidding?"

He shook his head. "Bull wasn't too happy about it at first, but he's come around. Venom treats Ridley like a queen. They have two kids, both girls."

"And Torch? The Prospect at the gate said he had a wife now."

"Isabella. She's like thirty years younger than him, but I've never seen two people meant for each other more than those two. They have a kid too."

"Definitely not drinking the water around here," I muttered as I swallowed more beer.

Tank chuckled. "Don't blame you, man."

"Got a lot of new members?" I asked.

"Since you left? Yeah. A lot of Prospects have come and gone over the years, but a few have patched in. Our newest is Coyote," he said with a nod toward a table in the corner.

The guy looked to be near my age, and he wasn't lacking for female attention. My dick didn't even stir as I looked at the mostly naked club sluts draped over Coyote. It had been so fucking long since I'd been laid,

I wasn't sure my cock even worked right anymore. When I was younger, I'd had a different woman every night. After joining the Army, the women hadn't been quite as plentiful, or more aptly put, my days hadn't been quite as free. Over the years, I'd soured toward females, not trusting them. Getting my dick wet hadn't been worth a possible STD or being trapped by some conniving bitch who got pregnant on purpose. So I'd abstained. Now I never even felt the urge anymore. I could probably walk onto the set of a porno and my dick wouldn't so much as twitch.

Pathetic. That's what I was. Thirty-five and my cock was fucking useless except to take a piss. Probably for the best. When it had been in good working order, I'd knocked up the girl I'd been seeing. Just hadn't realized at the time that she was sixteen and had been using a fake ID. Had I known she wasn't eighteen, I wouldn't have fucking touched her. I'd miraculously gotten off without jail time and had entered the Army a few days later. I had no clue what happened to that girl or my kid. I'd thought of looking them up a few times over the years, but the girl's parents had made me sign away my parental rights to my kid. Some days, I regretted doing that. Had she even kept the baby?

"What's that look?" Tank asked.

"Taking a trip down memory lane. It wasn't a happy memory."

He nodded. "There's someone you should meet. Come on."

Tank stood and I followed him down the hallway, past all the rooms that seemed to be occupied. At the last door, he knocked and a redheaded guy opened the door. A bank of computers lined the wall as we stepped inside, and I wondered who the fuck this guy was, and just what he was into.

"Tex, this is Wire. He's a fucking genius when it comes to computer shit." Tank paused. "I know you're thinking about that girl, about the kid you left behind. If you really want to know what's up, Wire can find whatever you need."

Wire grinned and held out a hand. "I've heard mention of you over the years. Good to put a face to the name."

I shook his hand, then looked at the computers again. "You can really find anyone on there?"

He snorted. "Find them? I can give you every detail of their life if you'd like, down to what they bought on their last trip to the grocery store."

"Before I left, I knocked up a girl named Sabrina Kilpatrick. Didn't know at the time she was underage, and her parents made me sign away my rights to the baby. I'd like to know what happened to them, and if I have a son or daughter out there somewhere."

Wire nodded. "How old was she, how long ago was this, and do you know her parents' names?"

"She was sixteen, even though I thought she was eighteen, and it happened fifteen years ago. We'd used condoms, but one broke. Her dad was Phillip Kilpatrick."

Wire's eyebrows shot up. "The ex-Chief of Police?"

"Yeah."

Wire whistled. "Man, some serious shit went down involving that man and his family. About seven years ago, Kilpatrick was killed, presumably during a drug bust gone wrong. Except it was discovered that he wasn't busting them. He was the ring leader of one of the biggest drug rings in the state. Had connections in every department statewide. The wife committed suicide."

My throat tightened. I'd left my kid with someone like that? "And the girl? Sabrina?"

"Dead," Wire said. "But she died a while before all that shit happened. I don't remember any mention of a kid, though. I'll do some digging and see what I can find."

I nodded and thanked him. Tank led me back out to the main part of the clubhouse. When I'd come back, I hadn't had any intention of looking up Sabrina or trying to find my kid. But if the Kilpatricks were all dead, where was the baby Sabrina was carrying fifteen years ago?

"I'll talk to Torch tomorrow about a place for you to stay. Tonight, you can crash in my guest room," Tank said. "He turned the rooms in the clubhouse over to the Prospects, so all the patched members either have a duplex or a house inside the compound."

"Thanks. Do you know what happened to my bike?"

He smiled. "Torch has it under lock and key. He's kept up the maintenance on it, took it for a joyride every now and then to make sure it was in perfect working condition. I don't think he ever doubted you'd eventually come home."

At least one thing in my life was going right.

I followed Tank out of the clubhouse, and we walked down the road that twisted through the compound. About six houses down, he turned up a small walkway and entered a one-story blue house. He left the door open, and I made my way inside. I didn't know what the hell my future looked like anymore, and I was too fucking tired to think much about it tonight.

But I did know one thing. If I had a kid out there, I wasn't stopping until I had custody. My impeccable Army record had to be good for something. Maybe it could at least make sure my kid had a good life. I could only imagine the hell they'd lived through with the Kilpatricks.

Whatever it took, I'd make it right.

* * *

I sat across from Torch the next day, still feeling like I had no control over my life. He'd passed a set of keys to me, but I hadn't really looked at them. My gaze was focused on the manila folder in the center of the table. I was leery of what I'd find inside. Part of me wanted answers, and the other half wondered if I was better off not knowing.

"You going to open it?" Torch asked. "Wire worked all night trying to piece this together for you."

I slid the folder closer and flipped it open. The first thing I saw was a birth certificate. Janessa Kilpatrick. I had a daughter, and she didn't even have my fucking name, all because I'd signed away my rights. I looked at the date of birth and knew she was mine. My daughter. I flipped the birth certificate over, and there was a picture of a baby swaddled in pink, a shock of dark hair standing up on her head.

I traced the lines of her face with my finger and ignored the tightness growing in my throat and the tears burning my eyes. There were more pictures, up until she'd turned seven. The next piece of paper was an admittance form for Hillview Asylum, and my heart nearly stopped. My baby girl was locked up in an asylum? What the fuck for? I flipped through the rest of the file, and when I got to the end, I stared at Torch, not sure what to say or do at this point.

"Do you want your daughter?" he asked.

"Yes," I said, my voice more of a croak than anything else.

He nodded. "Then between Wire and the club lawyer, I think we can get a judge to grant you custody. You were young when you signed away your rights, and since then, you've had quite the military career."

"But I'm unemployed now. And let's face it, the judges around here don't look too kindly on the Dixie Reapers."

"I'll take care of it, Tex. Family is important to the club, and Janessa is your daughter. Which makes her a Dixie Reaper by blood. I didn't agree with how things were handled all those years ago, but I know you did what you thought was right."

"It was sign away my rights or go to jail," I muttered.

"Maybe. You could have fought it, and you might have won. Or you could have gone to jail for statutory rape, even though you honestly had no idea she was sixteen."

It still sickened me that I'd slept with a teenage girl. Maybe the warning signs had been there, and I'd just ignored them. Fuck if I remembered. I'd still been a kid myself, but definitely too old for a sixteen-year-old girl. Screwing around with the Chief of Police's daughter had been my downfall, or it would have been if the Army hadn't saved me. I'd known she was in high school, but she'd shown me that stupid fake ID that said she was eighteen. Who the hell got a fake ID that didn't say they were twenty-one? I don't know what game she'd been playing, and now I never would. From Wire's research, she'd been dead a while and had taken her secrets with her.

"I'll have the club lawyer draw up the necessary paperwork. She can get whatever information she needs from Wire to build her case, and we'll get the ball rolling today. But, Tex, this might take some time," Torch said.

"I can't leave her there," I said. "She's in a fucking asylum!"

"Yes, and for all we know, she needs to be there," Torch said. "You have no idea what her mental state is right now. Maybe losing her mother damaged her in some way."

"I need to see her."

"Your bike key is on the ring I gave you. It's parked out back in the shed. The other keys are to a house in the compound. The house number is stamped onto the key. Just follow the road until you find it."

I nodded and stood. "Thank you, Torch. For everything. For welcoming me back, giving me a place to stay, keeping my bike… and for helping me get my daughter."

"We're family, Tex. We look out for our own."

I tapped the table with my knuckles, then went to get my bike. The engine roared to life, and with the bike vibrating between my legs, I felt like I'd finally come home. I didn't have my new cut yet, but I would, and then I'd finally feel like me again. Or so I hoped. Right now, I still felt like a soldier, but that wasn't who I was anymore. I twisted the throttle, and the bike shot out of the shed and toward the front gate. The Prospect guarding the entrance slid the gate open, and I drove through it, speeding up as I hit the streets. The asylum was just outside of town, and I didn't stop until I'd pulled into the outer parking lot.

I shut off the bike and approached the guard station. A tall fence surrounded the asylum, with sharp spikes along the top. I shivered at how ominous the place looked. The man in the guard booth was old and graying, but the gun on his hip said he was ready for anything.

"May I help you?" he asked as I approached.

"I'm here to see Janessa Kilpatrick."

"Do you have an appointment?" he asked.

"No, but I'm her father."

He studied me a moment, then held out his hand. "ID."

I handed him my license and wished I'd worn my dog tags outside my shirt. Even though I wasn't active duty anymore, I hadn't taken them off just yet. They still felt like they were a part of me. He looked it over, then stepped farther into the booth and picked up a phone. It felt like an eternity while I waited.

"I'm sorry, Mr. Rodriguez, but Janessa isn't accepting visitors today. Doctor's orders."

"Of course." I took my license back and gazed beyond the guard booth at the asylum rising into the sky. I gave the guard a nod and then went back to my bike.

As soon as I reached the compound, I found Wire.

"I need everything you can get on Hillview Asylum. Layout, security system, employees. I want it all," I told him.

"And why do you need that?" he asked.

"Because I'm going after my daughter. Something isn't right about that place, and I'm not leaving her there another second. Fuck the paperwork. That kid is mine."

He nodded. "I already spoke with the club's lawyer and gave her everything she needed. She may need your signature on a few things."

"And the asylum?" I asked.

"I'll have it for you by morning. If the lawyer can't get a judge to give you access to your daughter before the courthouse closes tomorrow, then we'll hit the asylum tomorrow night. With some luck, they'll be so embarrassed they were breached and someone escaped, they won't cause too much trouble for us."

"We?" I asked.

"Yeah, soldier boy," he said, grinning. "Dixie Reapers take care of their own. Janessa is yours, which means she's one of us. If she needs to be rescued from that place, we'll get it done."

The tension I hadn't realized was building inside me started to ease. I nodded and left him to find whatever he could about the creepy place outside of town. I'd trusted my gut the entire time I'd been in the military, and it had saved my ass more than once. And right now, my gut was telling me that my baby girl was in trouble. No way in hell I was leaving her at Hillview. One way or another, Janessa was coming home.

Chapter Two

Kalani

Everything was hazy as I slowly opened my eyes. The ugly gray walls seemed to close in on me, blurring and swirling, until the room snapped into place. I groaned and tried to roll onto my side, but I couldn't move. I closed my eyes again and breathed deeply, the smell of antiseptic burning my nose. When I looked around again, I gazed down my body and realized they'd strapped me to the bed. It wasn't the first time, and I knew it wouldn't be the last. Everything ached, but I couldn't remember what they'd done to me. Maybe that was for the best. At least I seemed to be clothed this time.

I knew better than to call out, but my bladder was full and I really didn't want to piss myself. They'd done this to me countless times, and often I ended up soiling the bed I was lying on, which only ended in punishment. A shuffling sound caught my attention and I tried to crane my neck toward the far corner near the window. A shadowy form was huddle on the floor. Janessa. I didn't know why she was here, and I doubted I wanted to know. I only hoped they hadn't hurt her.

"Kalani," she said softly, scooting forward, but clinging to the shadows.

When she reached the bed, I saw the bruise on her cheek. It was my fault. I hadn't been paying attention and hadn't reacted fast enough. I always watched out for Janessa, but I'd been distracted, and it had cost her. Had cost both of us. When she'd first arrived, she'd been so damn small and scared. It had been easy to befriend her. Now she was a teenager, and I knew if she didn't get out of this place soon, she'd be in big trouble. Even though she was still a kid, she was beautiful with her olive-colored skin and dark hair. Her wide, brown eyes still looked innocent even after everything she'd witnessed in this place.

The guards had started to notice. I distracted them as often as possible, but one day, I wouldn't be able to stop them. And my stomach clenched when I thought about what she'd suffer at their hands. No one should ever go through that, but then the inhabitants of Hillview were no longer seen as human. We were just toys for the doctors and staff. But unlike the other residents here, I'd never been anywhere else. My mother had been a patient at Hillview, and my father had been an asshole rapist masquerading in a white lab coat. The fact that dear ol' dad was one of the doctors didn't mean shit. He didn't love me, had never wanted me, so he didn't care what happened. The staff and other doctors could do whatever they wanted, and he'd just stare right through me like I didn't even exist. I fucking hated this place, but it was all I'd ever known. I was just one of their many dirty little secrets.

"Sorry," I said, or tried to. My voice barely worked, and the words were such a soft whisper I wasn't certain she'd heard me.

Booted steps were coming down the hallway, more than one set. My heart raced and I struggled, trying to break free. I no longer cared what they did to me, but I couldn't protect Janessa if I was tied down. They could hurt her, or take her away, and I'd be unable to stop them. The door to my room opened, and an orderly stepped inside. He was one of the nicer ones, or at least he'd never unfastened his pants around me. To me, that was nice.

More dark figures entered the room, two of them had to be the largest men I'd ever seen, and my fear spiked higher. I whimpered and fought some more. Janessa crowded closer to me, her hand reaching for mine. One of the men came closer, and the moonlight washed over him. Eyes a dark chocolate-brown focused on Janessa, but it was the look of wonder that made me stop fighting.

"Janessa," he said.

She clung tighter to me.

"Honey, I'm not here to hurt you," he said. "We're going to get you out of here. My name is Houston Rodriguez, but everyone calls me Tex. Do you know who I am?"

The tension in Janessa eased a little. "Tex?" she asked.

He nodded. "Yeah, honey. I'm your dad."

"She said you didn't want me," Janessa said.

"You need to hurry this up," the orderly said. "The guards will come through here again in the next twenty minutes, and you need to be long gone."

Tex nodded. "Come on, honey. We're going to go home. To my home. These are your uncles, Tank and Flicker."

Janessa smiled a little and giggled. "You all have silly names."

"Yeah, I guess we do."

Janessa sobered and moved closer to me again. "I'm not leaving Kalani."

Tears pricked my eyes as I gazed at the young girl. It was just like her to try to take me along, but I knew they couldn't do that. There was no way my father would ever let me out of this place. No, I'd been born in Hillview and I'd die here, probably sooner rather than later.

"Go," I said, my voice a little stronger this time.

"I won't leave you," she said stubbornly, her chin jutting out.

I flicked my gaze over to her father, who was regarding me with interest. "Take her. Make her leave."

The man looked from me to the orderly. "Why is she tied down?"

The orderly looked nervous and fidgeted, looking everywhere but at me or the man asking questions.

"They hurt her," Janessa said. "They're always hurting her. They make her do things."

My eyes closed and I fought hard not to cry. I'd hoped she wouldn't know what was happening to me, what would eventually happen to her. I should have known a smart girl like Janessa would figure it out. I heard her father curse, and then rough hands were yanking at the buckles on my restraints.

"You can't take her," the orderly said, panic rising in his voice.

"The fuck I can't," Tex said. "Flicker, how much time do we have?"

"Another five minutes, then the security footage will be back online and we'll be spotted if we're still inside. Wire gave us as much of a window as he could."

Tex nodded and finished releasing me. Then he gently lifted me into his arms and looked down at his daughter. Janessa seemed uncertain, but the man called Flicker reached for her hand.

"Come on, Janessa," Flicker said. "I'm your Uncle Flicker, and we're going to take you home. You never have to come back here again."

For the first time since meeting her, I saw Janessa smile a true smile. One that made her shine from the inside out.

"Kalani too," she said. "Promise. Kalani can come home too."

The men shared a look and Flicker nodded. "I promise. Kalani can come home too, and she doesn't have to come back here."

The orderly made a choking sound, his eyes wide, and I knew he was worried about what would happen once my father realized I was missing. I wanted to smile, not a pleasant smile but an evil one, because I knew the man's days were numbered. All the staff would be in trouble once my absence was noted, unless they found a way to hide that information from my father. Not like the man ever came to see me anyway.

Tex began walking with a ground-eating stride, the others walking beside him. When the fresh air outside hit me, I shivered and tried to suck in as much clean air as I could. I hadn't felt a breeze in so very long. When I'd been younger, they'd allowed me to walk the grounds for an hour every week. As time passed and I grew older, the outside trips grew more infrequent and eventually stopped all together. I couldn't remember the last time I'd felt a breeze on my face or seen the moon without looking at it through bars.

A large black truck was hidden in the shadows, and I hoped they knew how to get us out of here without being detected. Their five-minute window was about up, if it hadn't expired already. Tex climbed into the backseat with me still in his arms, and Janessa scooted in next to us. The other two men took the front seats, with the largest of them sliding behind the wheel.

"Get us home, Tank," Tex said. "And make it fast."

The big man nodded and floored it. I'd never been in a car before, and I wanted to look at everything, explore a little, but I was too scared to move. Now that I was no longer flat on the bed, my body hurt even more. I tried to relax against Tex, tried to put my faith in a man I'd never seen before. But he'd gotten me out of there, so that had to make him good, right?

The truck came to a stop just outside a metal gate. It slid open, and the truck pulled through. I didn't know where we were, and I didn't care, as long as it wasn't the asylum. Anything was better than being there. They drove down a winding road and stopped in front of a green house. Flicker got out and opened the back door. Tex held me tight as he stepped out of the truck and began carrying me toward the house. Janessa walked at his side.

"Call the doc," Tex said. "I think they both need to be checked out."

My body tensed, and I struggled against him. No, no more doctors. Doctors caused pain. I could feel the panic rising inside me, my heart racing and my lungs feeling like they'd seize at any moment.

"Hey, easy," Tex crooned at me. "No one's going to hurt you."

"Doctors do bad things," Janessa said softly. "Especially to Kalani."

Tex looked down at me and gave a slight nod. "All right. No doctors. Not for tonight anyway."

"Where are you going to put them?" Flicker asked. "Only two of the bedrooms are furnished."

"Kalani and I can share," Janessa said.

Tex carried me down a short hall and stepped into a blue bedroom. He eased me down onto the bed, and I winced as pain shot through me again. Janessa moved around to the other side of the bed and crawled in next to me. She stayed close, but not near enough that she'd hurt me.

"You're safe here," Tex said. "No one can get into the compound without our permission."

"Who are you?" I asked.

He smiled a little. "We're Dixie Reapers, and we take care of our own."

"But I'm not one of you. I don't belong to anyone."

He glanced at his daughter. "She thinks you belong to her, and since she's mine, I guess that makes you mine too."

A strange warmth worked its way through me at his words. I'd never been anyone's before, but as his gaze settled on me again, I decided I didn't mind being called his. With the bedroom lights on, I could see more details of the men who had rescued us. They were each handsome in their own way, but Tex took my breath away. I'd never considered a man attractive before, not when I knew what they were capable of, but these men had risked their lives to save us. And that made them different.

"Bathroom," I blurted, still feeling like my bladder would burst.

"It's down in the hall," Tex said.

I tried to stand, but my body wouldn't cooperate very well. He scooped me into his arms and carried me to the bathroom. He released me and went to turn away, but I nearly collapsed. With a curse, he grabbed me again.

"You're going to have to let me help you," he said.

I swallowed hard and nodded. It wouldn't be the first time a man had seen me naked. He helped me pull my pants down, and I sat to do my business. When I was finished, he helped me stand and pulled my pants back up, then carried me back to the bedroom and eased me back down onto the bed.

The men who had lingered filed out of the room, with Tex staying a moment. "I'll find you both some clothes, and then you can shower. I'm sure you'll want to wash that place off you."

He left the door open as he followed the others back down the hall, and I wondered if he'd known I would feel caged in with the door shut. Or had he left it open for his daughter? I glanced at Janessa, and she looked confused but hopeful. She'd never talked about her dad before, only her mom and what a horrible person she'd been. I didn't know why her father hadn't come to get her sooner, but I hoped that he was here to stay. He was all that stood between us and Hillview. And I'd rather die than ever go back to that hell.

When Tex returned, he had a woman with him. Was he married? Was she his wife? There was a band on her finger, but he wasn't wearing one.

The woman smiled and moved closer, the plastic sacks in her hands crinkling.

"My name's Ridley," she said. "I don't know if the things I brought will fit, but maybe they'll do for tonight. We can figure out your sizes in the morning and buy you some clothes and shoes."

Janessa eased off the bed and approached Ridley. "Are you my stepmom?"

Ridley threw her head back and laughed. "No. But your daddy is friends with my husband. I'm just here to help, then I'm going home to Venom and my daughters."

Janessa looked longingly at the sacks. "And those are for us?"

Ridley nodded and set the bags down.

"Flicker sent me a text after the two of you were rescued. I had to run to the nearest store, and I just grabbed a few different sizes of panties and flip-flops since I didn't know your sizes. I just got some one-size-fits-most shirts and leggings, and two nightgowns for the both of you to sleep in tonight. You can wear the shirts and leggings tomorrow with the flip-flops, and someone will take you shopping for clothes and shoes that fit better."

I tensed, knowing it wasn't a good idea for me to leave this place. If being behind the gate meant no one could get me, then I wanted to stay right where I was. Preferably forever. Venturing out to go shopping didn't sound like such a good idea, even if it was something I would have loved to experience one day.

"Janessa, you can use the hall bathroom," Tex said. "Ridley got you some girly soap and shampoo too."

His daughter grabbed her new items and practically ran for the bathroom. Ridley and Tex stared at me, and I tried to sit up, but pain shot through me, nearly stealing the breath from my lungs. I collapsed onto the bed and wondered if I could just stay in my asylum-issued clothes until I no longer felt like I'd been used as a punching bag. And it wasn't unthinkable that something like that had actually happened after I'd blacked out from whatever drugs they'd given me. Thankfully, I wasn't sore between my legs, so at least they hadn't raped me.

"Your name is Kalani?" Ridley asked.

I nodded.

"That's a beautiful name," she said.

"It's Hawaiian," I said. "That's where my mom said she was from, before she came to this town and got locked up."

"Your mom is in the asylum?" Tex asked.

"Not anymore," I said softly.

"Is your father still in Hawaii?" Ridley asked. "We can get word to him that you're safe."

I felt the blood drain from my face at the mention of my father, and a whimper escaped me before I could fight it back. No, if my father knew where I was, he'd come for me. And then he'd take me back to the asylum, and he'd make sure I never left again. Not unless it was in a body bag. Tex knelt beside the bed and slowly reached for my hand, giving it a gentle squeeze.

"Easy, Kalani. If you don't want us to contact your dad, we won't."

"He's a monster," I said. "He'll come for me if he knows where I am. He'll never stop looking. Not until I'm locked up again, where he'll make sure I disappear this time."

Ridley's brow furrowed. "Kalani, you're safe here."

"Never safe. Safe is an illusion," I said. "Dr. Whitby will find me. And then he'll make me pay."

Tex tilted his head and studied me. "Is this Dr. Whitby your father?"

I nodded slowly. "He raped my mom. She begged to keep me, and he let her. But then she didn't wake up one day."

Ridley gasped and as I looked at her, I saw tears running down her cheeks. "Kalani... have you... have you ever been outside the asylum before today?"

"No," I said softly.

She and Tex shared a look, then she fled the room.

"I didn't mean to upset her," I said.

"She's upset about what happened to you and to your mom." His jaw tightened. "You said they raped your mom. Kalani, have they ever…"

"I kept her safe," I told him. "I wouldn't let them do that to Janessa."

"But you let them do that to you. In order to protect her."

I didn't answer, but I didn't have to. He could see the truth when he looked at me, and it was like the weight of the world settled on his broad shoulders. He sighed and dropped his head, his hand tightening on mine a moment.

"I'm so fucking sorry," he said.

"What happened to me wasn't your fault," I told him. "I've lived at Hillview for twenty-two years. Saving Janessa gave me a reason to live. And I'd do it again without hesitation."

"Thank you," he said, his voice deep and gravelly. "I can never repay you for what you've done for my daughter. You can stay here as long as you want."

Janessa returned, her hair dripping wet, and her new nightgown covering her down to her ankles. She smiled broadly and looked almost like a different child. Being free of that place was already doing wonderful things for her, or maybe it was knowing that her dad was here and wanted her. I could only imagine what that would feel like, since my father was a monster who thrived on hurting people.

"Your turn, Kalani," she said.

"I'll take one tomorrow," I said.

Tex gave me a questioning look.

"I don't think I can stand yet," I said.

"I could get Ridley to help you," he offered.

"That's sweet, but she can't hold me up." I motioned to my body. "I may not be taller than her, but I'm quite a bit heavier. My mom was a big woman, and I guess I take after her."

"Then let me help you," Tex said. "I promise that you're safe with me. I would never hurt you the way they did. It will be just like earlier. I'll help however you need, and I won't touch you in any way that you don't want me to."

I could see the truth in his eyes, and it wasn't like men hadn't been looking at my naked body for as long as I could remember, and he'd already seen me half-naked. I nodded, and he lifted me into his arms again, carrying me the opposite direction down the hall.

"Where are we going?" I asked.

"My room. The shower is bigger."

I stayed silent as he set me down on the bathroom counter and started the shower. I could see he was conflicted, and I hated that he felt like he had to do this. Tex began stripping off his clothes, but left his underwear on. It molded to him and left little to the imagination, but I was too busy staring at his rather perfect chest and abs. I'd never seen a man like him before. Had never seen a naked man at all. Oh, I'd seen what they had hiding behind their zippers, but they never fully undressed. Even so, I doubted any of the men at the asylum looked anything like Tex. If there was such a thing as a perfect man, I'd imagine he would be it.

Tex came closer and slowly began undressing me, his gaze assessing, as if waiting to see if I would scream or freak out. Once I was completely naked, he carried me into the shower and eased me down onto my feet. His arm banded around my waist, pressing our bodies together, and I felt his quick indrawn breath. Looking up at him, I saw his eyes darken. I'd never seen a look quite like that before. Lust, yes, but there was something more in his gaze. I felt a tingle working its way through my body, and for the first time in my life, I knew what it was to desire someone. It was rather fucked-up, after everything I'd been through, but deep down I knew that Tex wouldn't hurt me. But no matter how much I wanted him, he was a man I knew that I could never have, because someone as perfect as he would never want someone as broken as me.

Chapter Three

Tex

The hot water beat against my shoulders as I braced my hand against the tiled wall. I'd been hard as a fucking post ever since I'd helped Kalani shower last night. I'd patrolled the house, checking on Kalani and Janessa frequently. I'd known sleep would be impossible, not after hearing what Kalani had endured in order to save my daughter. I owed her everything, and yet my hand was fisted around my cock as I thought about how fucking beautiful she'd been standing naked in my shower.

I'd helped her wash, then helped her dress, and put her to bed with my daughter. But I'd wanted to put her in my bed. I was sick, obviously, getting hard over a woman who had been so badly abused, but there'd been strength in her eyes despite the horrors she'd faced.

For one brief moment, as I'd washed her body last night, I'd looked into her eyes and thought she wanted me too. Then I'd shoved the thought aside as ridiculous and tried to focus on taking care of the two of them. If there was one woman in the world I shouldn't pursue, it was Kalani. Didn't stop me from wanting her, though. My eyes closed as I pictured her smiling at me softly, sliding to her knees at my feet. Those pretty lips of hers would part, and her tongue would flick out and tease the head of my cock.

I groaned as I stroked my dick faster, harder. Her mouth would be soft and wet. My control would be tested, until she begged me for more. I'd fist her hair and thrust into her mouth, fucking her with long, deep strokes. Those pretty brown eyes of hers would look up me, telling me how much she wanted my cum. I cried out as my release splashed against the tiles, and a shudder raked my body as I pictured Kalani, still at my feet, giving me a smile that told me there was much more to come.

Fuck. I was seriously screwed.

I finished with my shower and got dressed. Dr. Myron was due any minute, even though I knew both Janessa and Kalani were terrified of seeing a doctor. After being at Hillview, I didn't blame them. But then Dr. Myron wasn't at all like the doctors they'd been subjected to in that place of horrors.

The doorbell rang, and I went to let the good doctor in. Another man was with him, and I hesitated a moment.

"Tex, this is my partner. His name is Dr. Sykes, and he's a psychiatrist. But he's not here in a formal capacity."

Partner. Right. I'd forgotten Dr. Myron was gay.

"Come on in," I said, backing up.

The men stepped inside, and I shut the door. Janessa slowly approached from the living room where she'd been watching morning cartoons. Her gaze was wary, but I wasn't as worried about her reaction as I was about Kalani's. My daughter might not trust doctors, but Kalani had been abused by them, and had been fathered by a doctor who'd raped her mother. I could only imagine what she was going to say or do.

"Janessa, this is Dr. Myron, and his partner, Dr. Sykes. They're friends of the Dixie Reapers, which means they'll be friends of yours, if you'll let them," I said.

She eased a little closer. "You're not going to hurt Kalani, are you?"

"No," Dr. Sykes said. "Has Kalani been hurt by doctors before?"

Janessa nodded. "They do things to her. And sometimes she comes back covered in bruises or throwing up."

The men shared a glance before focusing on Janessa again. "Do you think Kalani would talk to us?" Dr. Myron asked. "We want to help the two of you, make sure you're healthy."

Janessa slowly reached out and took Dr. Myron's hand, then led the men down the hall toward the room she shared with Kalani. I followed, but kept my distance and stayed out of sight. I heard my daughter introduce the men and heard Dr. Myron ask if they could ask Kalani some questions. Alone. A moment later, Janessa came out of the room and moved down the hall toward the living room. And I was grateful when I heard what came out of Kalani's mouth for the next hour. Her words were stilted at times, and I could tell it was difficult for her. I doubted she'd had much reason to trust anyone before now. It killed me, hearing the fear in Kalani's voice, but as she opened up, what I felt quickly turned to rage. I wanted to burn Hillview to the fucking ground, with every employee locked inside the damn building.

The men talked to Kalani for a while, backing off when she seemed to shut down, then gradually getting her to talk again. When they were finished, they asked me to send Janessa back in. When they were finished talking to my daughter, they stepped out into the hall. The look in their eyes was enough to tell me they were every bit as furious as I was. I motioned for them to follow me, and we went to the kitchen, where I had some coffee keeping warm from this morning.

Dr. Myron sat across from me at the kitchen table, his partner next to him. Both men looked sickened, and I could understand why. I'd heard a little of what had been said between Janessa and them, and most of Kalani's story, and I'd fought hard not to throw up. My daughter hadn't suffered as much, but she'd known what was happening to Kalani, and it had likely done some psychological damage. The broken way Kalani had spoken to them, I knew she had a rough road to travel.

"Kalani is battered and bruised, but I don't think anything is broken," Dr. Myron said.

"Except her mind," his partner muttered. "She's separated herself from what happened at the asylum, probably as a way to protect herself. She knows she was violated, knows she was abused, but when she describes it, it's like she's talking about something that happened to someone else. There's a disconnect there, and that may be all that's keeping her from freaking the hell out."

Dr. Myron nodded. "If you can get her to attend therapy, it would be beneficial for her."

"And Janessa?" I asked.

"Your daughter is traumatized by what happened, but I think Kalani protected her enough that she'll bounce back. She saw things, heard things, that may give her nightmares. But thanks to Kalani, your daughter didn't suffer," Dr. Myron said. "Not physically anyway."

No, Janessa hadn't suffered, but Kalani had. A great deal. I had no idea what to do with her. Janessa seemed close to her, and if Kalani had truly been born at the asylum and never been out in the real world, she likely didn't have the skills required to survive. I couldn't just toss her out the front gate with a handful of cash and wish her well. She'd probably need someone to look after her just as much, if not more so, than Janessa. I'd told her that she was mine, and I meant it. I just wasn't certain how she would feel about it.

"Can I make a suggestion?" Dr. Myron asked.

"About my daughter?"

"No. Kalani. She's never had a chance to have a real life, and if the doctor who raped her mother wanted to hide his misdeeds, I'm thinking Kalani doesn't have a birth certificate or any other documentation on file anywhere. She's going to need those documents in order to have a life."

My brow furrowed as I thought about what that meant. She'd have no identification at all. While it didn't sound like she'd be ready to venture outside the compound anytime soon, she'd still need a paper trail of some sort. I didn't have a clue how to go about getting those things for her, or if I even should. If the doctor was looking for her, then I didn't want to give him any idea where Kalani might be hiding. I needed to talk to Torch and get a few things figured out, not just for Kalani but for Janessa too.

"Let them sleep as long as they'd like," Dr. Myron said. "I would imagine they didn't get much rest inside that place."

"How is it possible that Hillview is filled with so many horrors? Aren't there regulations in place to keep that from happening? This isn't the eighteen hundreds."

"If you have someone who can do some digging, you'll probably find that on the surface everything looks legit. And I'd be willing to bet that Kalani never existed. You likely won't find any records on her. On the one hand, that's a good thing. It means the asylum has no legal way to get her back. But…"

"It means they'll want her even more," I said. "Just to hide their dirty secrets."

Dr. Myron nodded.

"Thanks, both of you. If either of them needs medical attention, I'll be sure to call."

Dr. Myron and his partner rose, both shook my hand, and then I saw them to the door. After they left, I checked on Janessa and Kalani. They were both staring with rapt attention at the TV, and I couldn't help but smile. A cartoon was playing, but you'd think it was the most fascinating movie to have ever existed. I leaned against the doorway and watched them for a minute, then went back to the kitchen to make a call. Torch answered almost immediately.

"How are they?" he asked.

"They're watching TV, and Dr. Myron says they seem to be all right. He can't tell me much without being able to run tests at his clinic or sending them to the hospital."

"Probably not a good idea right now," Torch said.

"No, I didn't think so either. I need to talk to you, and I don't know if you want to have this conversation over the phone or in person. It's about Kalani and about the asylum."

"I can be there in a few minutes, but we should probably talk outside. If you have some things to say about Kalani, it would probably be better if she couldn't hear you," Torch said.

"Agreed."

We hung up, and I stepped out onto the porch, pulling the door shut behind me. I heard the rumble of Torch's bike a few minutes later, and I leaned against a porch post while I waited. He turned off the engine and made his way up the front steps.

"Start talking," Torch said.

"Kalani was born at Hillview. Her mother was raped by a doctor there. This is the first time she's ever left the asylum." My throat tightened. "She saved Janessa, kept her safe. By offering herself instead."

Torch cursed and folded his arms.

"Dr. Myron came with his partner, and they think she needs a therapist. They said the way she described what happened was like she'd watched it happen and it had been done to someone else," I said.

"Maybe that's a good thing," Torch said. "If it's helping her cope, then I say let her handle it that way at least for a little while longer. I'd imagine she's overwhelmed and scared being outside the asylum for the first time. At least inside those walls, she knew what to expect."

"Dr. Myron said she probably doesn't have a birth certificate or any other ID. It's his belief that the asylum hid any record of Kalani even existing."

Torch nodded. "Makes sense, considering the evil shit going on in there. Wire actually found a manual in Whitby's secret files, detailing how the staff should act while abusing the female patients. They were required to use condoms so there wouldn't be more pregnancies after Kalani. How sick is that fucking shit? I'll have Wire do some digging, see what he can find, and I'll hire someone to get some papers together for Kalani. Do you know if she has a last name? Or what her mother's name was?"

"I can ask."

"I don't want to scare your girls, but I'd like to meet both of them."

"My girls?" I asked.

Torch smirked. "You brought them both home, so they're both yours. At least for now."

I shook my head and led Torch into the house. Kalani and Janessa were watching TV, but they both looked up when we entered the room. I saw Kalani tense and slowly curl into the corner of the couch, making herself as small as possible. My heart ached, and I hated that she was so damn scared. Janessa just looked at Torch in curiosity. I was grateful that her time at the asylum hadn't damaged her as much as it had Kalani, even if it meant the terrified young woman had suffered in my daughter's place. It was a debt I would never be able to repay.

"Janessa, this is Torch. He's the President of the MC I belong to. We're Dixie Reapers, and this house in located inside the compound."

My daughter slowly came forward but stopped a few feet away.

Torch smiled at my daughter and relaxed his posture. "It's nice to meet you, Janessa. Welcome home."

Janessa studied him another moment, then smiled. But a whimper across the room made that smile drop from her face and she turned to face Kalani. I brushed past my daughter and approached the couch, moving slowly so I wouldn't spook the woman further. I crouched in front of her and slowly reached out a hand, placing it on her knee.

"Kalani, you're safe. No one here is going to hurt you. Torch would never hurt a woman or child. None of my brothers would."

She trembled under my touch, and I rubbed her leg before rising to my feet.

"Kalani," Torch said softly. "I'm sorry for everything that's happened to you, but you have my word that no harm will come to you while you're here."

Kalani glanced at Torch, then turned her gaze toward me. I could see the fear and uncertainty there, and I hated it. She'd only been free for one night, and I knew it was too much to hope that she'd settle in quickly. After all the years of abuse she'd been through, I knew it would take time. I'd give her as much as she needed.

"Kalani, I need to know your mother's name," I said. "It's important."

"Ulani Mahelona."

"And she told you she was from Hawaii?" I asked "Do you remember what part?"

Her brow wrinkled and mouth turned down as she thought about it. "Oahu? Is that a place?"

"Yeah, sweetheart. That's a place."

"Do you know when your birthday is?" Torch asked. "The month or day?"

"March seventh," she said. "I remember last year on my birthday, one of the doctors made a comment about it being my twenty-first birthday."

She grew quiet, and a darkness entered her eyes that I didn't like. I had no idea what had happened on her twenty-first birthday, but I could tell it hadn't been good. I wanted to help her heal, but I didn't even know where to start. And with Janessa always nearby, I didn't think Kalani would open up completely. My daughter might know some of what happened at Hillview, but I doubted she knew everything Kalani had done to protect her, and I wanted to keep it that way.

"Janessa, my wife was going shopping today. I have a few men going with her for protection. Would you like to go too?" Torch asked. "A few Dixie Reapers will be with them, so I don't think you'll have any problems. Never hurts to have protection, though."

"Can Kalani come?" Janessa asked, looking at the woman who was still cowering on the couch.

"I think Kalani would prefer to stay here," I told Janessa. "But I trust the Dixie Reapers to keep you safe. If you'd like to go shopping, I'll make sure you have money to buy some new things."

Her eyes widened. "You mean like at the mall?"

Torch chuckled. "Yeah, kid. At the mall."

Janessa let out a whoop and ran for the bedroom, coming back a minute later with her flip-flops on. She'd been dressed all morning, and the excitement in her eyes made me smile. She seemed normal in that moment, like she'd never been locked away in that awful place. And I hoped she'd have many more moments like this one.

"I'll head home and take over babysitting duties from Isabella and send her this way in the SUV. Tank will go with them, since he's familiar to Janessa. I'll leave it to him to decide who else goes," Torch said.

Janessa bounced around the living room until Isabella arrived to take her shopping. I hugged my daughter, made sure Isabella had my number, and then waved as they pulled down the driveway. It was amazing how Janessa was acting so normal considering what she'd been through.

After they were gone, I went back to Kalani, settling on the couch next to her. She chewed on her lip nervously and her gaze darted around the room.

"Do you want me to move?" I asked.

"No!" She winced at her outburst. "Please. Stay."

"Come here, sweetheart," I said, lifting my arm.

She hesitated only a moment before curling against my body. Her hand clutched at my shirt, and she held on tight, almost like she was worried I'd disappear. I was humbled that she trusted me this much. There were questions I wanted to ask, but I didn't want to push too hard too fast. She'd had enough for one day. Dr. Myron had been professional, but a bit invasive. I knew it was for her own good, but Kalani seemed fragile in the light of day. The tough girl from last night had disappeared.

"What's going to happen to me?" she asked, her voice so soft I almost didn't hear her.

"You're going to stay here with me and get better."

"I can't stay with you forever," she said.

"Let's just take things one day at a time. I'm not throwing you out anytime soon, Kalani. You protected my daughter. Let me protect you for a little while, okay?"

She nodded and relaxed into me a little more.

"Let's spend a quiet day watching movies while Janessa is out shopping." I frowned. "But you're going to need some clothes too."

"These are a little tight," she said, tugging on the leggings.

"We can measure you later and figure out what size pants and tops you need. If you want to stay inside the compound, I can order you some clothes online, or ask Ridley to pick up something the next time she goes out."

"Okay." She glanced up at me. "Thank you. For saving me."

"My pleasure, sweetheart. I'm only sorry I couldn't have gotten you out of there sooner."

Chapter Four

Kalani
Two Weeks Later

I still jumped at shadows and loud noises, but I thought I was improving. I was also adjusting to some of the men in the Dixie Reapers, but a few still scared me. Janessa had blossomed and settled into her new life with relative ease. I was a little jealous at how easily she'd adapted, but at the same time it meant I'd done a good job protecting her from the horrors of Hillview. And for that I was really grateful. Tex was amazing with her, and she seemed to sense that she was safe with him.

She'd been spending a lot of time with Isabella and Ridley and seemed fascinated with the smaller children in the compound. Most days, Janessa was gone from after breakfast until nearly dinnertime. Which left me a lot of time alone with Tex. I'd encouraged him to leave, to spend time with his friends, but he'd refused to leave me alone. I didn't know how he could tell that I needed him here, but I was glad he'd stayed with me every day. As long as Tex was here, it made me feel like the monsters would stay away a little while longer.

He was in the kitchen with two other Dixie Reapers having some sort of meeting, and I'd been watching romantic comedies on TV. I didn't know what they were discussing, but I had a feeling it was about Hillview. I knew Tex was worried they'd come for his daughter, and they might, but something told me they wanted me back far more. I wondered if he'd considered that the doctors at Hillview might be willing to trade. Me for his daughter's freedom. Being away from Hillview had been nice, but I didn't delude myself into thinking it was permanent. Did I want it to be? Hell yes! But I'd been born into that hell, and until the night Tex carried me out of there, I'd known I was never leaving. Going back would be hard for me, but I knew I could handle it better than Janessa. She needed her daddy, and I think he needed her too.

There was a knock at the door, but Tex never came to answer it. The knock sounded twice more before I got up. I pulled open the door and took a hasty step back. A fierce-looking man stood on the other side, his height towering over me even more so than Tex. His long, blond hair flowed over his shoulders and his gaze seemed to miss nothing. He took a step over the threshold, and I scrambled to put more distance between us. My heart hammered in my chest as the door shut and he came closer. He wore a Dixie Reapers cut, but I'd never met this man before. The hard look in his eyes reminded me too much of the men who had delighted in hurting me.

A whimper escaped me, and black dots swam across my vision. The man kept coming until I could nearly feel his breath in my face, and I cried out, falling to the floor and curling in on myself.

"What the fuck is going on?" Tex demanded, stomping into the front entry.

"I think I scared her," the other man said, his voice deep and gruff.

"Jesus, Bull. You should have called and let me know you were coming over. I could have prepared her," Tex said. "You're a big bastard and scare the shit out of grown men."

I felt strong hands grip my arms and pull me up. Tex's scent surrounded me, and I held on tight as he pulled me against his chest.

"Easy, Kalani," Tex murmured. "You're safe. Bull would never hurt you. I know he's huge and a little scary, but he'd never hurt a woman."

"I'm sorry," Bull said.

"Go into the kitchen. I'll be there in a minute," Tex said.

After we were alone again, he lifted me into his arms and carried me over to the couch. He sat down and held me close. I wasn't as scared as I'd been a minute ago, not with his arms around me.

"I need to finish talking to the guys," he said.

"Please don't leave me."

"Will you be all right sitting in there with all of them?"

I nodded slowly, but I wasn't sure I quite believed it myself. He carried me to the kitchen, then sat on one of the wooden chairs, settling me in his lap. I clutched tight to Tex's shirt and tried to slow my racing heart as I looked at the men sitting around the table. The redheaded man smiled slightly before looking down at the computer in front of him, and the others only gave me a brief glance.

"I think I know how to solve one of our problems," the redhead said.

"How?" Tex asked.

"You have the paperwork I gave you for Kalani? Her birth certificate and social security card?" the man asked.

I had those things? My brow furrowed. I didn't understand how any of that worked, but would my father have actually acknowledged my birth like that? I'd always thought I was a dirty little secret.

"Yeah. Why?" Tex sounded a little leery of what the man was about to say.

"Then getting a marriage license shouldn't be an issue."

My breath caught in my throat, and I glanced up at Tex. He looked completely stunned, and not in a good way. I'd watched enough TV the last few weeks, and read enough books, to understand that a marriage license meant a wedding would take place. But who was getting married and how was that going to fix anything?

"I don't understand," I said, drawing everyone's attention to me.

"You need to get married, darlin'," the redhead said softly. "After the things I've discovered by digging into Hillview's records, including the ones they don't want anyone to see, I don't think they'll let you just walk away. You're dangerous to them. Marrying one of us would give you some added protection. It's not going to be a magical fix by any means, but I honestly think it would help your situation."

"How?" I asked.

"If Hillview comes here looking for you, we could deny them entrance, but they would likely have some sort of forged documents saying they have the rights to decide what happens to you. They could call the cops, and the officers would send you back with them to Hillview, no questions asked. Right now, you have no living family except that asshole doctor. And he has the documentation to prove that you're his kid. I was surprised as fuck to find a form completed by a midwife. While it wasn't an official birth certificate, it might hold weight. As your only surviving relative, he could tell the police you need to be committed for your safety, or for the town's safety. But if you're married, then your husband could keep that from happening," the redhead said. "Theoretically, anyway."

"Who would I marry?" I asked. "I don't know any of you."

"Yeah, Wire," Tex said with a growl. "Who is she going to marry?"

"We kind of assumed it would be you," he said, smiling a little at Tex.

I felt Tex stiffen, and I knew he didn't like that idea. I couldn't really blame him. I was a complete wreck, jumping at every little sound, and I'd never been intimate with a man willingly. I wasn't certain I was capable of such a thing. If he married, he deserved a woman who didn't have my problems. Besides, if he'd thought I was attractive, he'd have said or done something by now, wouldn't he? It wasn't like he'd tried to steal kisses or get me naked all the times we'd been alone. That's what happened in the books I'd borrowed from Ridley. If my mother hadn't been part of my life the first eight years, I'd likely have never learned anything. She'd taught me what little she could. And from what I'd witnessed firsthand at Hillview, if a man wanted a woman, he didn't keep his distance. He took what he wanted. Didn't he? I felt so confused, and a headache was growing behind my eyes.

"I already have a woman, so it can't be me," Bull said.

"Ridley would kill me if I married another woman," Venom said. "But if you don't want to do it, Tex, we have quite a few single guys in the club. Including Wire."

They wanted me to marry a complete stranger? I didn't understand. I knew what happened between men and women, and if I were married, then my husband would want to do *that* all the time. What was the difference in being married and going back to Hillview? If a man was going to force himself on me, what did it matter if I was married and free or back in my prison? It was all the same thing, wasn't it? But then, Tex had been so sweet to me. I had a hard time picturing him treating me the way the staff and doctors at Hillview had, but he was still a man. I trusted him, for the most part, but I didn't know if I would ever completely trust a man, not after what I'd been through.

"What about Janessa?" I asked. "They won't be happy she's gone. She's seen too much."

"Tex already filed for custody of his daughter," Wire said. "Hillview is aware that Janessa is here, and for now, the lawyer has managed to get Tex temporary custody until the paperwork can be pushed through. That should be resolved within a few days. But your problem is more long-term."

"It won't matter if I'm married or not," I said quietly. "They'll get me back by any means necessary. You should just…"

"We should what?" Wire asked.

"Trade me. Give me back to Hillview to keep Janessa safe," I said.

Tex's arms tightened around me. "You're not going back there."

I looked up at him, and the fierce expression on his face made me feel… something. Being with Tex was unlike anything I'd ever experienced before, but he needed to be reasonable. His daughter was more important. At fourteen, she had her entire life ahead of her. I'd known from an early age that my days were numbered, that I was never supposed to exist. My father had made sure of that, and once my mom had died, there had been no one left who cared what happened to me. Janessa had a family here, people who loved her. I had nothing.

"Being here has been wonderful," I told him. "But I never expected to get out of Hillview. I've always known that I would die there, probably sooner rather than later. Save your daughter. You know it's the right thing."

Tex growled. Literally growled! Then he stood so abruptly, the chair fell over. He clutched me to his chest as he surveyed the room. "Do it. Get a minister or who the fuck ever."

"I have a better idea," Wire said.

"What?" Tex asked, pausing in the kitchen doorway.

"Take her to Vegas. You can get a license there and get married the same day. Just as legal, but faster. I can do a bit of magic here in Alabama, hack the state system and get a license for you in a few days, but do you really want to put this off?" Wire asked.

"No. But they'll be watching the airport and bus stations for her, and it's a long ass drive to Vegas from Alabama," Tex said. "Besides, I'm not sure how she'd handle all that noise and the crowds."

"You can't seriously be thinking about marrying me," I told him.

He glowered down at me, and that look said yes, that's exactly what he thought. Stubborn man. He was going to ruin his life if he married me. Dr. Whitby would never stop, not until I was back behind the gates of Hillview or dead. I knew that. Everyone in this room should know that, especially if Wire said he'd seen the files on me. Oh, God. My stomach nearly dropped.

"You... you said you saw my files?" I asked Wire, the blood draining from my face. I didn't know for certain what was in there, but I could only imagine. Had they documented everything they'd done to me?

"Yeah," he said softly, sympathy in his eyes. "I did, and I'm sorry as hell for everything you've been through. You should know there are videos of some of it, stored on what Whitby thought was a secret, secure server. But I found them, and I saved a copy in case we need leverage. I still think marrying Tex is your best bet, though."

"If you've seen all that, then you know why I can't marry him."

"What's going on?" Tex asked.

"Because Kalani was a favorite," Wire said, his face twisting with disgust, "Dr. Whitby had her tubes tied when she was only sixteen. He wanted to make sure she never got pregnant."

"You mean he did that to his daughter so the assholes who worked for him could..." Tex made a sound like he was strangling, and as I looked up, I saw an unholy light in his eyes, and possibly a sheen of tears. I didn't know what to make of that, but surely he could understand now that if he married me, he'd never have more children. And as wonderful as he was with Janessa, he deserved that chance.

"I'm tainted, Tex," I told him softly. "Do you really want to be stuck with me? I've read enough and watched enough movies since being freed that I know married couples..." My cheeks flamed, and I couldn't even finish the sentence.

"Everyone out," Tex said quietly.

Wire closed his laptop and hesitated after everyone else had filed out of the room. He looked from me to Tex and seemed to come to some sort of decision.

"If you want to go to Vegas, I can make it happen. Casper VanHorne can have a jet or chopper here probably within a few hours," Wire said. "No one at Hillview would even know you'd left."

Tex frowned. "Why the hell would Casper VanHorne help me?"

Wire smiled a little. "Because Isabella is his daughter."

Tex looked more than a little stunned, but I had no idea who Casper VanHorne was. I was going to assume he was someone important to get that kind of reaction from the man who still held me like he'd never let me go.

"Do it. Call me or text me with a time and location." He turned, then stopped. "Why exactly hasn't Hillview already sent someone to retrieve Kalani? They know I have Janessa, so they have to assume that Kalani is here too."

Wire shrugged. "Sadly, all the video footage from the night of her escape seems to have been magically erased, the orderly who helped you has gone missing, and everyone at the compound has played stupid when it comes to Kalani. Since she hasn't left your house, there's been no way for Hillview to see her roaming the compound. They can speculate that she's here, but there's no way for them to know for sure. Maybe she just ran off all on her own."

I stared at Wire. "And they actually believed that?"

Wire chuckled. "Probably not. Which is why I released a few viruses into their systems to keep them busy. One of them is really awesome. Every time they get close to figuring it out, the virus evolves, and they have to start over. Right now, they don't have access to at least half their records, including your files, which means they can't get their hands on anything that says you belong there."

"Then why do we have to get married?" I asked.

"Because the virus is temporary. Eventually, they'll hire someone who will fix their system, and then they'll come looking for you. I know what you've been through, I've seen what they did to you, and I won't let you go back," Wire said. "You protected Janessa, and it's obvious that she didn't want to leave you there. That makes you one of us."

My throat grew tight. I'd never belonged anywhere before.

"I'll see myself out," Wire said. "Be listening for that call."

Wire stepped past us, and Tex carried me down the hall. I'd thought he was taking me to the room I shared with Janessa, but he went right past it and continued into his bedroom. He kicked the door shut with his booted foot, then eased me down onto the bed. Tex paced for a moment, then stopped in front of me. Men towering over me still made me nervous and I tried not to fidget. My hands gripped the bedding tight, and I couldn't help but stare straight ahead, right at his zipper. Was this the moment that he made me…

He tipped my chin up with his hand, then he knelt to get closer to eye-level with me. "Whatever you're thinking, you can stop. I'm not going to hurt you, Kalani. I would *never* do anything to bring you harm."

"Then why are we in your room?" I asked, trying to hold his gaze.

"If we get married, this is going to be your room too. What part of getting married scares you the most?" he asked.

I glanced behind me at the expanse of the large bed.

"Darlin'," he said, turning my face back toward him. "I won't force myself on you. If all you want to do is sleep, then I'll lie next to you and let you sleep. I'm not going into this expecting us to have a normal marriage. I doubt that you're anywhere near ready for that, and that's okay. I haven't been with a woman in a while, truth be told. If I've lasted this long, I can wait longer."

"What if I'm never ready?" I asked, my gaze dropping from his. "What if I can't ever give you what you want, what you need? It's not fair for you to be stuck with a woman who may never want to be intimate with you."

"Seeing as how we're getting married, mind if I try something?" he asked. "I'll stop anytime you want me to."

"Try what?" I asked, looking at him again.

"I want to kiss you," he said, his gaze dropping to my lips. "And if you don't like it, or it scares you, then you push me away and I'll back off. I will never ask more of you than you're willing to give, Kalani. But I think, given time, that you could have a normal life. I know you've been through some dark shit, and no, I don't know all the details, but I know enough. Don't let them win. If you give up on life, if you never give living a chance, then they win."

I licked my lips and he groaned a little. "And kissing you will mean they aren't winning?"

"Yeah, darlin'. But if you don't want that, then I'll back off right now."

My heart was pounding, but I wasn't sure if it was because I was scared or because of something else. I might not be a virgin, but when it came to this, to kissing and someone *asking* if they could touch me, I was completely clueless. No one had ever kissed me. Not really. They'd ground their lips against mine as they fumbled with their pants, but I didn't think that was an actual kiss. Part of me was curious, even if I was little frightened of what might come after that.

"All right," I agreed. "You… you may kiss me."

Tex moved in closer, his hand sliding into my hair. His gaze met mine before he lowered his head and his lips lightly brushed across mine. He was so tender, his kiss so soft, that the tension and fear began to melt away. He kissed me slowly, his lips caressing mine, and when his tongue flicked out, I gasped. I didn't know what to think when his tongue slid into my mouth, but I tried to mimic what he was doing. When Tex pulled away, he rested his forehead against mine.

"Did I… did I do that right?" I asked.

He gave a gruff laugh and looked at me. "Yeah, darlin'. That was perfect."

I nibbled my lip, which tingled a little from his kiss. "Tex? Is… is all parts of being married like that kiss?"

"You mean the bedroom parts?" he asked.

My cheeks flushed and I nodded.

He cupped my cheek, his thumb rubbing lightly against my skin. "With us, yeah. All parts will be like that. I'll go as slow as you want, sweetheart. And I wasn't lying. If you decide you don't want that part of marriage at all, then it doesn't have to happen. Ever."

"You're giving up children," I reminded him.

"As many kids as we have running around this compound, I'm sure a few brothers won't mind loaning their kids out here and there. We'll just volunteer to babysit sometimes so they can go on date nights, and we can get our baby fix."

"You make it sound so easy, but I know it's not."

"Kalani," he said softly. "Torch referred to you and Janessa as my girls, and he was right. The moment I carried you out of that place, you became mine. We'll make this work, whatever it takes. All I want is for you to be happy and safe, and I will stop at nothing to make that happen."

"All right," I said, my voice so quiet I wasn't sure he heard me.

Slowly, he moved toward me again, and he kissed me once more. This time, I was able to kiss him back better than the first time. I had to admit that kissing Tex was nice, and I wouldn't mind doing that for the rest of my life. Maybe he was right. If kissing felt this nice, maybe other things between us would be good too. And hopefully, if things did get that far, I wouldn't freak out at the last minute.

His phone chimed with an incoming message and he drew back. He pulled the phone from his pocket and smiled. "It's Wire. Our flight will be ready within two hours. It seems we're taking a private jet to Las Vegas."

I rubbed my hands up and down my thighs. "I've never been on a plane before. I'd never been in a car until the night you rescued me."

"Everything's going to be fine."

"What about Janessa?" I asked. "Is she going too?"

He cursed under his breath. "Hang on. I don't think anyone thought that far ahead."

He tapped on his phone and smiled a moment later.

"Torch said Janessa can stay with them. He's ordered me to keep you in Vegas for a few days to give us some alone time."

"A few days?" I asked. "Where will we stay?"

"Wire said he was making arrangements for us. He'll text the information to me once everything is finalized."

"Tex, can you afford all this? Isn't something like traveling expensive?"

"I'm not a rich man," he said. "But I can take care of you. Want to see my account balance? Would that make you feel better?"

I shook my head. "It wouldn't mean anything to me. I've never dealt with money before."

"When we get back, I'll have you added to my account and get a debit card for you. I can teach you how it all works, and if you're ever worried that something costs too much, just ask. It's time for you to experience freedom, Kalani. I don't want to keep you behind these gates forever. Once Hillview is taken care of, you'll be able to come and go as you please, without fear of someone coming after you."

"How are you going to take care of Hillview?" I asked.

"Let me worry about that." His jaw tightened. "Those assholes are in for a reckoning. Dixie Reapers take care of our own, and you're one of us now, sweetheart. We won't stop until that place is shut down and the men who hurt you are either dead or in jail."

His words should have scared me, but they didn't. Maybe it was wrong, but I wanted those people to suffer. They were horrible, evil men and women, and every last one deserved whatever Tex did to them. I only hoped he didn't get in trouble. I'd come to rely on him, and I wasn't sure if I'd ever be ready to be out in the big wide world without him by my side.

He looked at me, a little pensive. "We didn't buy you anything appropriate for a wedding."

I glanced down at the T-shirt and leggings I had on. I'd found them comfortable, so when Tex had bought clothes for me online, I'd just ordered more of them. Getting a bra had been a little trickier, and my cheeks had never been so red as when he helped me measure. I'd tried to do it on my own, but hadn't know what the hell I was doing. Tex had fumbled a bit, but he'd remained a gentleman the entire time.

"We'll go order our license and then go shopping," he said. "I'm sure it will take a few hours to get the license so that will give us some time. You can get a wedding dress, and I'll get a suit. Even if we're doing this in Vegas, doesn't mean we can't do it in style."

I had no clue what that meant, but if he wanted to buy me a dress, I'd go along with it. I'd done what he called binge-watching with every show I could find since he'd brought me home, and Ridley had given me a few sacks of books. I'd watched TV a few times in the asylum, but it hadn't been often. We quickly packed our clothes, dropped some things off for Janessa, and then we headed to the airstrip. Wire drove us in a large truck, claiming it made more sense than having to leave a vehicle at the airstrip. As we boarded the jet, my stomach twisted and churned. I only hoped that Tex didn't wake up tomorrow and regret all this.

Chapter Five

Tex

I had to admit, I never thought I'd get married. Not after what happened with Janessa's mom. Trusting women after that had never been easy, and was probably why I'd never had a relationship after I'd left the Dixie Reapers and joined the Army. But as I watched Kalani walk down the short aisle of one of the Vegas chapels, I wasn't nervous, I wasn't scared... I just felt content. I knew that we might not ever have a normal marriage, but I hadn't lied to her. I was okay with that. She was an incredible woman, and I wanted to give her the world, wanted to keep her safe, and I wanted to prove to her that not all men were assholes. I didn't know what our wedding night would consist of, but as long as I got to spend time with her, then that's all that mattered.

"You're beautiful," I said as she stopped next to me.

Her cheeks flushed and there was a hesitant smile on her face. I knew she still thought I was making a mistake, that I would regret marrying her. But she couldn't have been more wrong. I'd thought she was pretty even from the beginning, but seeing her like this? She was stunning. And after this ceremony, she'd be mine.

She reached up and smoothed her hand down the lapel of the navy suit I'd purchased. Kalani had said I could get married wearing whatever I wanted, and maybe some other guy would have done just that. No way was I showing up to my wedding in my cut, jeans, and biker boots. Kalani deserved better than that, so if that meant I had to wear a suit and dress shoes, then that's what I'd do. I'd thought about taking my Army dress uniform, but the only uniforms she'd ever seen were in Hillview. I hadn't been sure how she'd react, and I wanted this day to be a good memory for her. So I'd left the uniform hanging in my closet at home. Not that an Army uniform was remotely close to what the staff and doctors wore at Hillview, but I hadn't been willing to take the chance.

I barely heard the words of the minister. Somehow, I'd managed to find one who didn't dress like Elvis. And I'd even arranged for Kalani to have a bouquet and for pictures to be taken before, during, and after the ceremony. I might not have ever been married before, but I remember how much my mom had loved her wedding pictures. Kalani had lived such a hard life, I wanted her to have a way to remember a happy day. Or what I hoped would be a happy day. So far, she'd been smiling through most of it, and hadn't seemed quite as scared as she normally was. I didn't know if that's because Hillview was so far away, or if she just trusted me to keep her safe.

The minister cleared his throat and I realized they were waiting on me.

"I do," I said, hoping that was the right thing to say. I hadn't been listening at all, too busy staring at the gorgeous woman in front of me.

"And do you Kalani Whitby take Houston Rodriguez to be your lawfully wedded husband? In sickness and in health, for richer or poorer, 'til death do you part?" the minister asked.

"I do," she said, without hesitation. My heart warmed as she smiled up at me.

"You may kiss the bride. Congratulations, Mr. and Mrs. Rodriguez."

I leaned down and softly brushed my lips against hers but pulled away quickly. The only kisses we'd shared had been at home in my bedroom, and that had only been about nine or ten hours ago. I didn't think she was ready for PDA at this stage, and might not ever like it. That and I really didn't want to get a hard-on while we were out in public. No, I hadn't reached my age and never sported wood out in public, but this wasn't just any woman. She was my wife, and I didn't want to embarrass her.

We posed for a few pictures, then waited while they were printed off. I even purchased a small wedding album they offered, and hoped I was doing the right thing. Wire had found us a hotel off the strip, agreeing with me that the lights and crowds might be too much for Kalani. But it was a nice hotel, and he'd booked the honeymoon suite, letting me know that the club was taking care of the cost as a wedding gift to us. I hadn't lied to Kalani about my finances. I was well enough off that she didn't need to worry about anything, but it was nice of the guys to do something like this for us. It would allow me to spend more money on my new wife.

We walked down the strip, with her hand clutched tightly in mine. Anytime someone brushed against us, she pressed even closer. While I hated that she was likely nervous around so many people, I had to admit that I didn't mind her getting as close as she wanted. My heart was pounding as I thought about the night ahead. I'd let the concierge know we were off to get married and that I'd like room service waiting when we returned, complete with champagne. I'd handed him a slip of paper with my order. The man had winked and said everything would be taken care of.

We turned off the strip and walked to our hotel, the crowd having thinned quite a bit. My new wife didn't clutch my hand quite as tightly, but she still held on. I scanned the area, making sure trouble wasn't lurking. In a place like this, it was probably a mugger's paradise. Despite the fact I was dressed up for the wedding, I had my Glock concealed under my suitcoat. I didn't care if Nevada was a reciprocity state for conceal and carry or not. When it came to Kalani's safety, I wasn't taking any chances.

The concierge gave me a thumbs-up as we walked past, which Kalani thankfully didn't notice. I wanted to surprise her. I only hoped she liked surprises. The elevator was empty as we stepped inside, and I pushed the button for our floor. Kalani had yet to release my hand, and I was fighting the urge to lean down and kiss her again. I had to remind myself to move slowly. Yes, we'd kissed three times now, but that didn't mean she'd be open to more of them right now.

The elevator stopped at our floor, and we stepped off and walked down to the honeymoon suite. Kalani's eyes had gone wide the first time she'd seen it, and I had to admit I was pretty impressed too. There was a living area with a black leather couch and two matching chairs. A large TV was mounted on the wall, and there was a roomy bedroom with a bathroom that had a large, jetted tub and a separate shower.

I pushed open the door to our suite, and Kalani gasped as she walked into the living area. The concierge had gone above and beyond. Candles were lit around the room, the champagne was chilling in a silver bucket on the glass-top coffee table, and he'd included strawberries with chocolate sauce. A wheeled cart held our meals, covered with silver domes, and I noticed a trail of red rose petals leading into the bedroom. I'd have to remember to give the man a good tip.

"This is..." Kalani spun around, taking everything in. "You did all this for me?"

"I wanted tonight to be special," I said.

"Tex, it's... it's beautiful."

I noticed the shine of tears in her eyes, but she wrapped her arms around me and hugged me tight. I just stood there, holding her, and hoping that tonight would be filled with happy memories, something to wash away all the evil she'd experienced. Not that I thought a wedding and a possibly G-rated honeymoon were going to make it all go away, but it was a step in the right direction.

"Come on, sweetheart. Let's get a glass of champagne and have some dinner. Then we can check out those strawberries for dessert."

She nodded and let go. There was a small table near the large floor-to-ceiling window. I carried our dinners to the table and poured each of us a glass of champagne. I was more a beer type of guy, but women liked this kind of shit, right? Kalani sat and took a tentative sip of her champagne. A drop clung to her lip, and before she could lick it away, I leaned over and kissed her, lapping up the droplet with my tongue. She inhaled sharply and I backed off, wondering if I'd pushed things too far already.

"Sorry," I said.

She blinked at me, looking a little dazed, then took another sip from her flute. From what I'd gathered, the food at Hillview had been severely lacking. I'd tried to introduce some new foods to Kalani over the last few weeks, and her stomach hadn't tolerated a lot of them very well. She looked healthier, though, and had even filled out a little more. She'd called herself heavy when I'd first brought her home, but she hadn't been. Now her curves were more pronounced, and fuck if she wasn't the sexiest woman I'd ever seen. I lifted the lid on her dinner and watched as her eyes went wide and mouth dropped open a little.

"We haven't really tried seafood yet. I'm hoping you aren't allergic," I told her.

"What is all this?"

I pointed out each thing. "Lobster, shrimp scampi, scallops, and rice pilaf. I was going to order calamari, but I thought we'd better save that for another day. All this might be too much for you as it is."

"Everything smells so good."

The lobster tail was already cracked open. "Just pull out a bite of the lobster and dip it in the butter sauce. And if you don't like something, then don't eat it. Hell, if you don't like any of this, we can order something else."

"I'm sure I'll love it," she said, giving me a slight smile. "You really didn't have to go to all this trouble. I know you didn't really want to marry me, and now you've done all this. It's too much, Tex."

"No, it's just the right amount," I assured her. "And I never said I didn't want to marry you."

She tried a bite of lobster, and the sexiest moan I've ever heard slipped past her lips. My dick got hard, and I quickly sat so she wouldn't notice. While I enjoyed my food, I think I enjoyed watching Kalani far more. The silence between us wasn't awkward, so I just let her eat her dinner. The look of rapture on her face was one I would remember for a long time. We both cleaned our plates, not having eaten for hours, then I led her over to the sofa.

I reached for a strawberry, then hesitated. "It's possible you could be allergic to these. Obviously, shellfish isn't an issue, so maybe you don't have any food allergies."

"What happens with a food allergy?" she asked.

"Um, well. I guess it depends on the severity. Some people just itch, get red splotches, or swell a little. Or you could stop breathing."

She just blinked at me, then slowly reached for a strawberry, dipped it into the chocolate, then took a bite. I watched and didn't see any sort of reaction, other than her eyes rolling into the back of her head with every bite. She'd polished off three strawberries before I grabbed one. All right, so no strawberry allergy either.

When the strawberries were gone, and we'd each had a second glass of champagne, I knew it was time to call it a night. I was starting to feel a slight buzz, which was ridiculous considering how much I typically drank. I stood and held out my hand for her, then helped her to her feet. I could feel the nervous energy running between us as we entered the bedroom. A silk nightgown was already laid out across the bed for her, and I wondered if she'd done that before we left earlier. I didn't remember her buying one, but maybe she'd gotten it when she picked out her wedding dress? It looked like one of those fancy bridal-type nightgowns I'd seen in stores before. I tried not to read anything into it.

"Do you want a shower or bath before bed?" I asked. "I could run some water in the tub for you."

"I think I'd rather just go to bed, if that's okay?"

"Sure. I'll just, uh, step out of the room so you can change."

I turned, but her voice stopped me.

"Tex, you've already seen me naked."

I swallowed hard. Yeah, but my dick hadn't been hard as a damn post the last time. Now she was healthy, and it was our wedding night. My cock hadn't gotten the message that this was a marriage in name only. All the big guy in my pants knew was that Kalani was my wife, and that should mean some fun time in the bedroom.

I heard the rustle of fabric and closed my eyes tight, trying not to imagine her undressing. When I heard her climb onto the bed, I turned and my heart nearly stopped. The ivory silk of her nightgown clung to her curves, and the swells of her breasts showed above the lacy V-neck. I couldn't help but stare.

"Are you coming to bed?" she asked.

I slowly eased my jacket down my arms and draped it over the chair in the corner. I removed my holster and gun, locking them in the hotel-provided safe, then kicked off my shoes. A glance in Kalani's direction showed that she was watching my every move, and it was enough to make me move even slower. Her gaze tracked my hands as I undid the front of my shirt, then pulled it free of my pants and tossed it on top of my jacket. I pulled off my socks and let them fall onto the floor, but I hesitated when I reached for my pants.

"Kalani, maybe I should sleep on the couch tonight."

She crawled down to the foot of the bed, then sat on her knees, watching me. I didn't know what she wanted, or needed, so I moved a little closer to her, making sure I didn't make any sudden movements. When she reached out and placed her hand on my chest, I damn near swallowed my tongue.

"Kalani…"

"I know I saw you without a shirt before, but I didn't get to really look. I thought seeing a naked man would scare me, but knowing it's you makes a difference. I know you won't hurt me. You would have already if you were going to."

"Have you never seen a man without his shirt on? Other than me?" I asked.

She shook her head, while she explored my chest and abs with her hand. Her fingers trailed down lower, pausing when she reached the waist of my pants. She stared for what felt like forever before she lifted her gaze to mine.

"You're…"

"Hard?" I asked. "Yeah, sweetheart. But I don't expect anything of you. Can't help what happens when a beautiful woman touches me."

I could see a hint of fear in her eyes, but it quickly vanished, and I didn't know how to make her feel more comfortable. I'd already offered to sleep on the couch. She said she didn't fear me, but I think she wasn't being completely honest with herself. After what she'd survived, I wouldn't expect her to just spread her legs and beg for my cock. She had every right to be scared, and I would never force her to have sex with me, even if we were married now.

"It's not the first time I've been hard around you, Kalani. Just looking at you is enough to do that to me."

Her face paled and she started to pull away, but I grabbed her hand.

"I didn't tell you that to scare you more. I did it to point out that I can be hard and not act on it. Have I ever touched you when you didn't want me to?" I asked.

She shook her head.

"And I never will." I released her hand and waited to see what she would do. She didn't run away, so I counted that as progress.

I unfastened my pants and let them fall to the floor. "I'm going to take a shower."

I walked around the side of the bed, wearing only my boxer briefs, stepped into the bathroom, shutting the door behind me. My heart was hammering in my chest as I started the shower, hoping it would be enough to drown out any sounds. There was no way I could get into bed with my new wife while my dick was this damn hard and not want to reach for her. The last thing I wanted to do was scare her, and having my cock tenting the sheets would likely do that. Even if I did have enough control not to fuck her senseless, she might not know that.

I stripped off my underwear and got under the spray. I just stood there a few minutes, letting the water beat down on me. The hotel offered small bottles of shower gel and I poured a generous amount onto my palm. I slicked my shaft and started stroking. It was nowhere near as good as being inside a woman, but this would likely be my life for the foreseeable future. Hell, maybe forever.

I fought not to make much noise, but a few grunts and moans escaped as I got closer. My hand moved faster, gripping my cock tighter. I thrust against my palm, imagining it was my wife I was fucking, and then I came, shouting out my release as jets of cum bathed my hand and the shower wall. I shuddered from the force of my release, but my dick was still semi-hard. I had a feeling I was cursed to walk around with a hard cock. Especially since my wife was the sexiest woman I'd ever met, and I couldn't touch her.

I got out of the shower, dried off, and pulled my underwear back on. I'd have preferred a clean pair, but I wasn't walking naked into the bedroom to get some. Kalani would probably freak the fuck out if I did that. I shut off the bathroom light and stood in the doorway a moment, then made my way around to my side of the bed. Sliding under the covers, I lay back and held as still as possible. All I wanted to do was reach for her, hold her against me, but I didn't think that would be welcome. I hated that she was so scared, that she'd been through so much, but I would do what I could to make things better, to give her a happier life.

Kalani stared at me for a few minutes before she crawled a little closer and lay back down. There was a look of uncertainty on her face, and I wondered if she'd heard me in there. Was that why she hadn't moved? I flicked off the lamp and tried to relax, which was really fucking hard with my wife lying next to me. A wife I wanted more than I'd ever wanted another woman. A wife who had been badly abused and would likely never welcome my touch.

I still didn't regret my decision. She needed me, and I was going to be there for her, in whatever capacity she would allow. If that meant I went to bed with a hard-on every night and couldn't touch her, then so be it. My hand would just have to take up the slack during my showers. I briefly wondered if you could get carpal tunnel from jacking off.

Chapter Six

Kalani

Two days in Vegas and I was getting to know my new husband better, but I didn't feel much like a wife. The other couples around us were kissing, hugging, and I had no doubt they were doing much more behind closed doors. Tex held my hand as we walked down the Strip, but I knew he wanted more from me. He'd likely be embarrassed if he knew I could hear him in the shower. My cheeks burned every time I heard him grunting out his pleasure. Other women might feel flattered their husband wanted them like that, but for me all I felt was this all-consuming fear when I thought about sex. And I hated that. I hated that the men at Hillview had so much power over me that even now I was afraid.

Rationally, I knew what happened to me wasn't sex. It wasn't about pleasure, but about control and pain. But the thought of seeing Tex completely naked made my heart nearly stop. Sometimes I wondered if I would ever get over what happened to me, or at least get to a point where I could lead a semi-normal life. I hated being like this, and it made me feel like Hillview had won. The last thing I wanted was for them to control me for the rest of my life. While I might not be physically locked behind those walls anymore, maybe my mind was.

"What do you want to do?" Tex asked.

I knew he meant more in the did-I-want-to-catch-a-show way, but his question made me halt in the middle of the sidewalk. What did I want? No one had ever asked what I wanted in the grand scheme of things. Before Tex had freed me, I'd never even been asked what I wanted to eat. But being with him, I faced new questions every day. What did I want to eat? Did I want to buy more clothes? Did I like a certain type of movie? I'd never really been given the opportunity to think about what I wanted or needed. Since the day I was born, my life had been dictated by doctors and staff at Hillview.

"I want to be free," I said.

Tex frowned down at me. "Free? You mean you want a divorce?"

Oh, he thought I meant I wanted to be away from him. No. The last thing I wanted was for Tex to go away. We'd talked a lot since I'd come to live with him, but maybe it was time for us to have a more serious conversation. He mostly steered clear of anything he thought might upset me, and I appreciated that, but it was time for me to face my problems head-on.

"Is there somewhere quiet where we can talk?" I asked.

He rubbed a hand along the whiskers on his jaw. "The hotel? I could order room service, if you're hungry."

The hotel might be perfect for what I had in mind. I nodded, and his hand tightened on mine, before he led me back the way we'd come. Tex stopped at the front desk to place an order for room service, then we rode the elevator up to our floor. One of these days, I'd make my own decisions and order my own food, but I had to admit that I'd enjoyed everything he'd selected for me so far. It wasn't like he hadn't asked me before, but I never knew what to say. Ordering for me probably made him feel like he was taking care of me. When we entered our suite, I clasped my hands in front of me, suddenly feeling extremely nervous.

"What's going on, Kalani?" he asked. "If all this is too much, if you want to go home, we can do that. I'll call and make the arrangements today."

"I want to stay."

He nodded and took a seat on the couch. I eased down next to him and wondered if I should just start talking, or if I should wait for our food to arrive. If we were interrupted in the middle of my emotional and mental purge, then I might not get all the way through it.

Tex didn't break the silence between us, just sat patiently waiting. When our food arrived, he took care of everything, then sat back down. He didn't push, didn't prod. And for that I was thankful. I took a deep breath and tried to figure out where I wanted to start.

"You know how me being naked around you doesn't seem to bother me, but I can't handle you being naked?" I asked.

He nodded.

"For as long as I can remember, someone has watched me shower, watched me dress. Some of the… experiments were even conducted with me being completely naked. While a lot of the things they did to me were painful, I guess I've suppressed a lot of it. I think my mind has boxed some of it up and packed it away. I mean, I know those things happened, I remember them. But the way I felt at the time seems… distant."

"Kalani, I…"

I held up a hand. "Just let me get through this. I'm not sure I'll have the courage if I stop now."

"All right."

"You know they raped me, and made me do… things. But I was usually dressed those times, and they'd just move my clothes enough to do what they wanted to me. The only times I've ever seen a man naked below the waist was when that was happening to me. Logically, I know you wouldn't hurt me, even if you were completely naked, but I think part of my brain doesn't understand that. The thought of seeing all of you makes my heart race and brings on a panic attack because I associate that part of a man with pain and humiliation."

There was understanding and compassion in his gaze as he looked at me.

"I don't want to be damaged all my life, Tex. I want what normal people have. A home. A family. I want to lie next to you in that bed and not be scared every time you move or accidentally touch me. I want to shower with you, with both of us naked, and not freak out. I want…" I bit my lip. "I want to know why the women in movies and books enjoy sex, even ask for it. Dr. Myron said he thought I should talk to a therapist, but after Hillview… I don't trust doctors. Your Dr. Myron seemed nice enough, and his partner, but I don't think I want to see a therapist anytime soon. Not officially. I know Dr. Myron's partner treats minds and not bodies, but I don't trust those kinds of doctors."

"What exactly are you asking, Kalani? I want to give you whatever you need, but I don't want to make the wrong move."

My heart warmed a little more toward him. If someone like me was capable of being in love, I thought I was on my way to falling for Tex. He'd been amazing, kind, and so supportive. I couldn't have ever asked for a better man to spend my life with, but first I had to fix what was broken inside me.

"It's not fair for me to ask this of you, but can we take things one step at a time?" I asked.

"Like what?"

I licked my lips. "I like it when you kiss me. The books and movies say that all parts of being intimate are nice like that."

"And you want to experiment a little? See if you like doing more than kissing?" he asked.

"Yes, but... I was hoping you would be okay with keeping your clothes on, or at least your pants."

Tex moved a little closer and slowly pulled me toward him. "Sweetheart, I'll give you anything you want or need. If all you ever want to do is give me a kiss here and there, then I'll be content with that. I don't want you to do this because you feel like it's what I want."

"I'm not. I want this too. I want to be normal, Tex." I swallowed hard. What I really wanted was to be loved. I wanted what those couples in the books and movies had.

He smiled a little. "Normal is overrated. But I'll do whatever you need me to."

My cheeks flushed. "The women are usually undressed. In those scenes."

"Why don't we start out with both of us being fully dressed? If you're ready for more after that, then we can go a little further. It's not a race, angel. You set the pace, and I'll follow your lead."

"You're really okay with this?" I asked. "I don't want you to feel like I'm being a... a tease. Is that the right word?"

"Baby, I would never consider you a tease."

"Could we start with a kiss?" I asked.

He smiled and leaned a little closer. "I'll be happy to kiss you anytime you want."

My heart fluttered as his lips pressed against mine. When Tex kissed me, I didn't feel afraid. I felt...

warm, and I just wanted to melt against him, let him hold me and make all the pain and bad memories go away. His tongue flicked against my lower lip, and I let him in. No one had ever kissed me before Tex, not a real kiss. I didn't know what I was doing, but I followed his lead. We'd shared a few kisses before now, but I still felt awkward.

"You're thinking too much," he said, concern in his gaze. "Are you thinking about... Hillview?"

I shook my head. "I'm worried I'm not doing this right, that you'll be disappointed."

He cupped my cheek and lightly stroked my skin. "Sweetheart, you could never disappoint me. Try to shut out all your doubts and worries, block out the memories, and just feel. There's no right or wrong way to do this."

I quirked an eyebrow.

"Okay," he amended. "So I guess if you slobbered all over me and your tongue went up my nose that wouldn't be much of a turn-on, but stop worrying about whether you're kissing me correctly. I can assure you, I have no complaints on your technique."

My gaze dropped and my cheeks warmed when I saw the ridge of his cock straining against his jeans. No, it didn't seem like he had any complaints at all. I fought back the fear that would normally surface, and slowly reached for him. I skimmed my fingers along his length, and Tex groaned, his eyes sliding shut. His jaw tensed and his body seemed strained, as if he was struggling not to react to my touch. It was... empowering. And a bit freeing. I'd touched him, on my own, and nothing bad had happened. He hadn't lost control and forced himself on me. He hadn't demanded that I do anything. I slid my hand up his abdomen, across his chest, and gripped his shoulder, pulling him closer again. This time, I was the one who kissed him.

I could feel him holding back, felt the tension in his muscles. Gripping one of his hands, I placed it on my waist. I knew there was more than just kissing, knew that he should touch me. Even if I wasn't entirely certain I was ready yet, I knew I needed to try. I broke the kiss and focused on him, seeing the heat in his eyes. There was blatant desire etched on his face, and yet he hadn't done anything but kiss me.

"You can touch me," I said.

"Are you sure?"

I slowly nodded.

As he leaned forward to kiss me again, he tightened his hand at my waist before drawing back a little. His touch turned light and almost tentative. I wanted to assure him that I wouldn't break, but I honestly wasn't sure that was true. The way he was treating me, I wasn't panicking. But if he became more forceful, I didn't know what would happen.

Tex slowly moved his hand around to my back and pulled me a little closer and I felt his other hand under my breast. My heart beat a little faster, but I wasn't afraid. If anything, his touch seemed to excite me. My nipples hardened against the cups of my bra, and a warmth started spreading through me. Tex used his thumb to lightly stroke the underside of my breast, making me tingle.

I'd never felt desire before, not really. When he'd kissed me, it had always been nice, and I'd felt like maybe I wanted more. But it had never been like this. Tex slowly explored my body, his touch remaining light, and I knew if I asked him to stop that he would. Deep down, I knew he was nothing like the men at

Hillview, and maybe that's what had given me the courage to even attempt something like this.

"You're thinking again," he murmured against my lips. "Just feel, Kalani."

We kissed a while longer, his hands never straying below my waist, but tempting me to want more. I pushed him away and took a deep breath, trying to settle my nerves. My gaze fastened on his as I slowly removed my shirt and let it fall to the floor. I reached for his hand, and placed it over my breast. His gaze darkened and he lightly stroked me with his fingers. I knew in that moment that if I ever wanted things to go further, I'd have to prove to him that I could handle it. He might be an ex-soldier, might be a tough-as-nails biker, but he was also a tender and caring man who was afraid of hurting me.

I removed my bra, then stood and slid my pants and panties down my legs. Tex didn't move. If anything, he seemed to be made of stone in that moment. I took his hand and led him to the bedroom. There was hope blazing in his eyes, but I could tell he was fighting himself. In any other circumstances, I'd bet he'd be the type to take charge, order me around, and just take what he wanted. But he didn't want to scare me, so he stood there, immobile. It was sweet.

It took a few tugs on his shirt before he got the message and pulled it over his head. His body really was beautiful. Hardened from his time as a soldier. I lightly touched the metal tags hanging around his neck. I didn't know why he still wore them if he was no longer a soldier, but I figured he had his reasons. I let my hand trail down his abdomen, and when my fingers brushed the top of his jeans, I popped the button free. Tex sucked in a breath, and I could feel the tension radiating off him, but I wasn't stopping this time. The rasp of his zipper was loud in the otherwise quiet room, and I worked his jeans down his hips. Kneeling at his feet, I pulled off his boots, then finished removing his pants.

"Kalani…"

I looked up at him and the stark hunger on his face made my heart race. My hands trembled a little as I peeled his boxer briefs down his thighs. His cock popped free, long and hard. Tex had his hands fisted at his sides, and his chest heaved with every breath, like he was barely hanging on. I slowly reached out and wrapped my fingers around his shaft. It was soft and smooth, like silk over steel. It was amazing that something like this had caused me to be afraid for so very long. I still worried that having sex with Tex would hurt, but as gentle as he'd been with me, maybe it would be okay.

"Kalani… You don't have to do this."

"I want to," I said. "But I don't know what to do. Men always took whatever they wanted from me. I've never willingly participated before."

"You can do whatever you want to me, sweetheart, and I can promise I'll love it."

I eyed his cock a moment, and decided if I was brave enough to have sex with Tex, then I was brave enough to do this too. I licked my lips and tightened my grip on his shaft, then leaned forward and wrapped my mouth around the head of his cock. Tex groaned and I glanced up to see his eyes shut tight, and his jaw clenched. I slowly took in more of him, my lips stretching wide around his shaft. I felt a flutter of panic for a moment, but squashed it. Tex wasn't like the others. He was my husband, had been kind to me, and would never hurt me.

It took me a few minutes to figure out how to use my hand and my mouth together in order to give him pleasure. His body was wound so tight, I thought he might snap at any moment, but he just stood there, never reaching for me, never forcing his cock farther down my throat. I could taste the drops of pre-cum with every suck and lick.

"Kalani, I can't... I ... I need you to stop, please, baby."

I pulled back and looked up at him, wondering if I'd done it wrong. He almost looked like he was in pain.

"Was that not right?" I asked.

He groaned. "Sweetheart, that was almost too damn good. I didn't want to come in your mouth, and my control was close to breaking. Do you think you'd be okay with me giving you pleasure now?"

I stood and eyed the bed before crawling to the center of the big mattress and lying down. I flung my arms out to my sides and waited to see what Tex would do. He stood at the foot of the bed, just watching me for a moment, then reached for my ankles and eased my legs apart. My breath caught and my heart raced. Tex placed a knee on the bed between my splayed legs and then stopped. His hands tightened on my ankles before sliding up my legs in a gentle caress.

"If I do anything that scares you, say something and I'll stop," he said. "I want to make you feel good, but I don't want you to be afraid of me."

"I'm not," I assured him.

Tex came closer, then braced his hands on either side of my body. His gaze locked on mine as he lowered his head and traced my nipple with his tongue. A strange sensation I'd never felt before seemed to travel from my nipple to the junction of my thighs. His lips closed around the rosy tip of my breast and he sucked, his tongue flicking against the hardened point.

"Oh, God!"

My hands seemed to move of their own volition, one landing on his shoulder, and the other threading through his hair and pressing him closer. Tex took his time, licking, sucking, tasting. Then he moved to the other breast and gave it the same treatment. I felt warm and slick between my thighs, something that I hadn't experienced before. Tex reached between our bodies and his fingers lightly stroked over the lips of my pussy. I gasped and arched against him as little sparks of pleasure shot through me.

His thumb pressed against my clit and rubbed back and forth. It was enough to make my body feel like it was taking off like a rocket, and I screamed out his name. His real name.

"Houston! Oh, God! Don't stop, please don't stop."

He sucked harder on my breast as his thumb continued to rub. I felt one of his fingers start to ease inside me, and I tensed for a moment. He thrust his finger in and out of my pussy, then added a second one. The sensations became almost unbearable and soon I was screaming out his name again. He overwhelmed me with pleasure again and again, until I was growing hoarse. I lost track of how many times I felt like fireworks were exploding around me.

My body trembled as he drew away from me, his fingers slowly sliding out of me. Tex looked down at me with such need, such desire, that I knew I was ready for what came next. I wanted him. I wanted to know if everything else could feel as incredible as what he'd just done to me.

"We can stop now," he said.

I shook my head. "Keep going. I want you. I want… I want to experience all of it, the way it should have been all this time. I wish you could have been my first."

His body came down over mine and I felt his cock brush against my pussy. My breath caught, but he didn't thrust hard and deep. Tex took his time, easing into me, and his gaze never leaving mine. I could feel his cock throbbing inside me, stretching me wide, but it didn't hurt.

"I want to feel you come on my cock," he said. "I've never taken anyone bare. Not even Janessa's mom. You'll be my first, and I want to be the first man to make you come like this. I've always worried about birth control before, but…"

I smiled a little. "It's okay. You don't have to tiptoe around what happened to me. And you're the first man who's made me come at all. I've never known pleasure until you."

Heat flared in his eyes, then he lowered his head and claimed my lips. As his tongue tangled with mine, he began thrusting his cock in and out of me. Slowly at first, then faster. I wrapped my legs around his waist, and Tex slid a little deeper with every stroke. I could feel something building inside me again. Every time he slid deep, his pelvic bone brushed my clit and set off shockwaves of pleasure. Soon, he was nearly pounding me into the mattress, the last of his control gone. But I didn't fear him, didn't fear what was happening between us.

Tex reached between us and I felt his fingers stroke my clit. It only took a few swipes, and then I was screaming out his name again. He groaned and buried his face in my neck, his hips jerking against me, all sense of rhythm gone. He ground against me, and I felt a splash of warmth inside me.

His breath came out in pants and his skin was slicked with sweat. I ran my hand down his back and he pushed his hips tighter to mine.

"Did I hurt you?" he asked, looking at me.

"No." I smiled softly. "That was wonderful."

"So, it's something you might want to do again?" he asked.

I leaned up and brushed my lips against his. "You can do that to me as often as you want."

"Oh, sweet girl. You shouldn't have said that. We may never leave this bed for the rest of our honeymoon."

A warmth spread through me and I flushed at his words. "I don't think I'd mind that at all."

Tex smiled, and for the first time since I'd met him, he seemed genuinely happy. I had to admit, I felt happy myself. Now that I'd overcome my fear of being intimate with him, maybe we could have a real marriage, become a real family. I couldn't think of anything I wanted more.

Chapter Seven

Tex
Two Weeks Later

I woke with Kalani pressed against my side, her hand on my chest. A smile lifted the corners of my lips as I thought about how insatiable she'd been after she'd overcome her fear. Being with Kalani was better than anything I'd ever experienced, and I hadn't lacked for female company over the years. Not having to use a condom might have had a little to do with it, but I knew it was mostly because she was mine. She'd trusted me to keep her safe, trusted me not only with her emotions but her body, and I wouldn't fail her. I'd never really thought about getting married before, but I didn't regret making Kalani my wife.

My phone buzzed from the pocket of my jeans, and I eased out from under Kalani so I could answer it. Preferably before it woke her up. We were only supposed to be here a few days, but we'd ended up extending our stay. It had taken some convincing, because I hadn't wanted to leave my daughter for so long, but Torch had assured me she was fine. And Janessa seemed excited to be around all the babies in the club. I had to admit that I'd loved every minute with my new wife, but I was missing my daughter.

I jerked the device from my jeans and stepped into the other room before I answered. Torch's name flashed across my screen and my gut clenched. Had something happened to Janessa? Or had Hillview come for Kalani? Last time I talked to the Pres, he'd said everything was fine. The paperwork was still in limbo for making Janessa my daughter legally, but at least I had temporary custody. It didn't mean something hadn't gone wrong though.

"Torch," I said as I answered the call.

"I know it's still early there, but this couldn't wait."

The feeling of unease intensified. Then I heard him hand the phone off to someone else.

"How are things with the new wife?" Wire asked.

"Good. I think. Unless you're about to tell me that shit has hit the fan."

Wire chuckled. "Nothing quite that bad. Have you, um, slept together yet? I know that wasn't a likely outcome of this trip with everything she's been through. We'd honestly hoped that by extending your trip maybe she'd warm up to you a bit more."

"Yeah, why?"

"Whitby has the cops looking for Kalani. It seems he's done keeping her his dirty little secret. The news is saying that Kalani Whitby is disturbed and is dangerous. There's a reward for her return to Hillview."

I cursed and started pacing. "What the fuck, Wire? I thought you said he'd want to keep things quiet as long as possible. Why come forward now?"

"A social worker stopped by the morning after you left for Vegas. I didn't want to mention it before, but something's come up. They talked to Janessa, making sure her needs were met. The woman didn't seem too thrilled that your daughter was hanging around a bunch of bikers, but I still had enough strings to pull that it wasn't an issue. We explained you were getting married and on a short honeymoon, but she insisted on talking to your daughter and seemed satisfied that Janessa was all right. We'd thought that was the end of it."

"And this has what to do with Kalani?" I asked.

"Janessa told the social worker about Kalani and how she'd been treated at Hillview. I think the state made an inquiry into Hillview after that visit, so now Whitby is scrambling to cover his tracks and seem like a concerned doctor and father."

"But there's nothing wrong with Kalani, except for the shit he put her through. He and his staff tortured her for her entire life. She was born because her mother was raped for fuck's sake. Does he really think he can get her back?" I asked. "She's not the insane one. He is."

"He's trying damn hard to get his hands on her and make Hillview look legit. The social worker came back to talk to Janessa again the other day, asking a lot of questions about Kalani. She's concerned that what Whitby says may hold some truth, but she's not one hundred percent in his corner. Janessa has told her what little she knows about Hillview, but Kalani kept her as sheltered as possible."

"So what do we do?" I asked. "I can't stay away forever, but I don't want to risk Kalani being taken back to that nightmare of a place. And why the fuck does that have anything to do with us sleeping together?"

"Because if she allowed you to touch her like that, then it means she's starting to heal. It's been a month since she's been away from Hillview. I'm going to send you the name and address of a psychiatrist in Vegas. I know how Kalani feels about doctors, but you need to get her to talk to this person. We need an evaluation that we can show to prove she's not crazy. I mean, I could manufacture one, or pay someone off," Wire said.

"I'm not putting her through that shit. If she doesn't want to see a doctor, she's not going to.

Anyone upsets her or makes her withdraw again, and I'll fucking kill them. She's made a lot of progress and I don't want it to be derailed."

"Torch and I have been talking. If you really don't want to make her see a shrink, there's another way to sort this out, but it means you and Kalani need to stay out of town a while longer."

"I don't like being away from Janessa for so long," I said. "I already feel like a bad father taking this two-week honeymoon."

"We can make arrangements for Janessa to meet you. Torch will smooth things over with social services. There's a club in the panhandle, not too far from here, that's helped us out before. Devil's Boneyard. You were gone when we first talked to them, but their VP helped Venom's old lady get to us safely. He's also Bull's father-in-law. I've already talked to Scratch and he said their club is willing to help your family. We can get Janessa to you once you've arrived and made contact with us," Wire said. "I can have the jet ready to take you there in a few hours."

"And Casper VanHorne is fine with us just commandeering his jet whenever we need it? Because from what I've heard of the man, that doesn't sound likely," I said.

Wire snorted. "He's Isabella's daddy. If she tells him we need his help, then he'll help. If that means we need his jet for a few days, or weeks, then I'm sure it won't be an issue."

I could hear Torch and someone else talking in the background. It sounded like Wire covered the phone, and I heard more murmuring. I didn't know what the fuck was going on, but I didn't like it. At all. My family was in trouble and I wanted to fix the problem. But I couldn't just leave Kalani with someone and head home to take care of Hillview and Whitby. She didn't trust just anyone, and I needed her to feel safe. Yes, she'd improved a lot since we'd been in Vegas, but she was still healing.

"Torch and I are working on something," Wire said. "It's going to take me a few days to get everything organized. Once it's all in place, Hillview won't be an issue anymore. And none of us are going to get our hands dirty. I know you want to take them out, trust me I get it, but I think the Dixie Reapers need to keep some distance from this one. We're already connected to that place through Janessa and Kalani."

"What are you going to do?" I asked.

"I'll tell you after the fact. That way you can deny that you knew anything about it if someone asks. I'll send a text when it's time to head to the jet, and I'll have a car waiting downstairs to take you to the airfield," Wire said. "And, Tex? You might think about how you're going to spin this so Kalani doesn't freak out. You've already seen that she's the type to sacrifice herself. If she thinks turning herself in to Whitby will keep him away from Janessa, then she'll do it. The man hasn't made a move for your daughter yet, but I'm sure Kalani is worried about it."

"I know."

"Watch for my message," Wire said, then hung up.

I tossed the phone onto the couch and rubbed my hands up and down my face. This situation was beyond fucked up. I wanted to tear Whitby apart with my bare hands, maybe arrange for him to get some justice behind bars as some big thug's plaything. But my club wasn't letting me anywhere near this, and while I appreciated their concern, I fucking hated it. It was my job to take care of my family, and the club wasn't letting me do that.

I didn't know how long it would be before Wire sent the car to pick us up, so I went to wake up Kalani. She needed her sleep, but she also needed to stay safe. I slid back under the sheets and pulled her against my chest, running my hand down her hair. The soft floral scent that seemed to cling to her teased my nose. We hadn't packed anything other than some clothes, and I knew the hotel soap didn't smell like that. It was just a unique scent that Kalani seemed to always have. Even when I'd carried her out of Hillview I'd noticed it.

She murmured in her sleep and burrowed closer to me. I smiled and wished we could spend the day in bed. I'd have loved to see how much she was willing to experiment, but I wasn't going to push her. It was a miracle she'd touched me that night, or let me touch her, much less stayed awake until the wee hours making love. We'd spent every night since then tangled up in the sheets with her screaming my name. My heart twisted in my chest as I realized that's exactly what we'd been doing all this time. I'd fucked plenty of women, but I'd never made love to one before.

"Kalani, we need to get up." I brushed a kiss on the top of her head. "Come on. Wire is sending the jet for us today."

I felt her freeze, then she bolted upright, eyes wide and I could see her heart pounding in her chest.

"What's wrong? Why is he sending for us? Did something happen to Janessa?"

I smoothed her hair behind her ear. "No, baby. Janessa is fine, but we need to go somewhere and lie low for a few days. Maybe a week. Wire said he'd make sure Janessa is brought to us once we reach Florida."

"Florida?" Her brow furrowed. "Why couldn't we just stay here?"

"The club has some allies in Florida, and that's where we're going. I know you still aren't used to being around a bunch of bikers, but the VP of this other club is related to one of my Dixie Reapers brothers, and he's helped the club out before. If Wire thinks we can trust him, I think we need to go."

"And Janessa will come to us?" she asked.

"That's the plan."

"How much time do we have?" she asked.

"I'm not certain. Wire thought it might take a few hours. I thought we could get up and dress. Maybe go somewhere for breakfast? I'd wanted to take you out to a nice dinner and a show tonight, but we'll have to plan another trip to Vegas sometime in the future."

"Florida?" she asked again. "It looks sunny in the movies. And the ocean is there. I've never seen the ocean."

"I'm not sure where we're going in the panhandle, but if the beach is anywhere nearby, I'll make sure we go at least once. And we can always plan a family vacation once all this is over." I leaned forward and kissed her softly. "Come on, baby. Let's enjoy our last little bit of time on our honeymoon. Once Janessa meets us in Florida, it won't be just the two of us anymore."

"I miss her," Kalani said.

I cupped her cheek. "I know you do. I miss her too, but we'll be seeing her soon. And we're going to have the rest of our lives with her, right?"

Kalani nodded.

"Now come on, Mrs. Rodriguez. Get your gorgeous ass into the shower."

She giggled and dashed into the bathroom. I couldn't help but smile as I thought about how different she was compared to our first day in Vegas. More open, less afraid. I knew us sleeping together was a huge deal, but it seemed to have fixed something that was broken inside Kalani. Or maybe it had just helped us grow even closer over the past two weeks. Whatever it was, I was thankful for that giggle and that smile. It meant she was healing.

Steam was billowing out of the shower, and I leaned against the wall a moment and just watched her. The shower wall and door were glass, and I could see every droplet of water run down Kalani's body. She was so damn beautiful, it almost hurt to look at her. Over the last month, with regular meals, she'd filled out nicely. She considered herself plump, and maybe she was a little, but I loved it. Her breasts were more than a handful, and so was her ass. Her waist nipped in, but her belly was slightly rounded. She was fucking adorable.

I stepped into the shower and let the door close behind me. My cock pointed straight up and might have scared her in the past, but not anymore. Thank fuck because I got hard every time I was near her. Hell, just thinking about her made me hard. The water soaked me as I reached for the soap and began lathering Kalani from head to toe, taking my time with all my favorite parts of her.

Her nipples were hard and there was a flush to her cheeks that told me she was just as turned on as I was. I didn't know for sure how long we had, but I didn't think either of us was getting out of this shower without some satisfaction first.

I nuzzled her ear and slowly turned her to face the wall. "Put your hands on the tile and stick that sweet ass out for me."

Her hands trembled a little but she did as I'd asked. I ran my hands down her side, then slipped one around her hip and dipped my fingers between her legs. I nudged her legs farther apart with my foot, then teased her clit until the tension in her body began to melt away. I hadn't taken her from behind yet because I'd wanted to make sure she knew it was me that was buried inside her. The way she'd tensed when I turned her around told me that had been the right thing to do, but now I wanted to prove to her that she was safe with me even this way.

I squeezed her breast and tweaked her nipple while I teased her clit. My cock nestled between her ass cheeks and I couldn't help but thrust between them, rubbing my dick against her. I slid two fingers inside her pussy and groaned at how fucking hot and wet she was.

She whimpered and I rubbed her clit some more, wanting to get her as close to coming as possible before I slipped inside her. My cock rubbed against her ass again, and I hoped one day she'd let me take her there too. I could only imagine how fucking tight she'd be.

Kalani trembled and pushed back against me. I lined my cock up with her sweet pussy and plunged inside, going balls deep. She cried out and I felt her channel squeeze my dick so damn good. I knew I wasn't going to last, so I kept teasing her clit as I stroked in and out of her.

The second I felt her coming, I let loose and thrust hard and deep again and again. My balls drew up and I felt a tingle in my spine right before I erupted inside her. I groaned and buried my face in her neck as

I plunged into her three more times, not stopping until the last drops of cum had been wrung from me.

She leaned her head against the tiled wall, but didn't try to pull away. If I could stay buried inside her indefinitely, I'd die a happy man. Even though I'd just come, my dick was still pretty fucking hard.

Only Kalani got that reaction from me. I rubbed her clit again, slowly. She shuddered in my arms, but I felt her spread her thighs a little farther. Oh yeah, my baby wanted more. I held still, my cock buried in her as far as I could go. I circled and pinched her clit until she was screaming out my name and coating my cock in her cream again.

"Fuck yeah, sweetheart. Give me all that cream."

She moaned.

"You like coming on my cock, don't you?"

Her cheeks flushed and she shyly nodded. "I never knew it could be like this. I mean, I'd read about it in books, but I didn't... I thought maybe it was all just made up. But every time with you is amazing."

"I'd make you come all morning long if we had more time."

I slipped free of her body and washed her again. We quickly dried off and dressed, then grabbed breakfast in the restaurant downstairs. We didn't have much to pack since we'd never really unpacked. We'd been living out of our suitcases since we'd arrived. After we ate, we took a short walk and I took a few pictures of her around Vegas, even asked an older couple to take a few of us together.

By the time Wire sent me a text, we were back in the hotel and Kalani was pacing nervously. I knew she was worried about the new bikers, but I'd never let anything happen to her.

A car was waiting at the curb when we stepped out of the hotel. The driver took our bags and placed them in the trunk, then held open the back door for us. I would have preferred to sit up front and watch for trouble, but I also wanted to reassure Kalani. The trip to the airfield was uneventful, and soon we were on our way to Florida.

Chapter Eight

Kalani

The men who met us when we landed in Florida were intimidating. Tex assured me that they were going to help us, but a chill skated down my spine as I looked them over. They wore those black leather vest things like Tex and his club had. A cut. That's what he'd called it. Except this crew had Devil's Boneyard MC stitched on theirs. The man I assumed was the leader had Scratch -- VP on his cut. His eyes looked hard, and his muscular arms were on display. I couldn't lie. I was nervous as hell. They outnumbered Tex and could take him out, then I'd be at their mercy.

"Welcome to Devil's Boneyard territory," Scratch said, shaking Tex's hand. His gaze slid to me and I shrank back a little.

"This is my wife, Kalani," Tex said, putting his arm around my waist. "And my daughter Janessa is coming soon."

Scratch nodded. "We have a small home on the compound that you can use while you're here. I made sure it was stocked with groceries to last a few days, but if you need anything, I'll have a Prospect assigned to you."

"We appreciate your assistance," Tex said. "My club thought it best if my family was out of town for a little bit."

"Wire told me a little about Hillview. Nasty place, but no worries. It will be taken care of soon enough. My daughter is now a Dixie Reaper, and Casper VanHorne's daughter is also a Dixie Reaper. Between the Dixie Reapers, my club, and Casper, that Dr. Whitby won't know what hit him," Scratch said. "Our hacker, Shade, is working with Wire to get some stuff set up. And that's as much as I'm allowed to tell you."

My heart stuttered at the name Whitby. I felt like I should have felt something for the man who shared my DNA, but all I could hope was that they made him suffer horribly for what he'd done to my mother and me. Not to mention all those other poor patients. I was certain there was a place reserved for him in hell, and it was my hope he'd be residing there soon enough. He might have provided the sperm that created me, but I wanted nothing to do with him.

I'd learned long ago that fighting made things worse, but being with Tex had given me the courage to fight once more. I didn't want to go back there, ever, and I never wanted another woman or child to be harmed by Whitby or his staff. I didn't know what had been planned for Hillview, but I hoped it was truly horrible. Each and every person who worked at Hillview deserved to be tortured, abused, and killed slowly. But I worried about the patients still trapped there. They didn't deserve to be hurt more than they already had been. Most were innocent. Some were completely crazy, but they didn't deserve what had been done to them.

"Since you don't have your bike, we brought an SUV," Scratch said. He motioned to a man with Prospect stitched on his cut. "This is Seamus. He'll be the one to take care of you during your stay. Make sure you get his number, and you can call him at any hour of the day. For anything."

Tex gave Seamus a nod. I couldn't tell his age very well, but he seemed younger than Tex, but older than me. He had rather striking green eyes, and a smile that set me at ease. His gaze didn't stay on me for long, but that might have had more to do with the giant man holding onto me. I'd noticed that Tex didn't like it when men looked at me for very long. I didn't think he was necessarily possessive, but he probably thought he was protecting me. Even though I'd had a major breakthrough, I was still damaged from my years at Hillview, and I was thankful that he was watching over me.

Seamus led the way to a black SUV, and Tex slid into the backseat with me. His hand gripped mine, and I tuned him and Seamus out as we drove out of the airfield and down a highway. I didn't see the ocean, but I wondered if it was close enough to visit. It seemed a shame to be so close, yet not get to see something so wonderful. I'd seen pictures of the sun setting over the water on TV and on Tex's computer, but I doubted it could hold a candle to the real thing. Maybe I'd get a chance to find out before we went home.

The Devil's Boneyard compound didn't look much different from the Dixie Reapers. Except their clubhouse looked more like a warehouse and was two stories. We drove past the clubhouse, but all I could see were grass and palm trees. In the distance were small dots that I soon learned were homes. They'd built their houses farther away from the clubhouse than the Dixie Reapers had, and I wondered why they'd done it that way. Not enough to ask, though.

The SUV pulled to a stop in front of a small one-story blue home. There were two palm trees in the front yard and a cobbled walkway that led to the front door. It didn't have shutters, but had some sort of awning over each window, and the door was painted a bright red. I wondered if someone normally lived here or if it remained vacant for times like this. Had we kicked someone out of their home?

Seamus seemed to read my mind as his gaze clashed with mine.

"We keep a few empty homes for visitors who are here with their families. There are a few rooms at the clubhouse too for single men who stop by. Scratch didn't think you'd want to stay at the clubhouse, though," Seamus said.

"Thanks," Tex said. "I don't think Kalani could handle what goes on in the clubhouse, and I definitely don't want my daughter around that shit. She's only fourteen."

Seamus nodded. "The Pres would have been here to greet you, but he's taking care of some business out of state. The house's unlocked, and you should have everything you need."

Tex gripped my hand and started leading me to the front door, but Seamus' voice stopped us.

"Here's my number, in case you need something. Doesn't matter what time of day it is," he said, handing Tex a small piece of paper. His gaze shot toward me again, then he quickly looked away. "We want y'all to be comfortable during your stay."

At first, I'd thought he wouldn't look at me for long because of Tex, but now I had to wonder if everyone in the club knew what had happened to me. Did he not want to look at me because he felt I was tainted? I began to feel a little sick to my stomach and hoped that Seamus would move along.

"Appreciate it," Tex said. "We'll probably settle in and wait for our daughter to get here."

Our. Daughter. My heart stuttered and I looked up at him. I knew we were married and that made me Janessa's stepmom, but he hadn't called her ours before now. I liked the sound of that. We'd grown close at Hillview, and I hoped she wouldn't think I was trying to take her dad from her. We hadn't had a chance to really talk since Tex had taken me to Vegas. He'd called to check on her a few times, but they had been brief conversations. We'd left for Vegas so suddenly I really had no idea what she thought about all of this.

Tex shut the door and set our bags down. The house wasn't very big. There was a small tiled section at the front door, then you pretty much stepped into the living room when you entered the house. There was an archway that led to the dining room, and I saw a door off to the right. A door opened on the left of the living room and I saw a square hallway. Tex released my hand and I decided to explore a little. The bathroom was rather tiny with a shower/tub combination, but it was bigger than the bathroom I'd had at Hillview. The other two doors led to bedrooms. One looked out over the front yard and the other had backyard views. I opened one of the doors off the back bedroom and was pleasantly surprised to find a sunroom.

"Is this the room you want?" Tex asked from the bedroom doorway, motioning toward the queen-sized bed.

"That one's fine." I ran my hand along the back of the white wicker sofa that faced a wall of windows. "This is nice. I bet it's a great place to read."

Tex set our bags on the bed, then joined me, his arm sliding around my waist. "You want a sunroom? I'm sure I could add one off the kitchen. Or we could ask Torch for a bigger home. Three bedrooms is plenty of space right now, but we might want more space later."

His words made me freeze. I felt every muscle in my body tense as I started counting off the weeks I'd been with Tex. I might not be the smartest person in the world, but I knew I had a period every four weeks and that not having one could mean I was pregnant. I hadn't had one since two weeks before Tex carried me out of the asylum. My heart started pounding and I wondered if it was too soon to take a pregnancy test. We'd only been sleeping together for two weeks. Tex tightened his hold on me. It wasn't possible, right? I knew I'd been sterilized. That was a permanent thing, wasn't it?

"What's wrong, Kalani?"

"You want more children?" I asked.

"I'd never really thought about it. I mean, it might have been nice, but since you can't have children I'm okay with just having Janessa. Unless you want to adopt later." He released me and took a step back. "You're really great with Janessa. If you want more children, we'll figure it out."

I turned to face him, and I could tell he was disappointed at the thought of not having more children. "I'm late."

He stared.

"Um, I should have started my period by now, and I haven't, so…"

He pulled his phone out and the scrap of paper Seamus had given him.

"Seamus, I need a local doctor for Kalani. And I need a way to get her there as soon as possible."

He growled and his eyes narrowed.

"Just get a damn car to me and the name and location of a doctor. Don't worry about why she needs one." He ended the call and glared at the phone. "Nosy fucker."

"You probably scared him," I said. "Isn't he responsible for making sure everything is fine here?

With us I mean. He probably thinks I got hurt or something and is worried that scary guy in charge will kick his ass."

"He needs to worry about me kicking his ass."

"I'm fine. And it's probably too soon to tell if I'm pregnant. Maybe I just missed it this time because of all the stress."

He came toward me and pulled me tight against his chest. "I want the doctor to look you over. I wish we were home and you could see Dr. Myron."

I wasn't too thrilled over seeing anyone in a white lab coat, but I knew I'd have to get over it eventually. Not everyone was like Whitby and his minions. I knew that, I really did, but just the sight of one of those coats, or someone in scrubs, was enough to make me panic.

Tex kissed me, and I had to admit that as distractions went, it was a good one. The doorbell rang a moment later, and Tex practically dragged me through the house. Seamus was out front, the SUV parked in the driveway. He looked worried as his gaze flicked over to me, then back to Tex.

"The club uses Dr. Kameron. I've already called and told him we were coming in, but I didn't know the reason to give him," Seamus said.

Tex didn't say anything, just led me over to the SUV and climbed in back with me. Seamus looked at us in the rearview mirror every few minutes as he drove through the small town. He parked outside a non-descript brick building. If it weren't for the metal plaque next to the door that said Dr. Kameron, I'd have never known it was a doctor's office.

We followed Seamus inside. A blonde, bubbly receptionist greeted him. If the amount of cleavage she showed was any indication, she had a thing for the biker. I almost felt sorry for her since Seamus was polite but obviously not interested.

"Dr. Kameron said she could go straight back to room three. I'll let him know you're here," the receptionist said. She picked up a clipboard and handed it to me. "You'll need to fill this out, but you can do it in the room while you wait."

Seamus remained in the waiting room, but Tex went back with me. He helped me onto the padded table, but as I stared at the blank forms, I had no idea what to put for most of the information. Tex eventually took the clipboard from me and started filling in most of the blanks. He'd just finished when the door opened and a blond man walked in. He had on the dreaded white coat, but there was kindness in his eyes and his smile was genuine.

"I'm Dr. Kameron," he said, holding out his hand first to me, then Tex. "What can I help you with today?"

"We're just visiting the Devil's Boneyard," Tex said. "My wife thinks she might be pregnant, and I didn't want to wait to find out. We could be here a few days or a week. If she needs a special diet or anything, I'd rather know now."

"Um. There's something else, though. I was told my tubes were tied, so I didn't think it was possible for this to happen," I said.

Dr. Kameron nodded.

"Mrs...." He picked up the clipboard and scanned it. "Mrs. Rodriguez, while having your tubes tied usually works pretty well, there are cases where they have grown back. So, yes, it's possible you could be pregnant if you've been having unprotected sex. When was your last cycle?"

"About six weeks ago. I don't know the exact date, but I'm pretty sure it's been about that long."

The doctor nodded and pulled his stethoscope from around his neck.

"Well, let me check you over and I'll order a blood test. We can run the lab work here in house, so you won't have to wait long for the results. If you are pregnant, I can give you a prescription for prenatal vitamins."

Dr. Kameron listened to my heart, checked my eyes, ears, and throat. He asked questions along the way, some of which I didn't know the answer to, but I told him what I could. I didn't know if Tex wanted him to know about Hillview or why we were in Florida, so I didn't volunteer the information. Knowing my husband, he'd insist that I see Dr. Myron when we got back home anyway.

When Dr. Kameron was finished with his exam, he said everything sounded and looked great, then he ordered a nurse to come take blood. I was no stranger to needles, but I had a strong dislike for them. She took several vials of blood, which I didn't understand. I'd have thought a pregnancy test would only need one vial of blood. The nurse left and Tex and I had nothing to do but wait. He paced the room for what seemed like forever before Dr. Kameron returned.

"Why did you need so much blood?" I asked.

"I wanted to check a few things. You're a little low on iron. I'll prescribe some iron pills, along with the prenatal vitamins. Your regular doctor will probably test you again in a few weeks and see if your iron levels are higher. I can send him the results of today's lab work and visit. Aside from the anemia, everything looks great," Dr. Kameron said.

"So, she is pregnant?" Tex asked, moving closer to me and reaching for my hand.

"That she is." Dr. Kameron smiled. "Congratulations to both of you. She'll need to schedule an appointment with her regular OB-GYN when you get back home. They may even run another pregnancy test. Some doctors prefer to have their own results, especially in the case of specialists."

"Are there any dietary changes we should be aware of?" Tex asked.

"She should limit her caffeine intake, eat plenty of fruits and vegetables. Increasing how much milk and water she drinks wouldn't hurt. I'm sure her doctor will have more details of how they want to handle the pregnancy," Dr. Kameron said.

"Thank you, doctor," I said.

"It was very nice to meet both of you. If you have any medical needs while you're visiting the Devil's Boneyard, I hope you'll come back and see me."

"I haven't had a chance to figure out health insurance yet," Tex said. "We were just married a few weeks ago. But I can either write a check or pay with my bank card for today's visit."

Dr. Kameron waved a hand. "Devil's Boneyard has already covered it. I owe them a few favors, and they called in one of them. But you'll probably want to call about insurance sooner rather than later. Having a baby can be very expensive."

"Thanks again, Doc," Tex said, shaking the man's hand.

Dr. Kameron left and we made our way back to the waiting room. Seamus looked a little worried and like he'd been running his hands through his hair. He stood when we approached, but he still wouldn't look at me for very long.

"Everything all right?" Seamus asked.

"More than all right. It seems we're having a baby," Tex said, a huge smile on his face.

Seamus seemed to relax almost immediately, the tension in his shoulders easing. "Congratulations. I was worried something was really wrong when I heard them say something about blood work."

"Dr. Kameron said he was giving us two prescriptions," Tex said.

Seamus nodded toward the front desk. "Anna will have them most likely. There's a pharmacy up the road. We can go there and drop them off, and I can swing by when they're ready and pick them up for you. I'm sure you'd rather get home than wait around for them."

"Thank you," I said softly.

Seamus looked at me and smiled a little, then quickly looked back to Tex.

"Is there something wrong with me?" I asked.

Seamus jerked his head my way, his eyes wide. "What?"

"You never look at me for more than a few seconds. Are you disgusted because of what happened to me? Am I so hideous you can't stand to look at me?"

He groaned and closed his eyes. "Fuck." He opened his eyes and focused on me. "I wasn't trying to make you feel bad. We were told that you didn't trust men. I didn't want to make you uncomfortable or scared."

"Oh." I bit my lip. "It won't bother me if you make eye contact for longer than a few seconds. Just don't move too quickly, especially if you're reaching for me."

"Or better yet, don't fucking touch my wife," Tex said, his gaze narrowed and a hint of growl in his voice.

Seamus held up his hands and took a step back. "No problem. She's perfectly safe from me."

"Can we go back to the house?" I asked. "After that long flight, I'm a little tired."

Tex kissed my cheek. "We can go take a nap while Seamus gets your pills. I'll leave the front door unlocked and he can leave them in the living room."

"I can take you back to the compound first," Seamus offered. "I have some things I can do around town while I wait for the pharmacy to fill the scripts. And if you need anything in the meantime, you can call or text."

Tex nodded, then went over to the receptionist to get my prescriptions, leaving me with a Seamus who looked like he felt all kinds of awkward. I almost felt sorry for him.

"For the record," Seamus said. "I heard about what happened, and I think you're really brave. A lot of people wouldn't have survived all that. It either would have killed them or they'd have felt the need to end their lives. The fact you're here, married, and starting a family shows that you're really strong."

"Thanks. I don't feel very strong most days, but I'm getting better. Tex has helped me a lot. I trust him, and I know he'd never hurt me. It's being around other men that is still a little bit of a problem for me."

He nodded. "That's understandable. But I think you're doing great."

I smiled. Tex returned to my side and handed a piece of paper to Seamus. He placed a hand on my waist, and I had to admit that I liked it when he got a bit possessive. I'd thought he was just being protective, but maybe I'd had it wrong. After everything I'd been through, an alpha male should have been the last thing I wanted, but maybe it's exactly what I'd needed.

We rode back to the little house in silence, and Seamus didn't even get out of the car when we pulled up. Tex led me into the house and straight back to the bedroom. He knelt at my feet and removed my shoes, then helped me into bed. I scooted over to give him room, and after he pulled off his boots, he slid in next to me. With his arms around me, and my cheek pressed to his chest, I drifted off within minutes. I vaguely remembering Seamus returning a few hours later, and think I heard the phone when it rang. The only thing that woke me completely was Tex slipping out of the bed after the sun had set.

Chapter Nine

Tex

I'd tried to get out of bed without waking Kalani, but I'd failed. The doorbell rang for the third time and I hurried to answer it. Either something urgent was going on, or Janessa had finally arrived. Before I'd fallen asleep, I'd sent a text to Wire, letting him know that we were here and as settled as we were getting. I had no idea how my daughter was getting here, but I trusted my club to take care of her.

When I flung open the door, my daughter launched herself into my arms. I smiled as I hugged her tight.

"Did you have a good trip?" I asked.

"Yeah. Gabe brought me," she said, motioning to the Prospect behind her. "Torch told him to stay the night and head back tomorrow. But if you need him for backup or something, I'm sure he could stay."

"Thanks," I told the man and gave him a nod.

I pulled Janessa into the house and took her bag from her. If my daughter thought I needed backup, I wondered just what Torch had told her. Did she know why she was here? I wanted to keep her as innocent of club dealings as possible, but I knew she'd hear things eventually. I didn't want her to think I was some criminal. Yeah, the Dixie Reapers sometimes did things that weren't necessarily legal -- or were a fuck ton illegal -- but they never hurt anyone who didn't deserve it. I'd trust them with my life, and with the lives of my family.

Kalani came into the room and was tackled by our daughter.

"Easy," I told Janessa. "She's carrying precious cargo."

Kalani's eyes went wide and I wondered if she'd wanted to keep it a secret longer. We hadn't had a chance to discuss it, but I didn't see the harm in people knowing she was pregnant. Hell, I wanted to shout it from the rooftops. My wife was carrying my second kid. I couldn't think of anything more wonderful. I only wished Janessa's mom had been half as great as Kalani. But then, if she had been, I never would have found Kalani.

Janessa released Kalani and gave me a confused look.

"How do you feel about being a big sister?" I asked.

Janessa seemed to freeze for a second, and then she started screaming and bouncing around the room. She clapped her hands and smiled so widely I thought her face might crack. I honestly hadn't seen her that excited or happy about anything.

"Seriously? We're having a baby?" Janessa asked.

"You're all right with that?" Kalani asked, coming to stand by my side.

"All right? I think it's awesome," Janessa said. "I get a mom and a brother or sister! Oh! What if it's both? Maybe you're having twins!"

Janessa started squealing and bouncing again.

"So you're not upset I married your dad or that we're having a baby?" Kalani asked, looking uncertain.

"Why would I be upset?" Janessa asked, coming to a stop. "You've been like a mom to me the last seven years. Now it's just official. And I'd always wanted a brother or sister. Growing up it was kind of lonely. My family never really wanted me. Until I met you, I hadn't known what it was like for someone to care about me."

My throat tightened at her admission. I felt like the worst fucking father on the planet for having abandoned her all those years ago. If I'd had any idea how her life would turn out, I might have done things differently, but when the Chief of Police threatens you with prison and has the entire town backing him? Yeah, you get the fuck out of town and do what the big man says. I hated that he'd ruined so many lives, and I'd let him. He'd had my baby girl committed to Hillview on some bogus charge just so he wouldn't have to look at her. If the fates hadn't already taken care of his ass, we'd be having a lengthy, painful conversation.

Tears gathered in Kalani's eyes, and it looked like a weight had been lifted from her shoulders. Her body relaxed and it made me realize that I hadn't even noticed how tense she was. Janessa hugged her, and then I wrapped my arms around both of them. I wished Kalani had said something about her concerns before now, and I wondered if she'd been carrying that around with her ever since we'd arrived in Vegas. It had never occurred to me that she would worry. Janessa knew why we were leaving that day, and while we hadn't had much time together, I felt I had gotten to know my daughter well enough to know she'd have said something if she was unhappy. The way my daughter asked Kalani's opinion, and even seemed protective when my brothers were around, I'd never had any doubts that Janessa would accept Kalani into our family. It had been clear from the beginning my daughter loved Kalani.

"What would my girls like to do tonight?" I asked. "We could order in some Chinese, assuming this town has Chinese food, and then binge-watch some movies. The TV in the living room looks like one of those Smart TVs so I'm sure we can access Netflix or something. Or do you want to go out to eat?"

"How are we going anywhere?" Janessa asked. "You don't have a car."

"There's a Prospect assigned to help us out while we're here," I said. "I can give Seamus a call. I think we passed an Italian place earlier today and a Mexican restaurant. Either of those sound good?"

Kalani rubbed her stomach. "Lasagna? With extra cheese?"

My lips twitched, but I didn't dare laugh. Was she already feeling pregnancy cravings? I'd have thought it was too soon, but if she wanted lasagna, I'd make sure she got it. Hell, if she wanted to put ice cream on it, I'd make it happen, just as long as I didn't have to watch her eat it. Some of the guys I'd served with had talked about the insane things their women had eaten while pregnant, and how emotional they became. One soldier had described it as PMS on crack. I was pretty sure if his wife had heard that, he wouldn't have been able to walk for a week. I'd met her a few times and she seemed like the ball-buster type.

"Italian sounds good," Janessa said. "We should make sure Kalani eats whatever she wants so the baby will get nice and fat."

Kalani snorted. "More like I'll get nice and fat."

I brushed a kiss against her temple. "You're beautiful and you're going to be a beautiful pregnant lady. Even when you're about to pop, you'll be the most gorgeous woman I've ever seen."

Kalani flushed with pleasure.

"I'll call Seamus. Do either of you need to do anything before we leave? Wash your faces, use the bathroom? Do you want to change or something?" I asked.

Janessa rolled her eyes at me. "Go to the bathroom? Really, Dad? Are we five?"

I shrugged, not having a clue what the fuck I was doing most days, but I was trying. That had to count for something. I knew there would be a steep learning curve during Kalani's pregnancy and definitely after the baby arrived, but I'd buy every book I could find if I thought it would help prepare me. This was my second chance, an opportunity to not fuck things up, and I was determined to do all the right things. Starting with feeding my girls.

I shot off a text to Seamus and hoped he was inside the compound. If he was out on a job for the club, or partying, it could take him a while to get here. Since he was trying to prove himself to Devil's Boneyard in hopes of patching in, I knew he'd drop whatever he was doing to come chauffeur us around town. It sucked, but every patched member went through the same shit.

A knock sounded about ten minutes later and before I could even move, Janessa had bounded over to the door and flung it open.

Seamus blinked at her a moment, and my daughter looked a little stunned. For the first time, I realized my little girl was on the cusp of becoming a woman, and she was already getting the curves to prove it. With a mix of my heritage and her mother's Irish background, she had a golden honey glow with my dark hair. Fuck. I wasn't ready for this shit.

Seamus, to his credit, was the first to look away, but even he looked a little dazed. I glared at him and hoped it would put the fear of God into him. My baby girl was only fourteen, and Seamus had to be in his twenties. In ten years, that wouldn't be such big difference, but right now? Fuck no. And if he was one of those sickos who got off on being with a kid, I'd be happy to set him straight.

"I have the SUV out front. We can leave whenever you're ready," Seamus said. His gaze cut toward Janessa for split second, then he looked away again.

Kalani looked a little amused by the entire thing, which earned her a glower too. Not that she backed down. It seemed my wife had finally realized I wasn't going to ever hurt her. Part of me was elated that she wasn't scared of me, and the other half realized that she was going to make my life hell. With two females under my roof already, I was seriously hoping the little bun in the oven was a boy. Hell, Janessa had the right idea. I was going to hope for twins. Boy twins!

"I think we're ready," I said.

Janessa darted out the door and jumped into the front seat of the SUV. Seamus looked a little nervous and rubbed the back of his neck. I should probably cut him a little slack. Hell, Janessa's mom had only been two years older when she'd gotten pregnant with our daughter. But if I'd have had any idea she was sixteen, I'd have stayed the fuck away from her. The way Seamus twitched as he glanced at the SUV told me enough. He knew Janessa was just a kid and was going to do his damnedest to avoid her. Good.

Kalani leaned a little closer. "We're going to have to watch her. Poor Seamus looks ready to bolt, but I do believe our daughter would just run him to ground like a hound after a rabbit."

I snorted. Yeah, she wasn't wrong.

"Maybe it's time for that birds and the bees discussion," I said.

"Which one would that be?"

"The one where any guy looks at her, touches her, or even thinks of having sex with her will end with him being in a shallow grave at the back of the compound."

Kalani patted my arm. "Good luck with that. Maybe instead of trying to chase all the males off, you could just steer her toward more appropriate ones. Poor Seamus looks like he's been trapped and wants to gnaw off his leg to escape."

"Is there such a thing as an appropriate guy? I remember being her age. I was one big hormone and all I thought about was sex."

Kalani's eyebrows lifted. "So not much different from now?"

I swatted her on her ass. "Watch it, woman. If my wife weren't so sexy, maybe I wouldn't think about sex so much."

"Nice save." Kalani smiled and left me standing in the house. She slid into the back of the SUV, and poor Seamus stood next to the vehicle looking like he might bolt at any moment.

I should probably save the guy. It would be the brotherly thing to do. And then have a nice, long talk with my daughter. And make sure Seamus knew not to ever look her way again. I wasn't ready for this shit. At all. Why the fuck couldn't I have had a boy?

I left the house, shutting the door behind me, then practically yanked my daughter out of the front of the SUV and shoved her into the backseat with Kalani. Before Janessa could get back out, I engaged the child lock and slammed the door shut. She gave me a mutinous glare as I climbed into the front seat.

"Thank you," Seamus muttered under his breath as he started the SUV.

"Look at my daughter again the way you did when she opened the door, and they'll never find your body."

He gave a jerky nod and pulled out of the driveway.

"I'm going to marry a biker when I grow up," Janessa said from the backseat.

I growled and turned to look at her. She gave me a look that somehow managed to be both innocent and sassy at the same time, and I knew that whoever she ended up with would have their hands full. I just hoped I didn't have to deal with that for another five or six years. Hell, she was my kid. I didn't kid myself into thinking she'd be a virgin forever. The way she was acting over Seamus, I'd be lucky if she remained a virgin past the age of sixteen.

"You can marry whoever you want," Kalani said. "After you've graduated high school and at least given college a try. Your dad didn't pull you out of that hellhole just for you to run off and marry the first guy you think is cute."

"Didn't you?" Janessa asked.

Kalani paled a little, and if we weren't in a moving car, I'd have pulled my daughter over my knee and spanked her ass for that comment.

"Kalani's situation is different from yours, Janessa. She needed my protection," I said. "And I care about her. I'll do anything I can to make her happy and keep her safe. Most guys will just want in your pants. Don't think a few kisses and handholding means they want forever with you."

Seamus cleared his throat. "You should probably wait until you're married. If a guy's willing to wait until after the wedding, then you'll know he really wants to be with you and isn't just after a good time."

As much as I wanted to tell him to shut up, I had to admit he made a good point. And my daughter seemed to be listening to Seamus.

"Did you wait?" she asked Seamus.

His cheeks flushed. "Um, no. But if I met the right woman and she wanted to wait, then I'd respect her enough to abstain."

Janessa seemed to think it over. "So, you're saying the women you've been with were just a good time and not the kind of woman you keep forever?"

Seamus nodded. "Right. I haven't met the forever type yet. Maybe one day I will."

Janessa got an almost sly look in her eyes. "Or maybe you already have and you just don't realize it."

Oh, fucking hell. No she didn't!

"Janessa!" I leveled another glare at her. "Stop flirting with Seamus. He's a grown-ass man and you're still a kid."

"Fine." She folded her arms and sulked. "But I won't be a kid forever."

Seamus glanced my way before looking at Janessa in the rearview mirror. "Tell you what. When you're all grown up, you come look me up. If I'm still single, I'll take you out on a date."

Janessa fairly glowed, and I wasn't certain if I admired the way he'd handled that, or if I wanted to punch him. Either way, his words seemed to settle Janessa down enough that the issue was buried for the moment. I could only hope she'd forget all about this over time. Something told me that if she ever hooked up with the Prospect sitting next to me, that nothing but trouble would come of it.

Seamus looked at me before returning his gaze to the road. "Army, right?"

"Yeah. Fifteen years of service," I said.

Seamus reached for his arm and lifted the sleeve of his tee. A fucking SEALs logo. Jesus. My baby girl was flirting with a damn Navy SEAL.

"Just got out six months ago," Seamus said.

"What does your tattoo mean?" Janessa asked from the backseat.

"It means your flirt buddy here is a badass," I muttered.

"And it means you have my word that I would never touch her while she's underage," Seamus said. "I might have been momentarily out of sorts when she opened the door, but I would never, ever go there. I'm not that kind of man. If it would make you feel better, I can request someone else to help you while you're in our territory."

"Your word is good enough," I said. "Just keep your eyes off my daughter."

"Not a problem. I'm not into kids."

Seamus dropped us off at the restaurant and promised to return as soon as we were ready to leave. Janessa pouted when she realized he wasn't joining us, and I knew I needed to have that talk with her sooner rather than later. After being at Hillview, and seeing the bad things that happened, I would have never thought she'd go crazy over some guy she just met. Especially one who was too fucking old for her.

"He's too old for you," I said after we were seated and had placed our order. "You need to leave him alone. Do you really think Kalani acted like that around me?"

She cut her gaze toward Kalani, then shook her head. "I know she didn't. You make her feel safe."

"I'm glad that Hillview didn't permanently damage you," I said. "But you can't go chasing after guys. Did your mother ever tell you about me or how we met?"

"No."

"Your mom was sixteen and I was nineteen. But I didn't know how old she was. I'd thought she was eighteen, until she ended up pregnant with you, and your grandfather threatened to have me arrested for statutory rape."

Her eyes widened and her jaw dropped a little.

"I'm not telling you this so you'll think badly of your mom and her family, but I want you to understand how dangerous it is for you to act like that around Seamus. Until you're eighteen, you're jailbait, for lack of a better word. And that means if you think you want to hang out with boys, then you need to make sure it's guys your age."

"There's no one my age at the compound," she said.

"Maybe not, but I'm going to enroll you in school, and you'll make some friends there. They don't have to know about your past unless you decide to tell them. You can always just say that your grandparents sent you out of town when your mom died," I said.

"May I say something?" Kalani asked.

"Sweetheart, you're her stepmother and my wife. You don't need permission to say anything."

Kalani nodded and faced Janessa. "You know some of what happened to me at Hillview, and you know I don't trust men. I wouldn't have let just anyone take me out of there, even if it meant freedom from the doctors and staff."

"Then why did you let my dad take you from that place?" Janessa asked.

"Because when I looked into his eyes, I saw his love and concern for you. And I knew that anyone who felt that way about his daughter couldn't be all bad. Your father protected me, kept me hidden from Hillview, and even married me to make sure I never had to go back. He's the first man I've ever let touch me. Do you think it would have been wise for me to trust just anyone like that?" Kalani asked.

"No?" Janessa's forehead wrinkled like she wasn't certain of her answer.

"There are men in the world, and probably even boys your age, who are like the staff and doctors at Hillview. They'll take what they want because they think it's their right. They don't care if they hurt someone, and might even enjoy causing pain to other people. Be careful who you trust, Janessa. I never want to see you hurt the way I've been hurt."

Janessa nodded and hugged Kalani. "I promise I'll be careful. And I won't go chasing after guys, even if I am curious what it's like to go on a date and have my first kiss."

"It will happen when it's supposed to," Kalani said. "Don't rush it, and don't force it. When you meet the right guy, you'll know. He'll treat you with respect and kindness. He'll put your needs before his."

"And my dad does all that for you?" she asked.

Kalani nodded. "He does. Your dad gave me space and waited until I told him I was ready for more. He was patient, kind, and never once acted like I owed him something. Maybe he's one of a kind, but I think when the time is right, you'll meet a guy just as wonderful as your father."

My throat grew a little tight, and my heart felt like it might burst. Ah, fuck. I didn't know when it had happened, but I'd fallen in love with my wife. Now wasn't the time to tell her, though. I'd save that for a special moment when it was just the two of us, and if I was lucky, one day she'd love me too.

The rest of the night passed without incident, until my phone jingled with a text that made my blood run cold.

Whitby escaped. What the fuck did that even mean? Escaped from where? My heart hammered as I called Torch. "What the fuck do you mean he escaped?" I asked.

"Wire managed to have all the patients transferred to other facilities. In the chaos, Whitby disappeared. The police anonymously received copies of Whitby's personal files with all the corrupt and abusive things that have happened at Hillview. The rest of the staff were arrested, but Whitby slipped through their fingers," Torch said.

"What does that mean for my family?" I asked.

"It means you need to keep your eyes open. I've already contacted Scratch to give him a heads-up. He's doubling the guards at the gate, and there will be two Prospects watching the house you're in. It's the best we can do until Wire and Shade can work their magic and locate Whitby," Torch said.

"If that fucker touches one hair on my wife or daughter's heads, I'll kill him," I said, my voice more growl than usual.

"I'm sending Johnny and Ivan your way. They're only Prospects, but they'll both be patched in soon enough. Don't leave the compound for anything," Torch said.

"Fine." My hand tightened on the phone. "Find that asshole."

"We're on it. We've got three clubs and Casper VanHorne working on this. You just keep your girls close," Torch said. "I'll call when I know more or the situation is resolved."

The line went dead and I stared into the darkness for a few minutes. Kalani was asleep. Watching her, I vowed that Whitby would never touch her. She'd suffered enough, and I wasn't about to let any more ugliness come near her. I checked on Janessa, then prowled the house. My hands clenched and unclenched, wishing I had my weapons. There was a gun in my bag, and I retrieved it just in case. Whatever happened, I'd keep my family safe, at all costs.

Nothing was more important than the two girls sleeping down the hall. Nothing.

Chapter Ten

Kalani

When I woke up alone, I knew something was wrong. Tex wasn't in bed and there was an ominous feeling in the air, like something bad was coming. I threw off the covers and checked on Janessa. She was still sleeping soundly in the bedroom across the hall. Slowly, I crept through the house, listening for anything that seemed out of place. I found Tex in the kitchen, downing a cup of coffee.

"What's wrong?" I asked.

His gaze was troubled as he faced me. "The police arrested the staff and doctors at Hillview."

"That's a good thing, right?" I asked. "It means it's all over?"

"Not quite. Whitby escaped."

I froze at his words. I knew deep down that the man would hunt me down. He might have been the sperm donor who helped create me, but he'd never loved me. And now I was a danger to his very existence. I didn't know what the police had that would have led to them arresting everyone. Maybe I was overreacting and Whitby was five states away heading in the other direction. But what if I wasn't? What if he was searching for me? After being his dirty little secret for so long, he had to be furious that I'd not only escaped, but the police were now hunting him.

Tex gripped my arms and I looked up. There was concern in his gaze, but also determination. My heart rate slowed and I took a deep breath. He'd kept me safe so far, and now that I was carrying his baby, I had no doubt he'd be twice as protective. I was behind locked gates, surrounded by bikers. I couldn't think of a safer place to be.

"Everything will be fine," Tex assured me. "We have two Prospects watching the house, and Torch is sending a few of our men as well... Prospects. And of course, Gabe is already here. I know they aren't patched members, but I have a feeling they can hold their own. Besides, they have something to prove. Screwing up isn't an option."

I nodded. He was right. I knew he was right. "So, we're on lockdown for now?" I asked.

"Yeah. I know it sucks. You've been locked up for so long and now I'm having to cage you again. I hate that, but I refuse to let anything happen to you."

"Or the baby," I said, placing a hand over my stomach.

"Hey." He tipped my chin up and lightly pressed his lips to mine. "I would worry about you whether you were pregnant or not. You know that, right? I care what happens to you, Kalani. I know we haven't been together all that long, but you mean so much to me. Yes, I'm thrilled we're having a baby. But even if there wasn't a baby, I'd still be glad you're part of my life."

I bit my tongue to keep the words *I love you* from spilling out. I didn't think he'd want to hear that right now, but I couldn't lie to myself. Somewhere along the way, I'd fallen for Tex. He was always so sweet to me, it was hard not to love him.

"Are you hungry?" he asked. "I'm not the greatest cook, but even I can manage bacon, eggs, and biscuits that come in a can. I checked the fridge and it's stocked with the basics."

I studied him and could see the tension lines bracketing his mouth. His body was strung tight, and even though he was saying and doing all the right things, I could tell that something was off with him. I just didn't know what.

"Why are you staring at me?" he asked.

"Because I feel like you aren't telling me something."

He sighed and ran a hand through his hair. "I'm fine, sweetheart. I just wish I was out there hunting Whitby. I'm not used to sitting on the sidelines when trouble comes knocking. For fifteen years, I've been the one kicking in the door on the bad guy, and it's hard to set all that aside and just... wait."

"Are you staying here because of me and Janessa, or because you were ordered to?" I asked.

"You see far too much," he murmured, then smiled faintly. "A little of both. I don't like the idea of leaving either of you, but yeah, I was ordered to stay put. After what Whitby did to you, and the way he ran Hillview, I want to be the one to put him in the ground. If he hadn't been so crooked, Janessa never would have been held in that place, and you wouldn't have been put in a position where you felt the need to protect her."

"I love Janessa, and I'd do it all again if I had to," I said. "I don't regret keeping her safe, no matter what they did to me. And I don't blame her or you for what happened. Whitby is an evil man, and so were the people who worked for him. No one is responsible for his actions except him."

A smile tugged at his lips. "Only you would see through all that and realize I feel guilty as hell that she ended up in that place. But I'm glad that by finding her there, I was able to get you out of that place, too."

"I was scared when I saw all of you come into the room. You're all so big I knew I wouldn't be able to defend myself against you. But then I saw the way you looked at your daughter, and the way you spoke to her told me that you weren't a bad man. I wasn't so sure about the others, though."

"Yeah, I guess we can be an intimidating lot." He rubbed a hand along his jaw. "But every one of my brothers would lay down his life for you or Janessa. You're family. You know that right? The first time Torch showed up at the house he asked to see my girls. He knew even then both of you were mine."

I pressed my cheek to his chest and held on tight. "I like being yours."

"That's good, sweetheart, because I'm never letting you go."

His words warmed me, and despite the fact a deranged doctor was out there lurking, I couldn't have been happier than I was in that moment. We just stood there for a while, his arms around me, as the sun began to rise and fill the kitchen with its warm, golden rays. I still battled my demons, but I was getting better. With every day that passed, I healed a little more. Maybe one day I'd be as close to normal as anyone could ever get. Tex insisted there was no such thing as normal, but for me, being normal meant I wouldn't jump at shadows, I wouldn't relive the moments from Hillview on a nightly basis, and I wouldn't distrust every man on sight because of what a handful of men had done to me. While every staff member at Hillview was a monster, I could count on one hand the men who had ever physically hurt me.

I sat at the table and sipped on some juice while Tex made breakfast. I watched him, wondering how hard it would be to do something so mundane as make breakfast. Even though I'd been free for a month now, I'd never attempted to cook anything. With my luck, I'd burn down the house and half the compound along with it. But some day I wanted to try. I wanted to get up one morning and cook breakfast for my family. It sounded simple enough, but the stove scared me a little.

Janessa still hadn't joined us by the time Tex had finished making the eggs, bacon, and biscuits. He joined me at the table after setting two full plates down. My stomach rumbled, but before I could take a bite, Tex was doctoring my eggs with salt and pepper.

"You only get a little bit of salt since you're pregnant, but I promise it will make the eggs taste better," he said, giving me a wink.

"One day, when all of this is officially over, will you teach me to cook a few things?" I asked. "There's so much I don't know how to do."

He nodded. "I'll teach you whatever you want. Once we're back home, you can even ask the other old ladies. I've heard quite a few of my brothers have settled down and started families."

"I think I'm ready to meet everyone," I said. "I know I was skittish before. I didn't really trust people."

Tex reached over and ran his fingers down my cheek. "One day at a time, sweetheart. No one is going to push you into doing something you're not ready for. Least of all me."

"I want to make some friends," I said.

"Then I'll make sure that happens. Everyone is going to love you, so don't worry about it. The Dixie Reapers are one big family. We accept each other, flaws and all. You're not the only one who's had to overcome something."

I was mid-bite when the front door was flung open so hard I thought it might have dented the wall. Three men wearing Dixie Reapers cuts stormed into the kitchen, then visibly relaxed when they saw us.

"What's going on?" Tex asked, his grip on his fork tightened until his knuckles turned white.

"Someone managed to get their hands on the information Wire and Shade sent the police. It's all over the Internet and TV, all Whitby's experiments, the abuse of the patients." Their gazes cut to me. "And everyone knows your wife is Whitby's daughter. They know everything about her."

Tex rose, his chair falling to the ground. "What the fuck is that supposed to mean?"

"It means they know everything that happened and was documented at Hillview. It's out there, for anyone to read on the Internet, and several news stations are broadcasting it. Hillview is the number one story nationwide right now," one of the men said.

"What does all that mean?" I asked.

"It means people are outraged, and the shit has hit the fan," one guy said. "I'm Ivan by the way. This is Gabe and Johnny," he said pointing to the other two.

"Anyone seen Whitby?" Tex asked.

"There have been reports of sightings, but they're all over the place. His picture is splashed all over the news and social media. It's a nationwide manhunt at this point, so there's not many places he can hide. Unless he's managed to leave the country already," Gabe said.

"It's good that people know, right?" I asked.

Tex placed a hand on my shoulder. "It's good and bad. I don't like that your information is out there. There are a lot of people who will be sympathetic for all you suffered, but there are those who will look at you differently. And not in a good way."

"Torch is already reaching out to clubs across the nation. And Casper VanHorne is getting the word out through his channels. Your family is to be protected at all costs, and Whitby brought to justice," Johnny said.

"Legal justice or our justice?" Tex asked.

"Torch wants to keep things legal this time," Ivan said. "He said it's such a high profile case it would bring too much heat down on us if we were to get our hands dirty. We're only allowed to hurt him if he makes an attempt on your family. And since no one knows where you are right now I don't think you have to worry too much. Wire and Shade made sure there wasn't a paper trail leading here."

"If we aren't getting our hands dirty, why is Torch rallying the clubs?" Tex asked.

"More eyes watching for Whitby. The average person might be looking, but they won't be able to check the underground places. Between the clubs and Casper, there won't be anywhere Whitby can hide. But until he's apprehended, we're your shadows," Ivan said.

"I'll watch the front," Gabe offered.

"And I'll take the back," said Ivan.

"You really think he'll get into the compound?" I asked. "It would be suicidal to come in a place surrounded by armed bikers."

Johnny shrugged. "We're not taking any chances. I'll stay inside with the three of you, just in case something does go down."

"Where is your daughter anyway?" Ivan asked.

"Sleeping," Tex said.

"Do you want some breakfast? Or something to drink?" I asked the men.

"We grabbed some food on the way here," Ivan said. "It's out in my saddlebags, but if you have some coffee, that would be great."

"I already drank most of it," Tex said. "But you can have what's left and we can make some more. There's enough food here to last a short time, but with more of us here, it's not going to stretch as far."

"We'll arrange a grocery run," Johnny said. "If there's anything in particular you want, just let us know and we'll make sure you get it."

"Chocolate milk?" I asked. "And maybe some Oreos?"

Tex arched a brow and looked at me, amusement sparking in his eyes. "I think the pregnancy cravings really are starting already."

The three Prospects grinned.

"Congratulations," Johnny said.

"Thank you," I said. "And thank you for letting us know what's going on. I'm sorry I dragged all of you into this mess. If I'd just stayed at Hillview, or turned myself in that first week, all of this could have been avoided."

Ivan's face darkened and his eyes turned stormy. "There is no way in hell we would have ever let you go back to that place. I'm glad Tex pulled you out of there, and even more so that he claimed you. You're one of us now, and we protect our women."

My eyes misted with tears and I nodded. I was going to blame my pregnancy on the number of times I'd wanted to cry lately, but I knew I was overly emotional. It was a little strange, having so many people care what happened to me, willing to risk their lives to protect me. I honestly didn't feel worthy.

"I bet we're heading home in the next day or two," Gabe said. "Whitby can't hide for long, not considering the types of people watching for him. Wire and Shade are going to keep us updated. I'm not sure you want to see the news. It's not pretty."

"I can handle it," I assured them.

Tex curled his arm around my waist. "I know you can, sweetheart, but it doesn't mean you should have to."

"I'll get any alerts on my phone if they report anything new," Johnny said. "I promise I'll let you know the second Whitby has been apprehended."

Janessa stumbled into the kitchen rubbing her eyes, and froze mid-step when she saw the three men standing near the table. "What's going on?" she asked.

"We'll talk about it while you eat," Tex said.

While he fixed her plate and got her caught up on everything, I slipped out of the kitchen and went to shower and change. As respectable as my pajamas were, I didn't think Tex wanted me hanging out around the other men without some actual clothes on. I had noticed all of them kept their gazes on my eyes when they looked my way. I didn't know if it was out of respect for Tex, or for me, or maybe both of us. But it was something I could easily get used to.

When I got out of the shower, I pulled on a pair of gray leggings and a plain blue tee. My hair was still wet, but I ran a brush through it and left it down. I could hear Janessa and Tex talking in the kitchen, and I decided to let them have some father-daughter time. Johnny was in the living room, staring out the front window.

He glanced my way as I entered the room, gave me a slight smile, then went back to looking out the window.

"Will it bother you if I turn on the TV?" I asked.

"Just pretend I'm not even here," he said.

I flipped through some channels and picked a movie, but I found myself studying Johnny. "Are you the youngest of the Dixie Reapers?"

He turned to face me. "For the moment. Ivan is only a few years older than me, but most of the guys are late-twenties to mid-fifties."

"So you're close to my age, then?" I asked.

He nodded. "A year younger. Don't let my age fool you. I've been prospecting for the Dixie Reapers for a few years now. I'll keep you safe."

"If you've been with them for so long, why are you still a Prospect?" I asked. "Or is that a rude thing to ask?"

"It's fine. I think Torch has been giving me time to grow up a bit. I know he trusts me, because I'm his first choice when it comes to protecting his wife and daughter. I don't mind being a Prospect. I know my time will come." He smiled. "It's actually not uncommon for guys to Prospect for a few years before they're either voted in or asked to leave. Some are lucky and get in within a year, but I think it depends on the club."

"Why did you want to join them?" I asked. Tex and I hadn't really talked about the Dixie Reapers before. I didn't really understand the MC world, or why people joined.

"My home life wasn't the best," Johnny said. "We live in a small town, and I'd grown up knowing who the Dixie Reapers were. When I was old enough, I asked if I could prospect for them. I haven't regretted it. Even my sister is part of the Dixie Reapers family."

"Because she's related to you?" I asked.

He grinned. "No, because Preacher claimed her. Actually, he knocked her up, then he claimed her. Best thing that could have ever happened to both of them. I guess you could say they saved each other."

"How so?"

"There's a pimp who pretty much controls my old neighborhood. He was after my sister, so she wasn't safe living there anymore. I tried to send her away, but it didn't work out. She fell in love with a patched member, Preacher, and he seems just as crazy about her," Johnny said. "One day I'll have what they have. But I don't think I'm ready just yet."

"Then I should probably warn you that Janessa, it seems, is going to be a little boy crazy. I think that's the term? I heard it on TV. Anyway, she may try flirting with you."

Johnny chuckled. "Sounds like my sister when she was that age. Janessa's fourteen, right?"

"Yeah."

"You're going to have a rough few years if she's anything like my baby sister. Don't worry. We'll all watch out for her, make sure she doesn't bite off more than she can chew. And she can flirt all she wants. None of us would ever touch her."

"Thanks, Johnny."

He nodded and went back to watching the window.

After a while, Tex and Janessa joined me. We had a movie marathon, letting Janessa choose what we watched. We even convinced Johnny to sit with us for short period of time, when he wasn't prowling through the house, waiting on the Boogie man to jump out.

Night had fallen and we'd finished dinner, convincing the three Prospects to sit down with us, when all the cell phones started going off at once. They each looked at their screens.

"We need to turn on the TV," Ivan said.

We left the dishes on the table and headed into the living room. Ivan turned on the TV and found a news station. A sea of blue lights filled the screen, along with a few fire trucks and an ambulance. I didn't understand what I was seeing at first, couldn't make sense of the text scrolling across the bottom of the screen.

A blonde woman with a microphone came on screen, with all the action behind her. "The manhunt for Dr. Whitby of Hillview is currently at a standoff. The man who ran Hillview Asylum, responsible for countless acts of violence against patients, has been cornered in Miami, Florida, where he was trying to stowaway on a boat and flee the country."

I gasped and stared at the screen, leaning a little closer.

"Dr. Whitby is armed and has taken a hostage. The crew of the ship *Marionne* discovered the doctor trying to sneak into the cargo hold. According to the manifest, the ship was carrying a load of textiles and was scheduled to make several stops outside the US. It's believed Whitby was trying to reach a non-extradition country, in hopes of escaping justice for his crimes," the reporter said.

Gunshots went off and the reporter dove for the ground. The camera jostled and bounced, finally zooming in on the reporter again.

"Shot have been fired," the reporter said. "Dr. Whitby is shooting at the officers on scene, and now it sounds like we're in the middle of a war zone. I can't see the hostage, but all of this may be over soon."

Everything went still and quiet, and the reporter slowly rose to her feet, the camera following her. They tried to get closer to the police line, but an officer was pushing everyone back. The crowd of officers parted and a bloody Dr. Whitby was pushed through, his hands cuffed behind his back.

The reporter rushed forward again, shoving the microphone in an officer's face. "Can you tell us what happened? Is the hostage still alive?"

The office shoved the microphone. "No comment."

The reporter jogged after Whitby, getting as close as she could, and the camera stayed on the man I hated more than anyone else on the planet. I couldn't tell if the blood on him was his or someone else's.

We watched the news a while longer, waiting to find out exactly what had happened, but just knowing he wasn't out on the streets anymore filled me with a sense of peace. No one else would come to harm at Whitby's hands.

My hand tightened on Tex's and he lifted our clasped hands to kiss mine. "That's it?" I asked. "It's all over?"

"They'll probably make a statement if we watch a few more minutes," Ivan said.

Sure enough, a man approached the press and held up his hands to quiet everyone. "I'm Chief Jacobs. As you know, there has been a nationwide manhunt for Dr. Whitby, the man who ran Hillview Asylum in Alabama. Dr. Whitby has been apprehended, but not before he shot his hostage and three officers. The hostage didn't survive, and the three wounded officers are undergoing medical care. Their names will not be released at this time as their families are still being notified."

The reporters all yelled out questions to the police chief, but I tuned them out, waiting to see if he'd say anything else.

"Dr. Whitby will remain in custody until his trial. Considering his numerous and heinous crimes, it's doubtful he'd be granted bail, but that will be a judge's decision. That's all the information we have at this time. I know that information was released on Whitby's victims, and I would like to ask that you please leave them in peace. Most have been transferred to other facilities to undergo therapy and evaluation. Those determined to be of sound mind will be released. I know that you're all aware of Whitby's daughter, Kalani. Her whereabouts at this time are unknown, but a medical professional has reached out to assure the local law enforcement that Kalani Whitby isn't a danger to anyone," Chief Jacobs said.

"Kalani Rodriguez," Tex said. "Asshole."

I snickered, but I was also thankful they didn't know I'd gotten married. It might make it harder for people to find me.

Ivan flicked off the TV. "So, it looks like we're free to go home. Whenever you're ready. We'll escort you home."

"It's getting late," I said. "Should we wait until tomorrow?"

"If you want to wait, we'll wait," Tex said. "But if you think you can handle the trip, it would be nice to be in our own house again."

"About that," Gabe said. "You won't be returning to the same house. When Torch heard about the baby, he decided you needed more room."

"I was going to talk to him about that, but I was waiting until all this had been settled," Tex said.

Gabe shrugged. "Your things were already moved to the new house. And um... the old ladies put together a surprise for you. They're anxious to get to know Kalani."

"Let's go home," I said.

"I'll notify Seamus," Johnny said. "He's lurking somewhere outside. I'm sure Devil's Boneyard has already been notified that they can stand down."

"Thanks," Tex said. "We never unpacked, so it won't take us long to load up."

"I'll unlock the car," Gabe said.

And once more we were piling into a car and hitting the road. I had to admit, getting back home, and not having to leave again in the near future, sounded rather nice. Seeing new places had been a little fun, but I was ready to meet all the Dixie Reapers. It was time to start my new life, with my new family, and leave Hillview firmly in my past.

Epilogue

Tex
One Month Later

The field behind the clubhouse was filled with canopies, picnic tables, and every member of the Dixie Reapers, from the oldest to the youngest. Kalani stood in a small group with Bull's woman, Darian, and the VP's old lady, Ridley. Preacher and his wife, Kayla, were sprawled on a blanket nearby with their twins in their arms. The sun was shining, the music was going, and everyone was having a good time.

Flicker slapped me on the back. "How's family life treating you?"

"Good. Kalani gets some weird ass cravings, though," I said with a chuckle. "She asked for mashed potatoes with gravy at three o'clock the other morning, and then sliced a dill pickle to put on top."

"Remind me not to eat at your house anytime soon," Flicker said.

I punched his arm, but he was grinning. He nodded toward Janessa. "What's up with that?"

I tried not to growl. My little girl had started school the week after we'd returned home. Much to my horror, she was popular -- with the boys. One in particular seemed to be a regular fixture in our home. He seemed like a good enough kid, but I wasn't ready for her to grow up and go on dates.

"We had the talk the first time she asked him to come over," I said. "He assures me they're just friends, but Kalani thinks Janessa likes him as a boyfriend."

"You going to let her date?"

I shrugged. "I think she's too young. Kalani said Janessa was exposed to more than most kids her age because of what happened with her mom and being locked up at Hillview. I asked Dr. Myron's partner to talk to her. While he agreed that Janessa is more mature for her age, he didn't think she was emotionally ready to date."

"I'm sure that went over well with her," Flicker said.

"Kalani talked to her. Said it might be better coming from a woman. Janessa agreed to not push the dating thing until she's sixteen. In the meantime, I'm letting her invite friends over whenever she wants. I'd rather have that kid at our house where I can watch him."

"At least she's not chasing after grown men," Flicker said.

"Don't remind me. I'm hoping in another few weeks, she won't even remember her infatuation with Seamus. I think she lacked for affection for so long, she's eager to latch onto just about anyone."

"Makes sense. Well, she has you, Kalani, and the rest of us to keep an eye on her. She'll stay safe, papa bear. We'll make sure of it."

"Thanks."

Flicker nodded and pointed his beer bottle toward his sister and her man. "I'm going to go hassle my sister. Don't stand here by yourself. It makes you look creepy."

I smirked as he walked off, my gaze straying to his sister and Ryker. I'd talked to Ryker a few times, but the situation was a little strange to me. He wasn't a Dixie Reaper, but he lived here at the compound. Torch seemed to trust him, so that was good enough for me.

Coyote joined me, a black leather cut clutched in his hand. "Got what you asked for."

I took it from him and headed toward Kalani. We'd been married a month now, and while she wore my ring, I hadn't claimed her the way a Dixie Reaper should claim his woman. I'd talked to Zipper and we'd agreed that it would be better to wait and ink her after the baby arrived. Kalani had improved tremendously over the last month, but she was still healing.

I stopped next to her, took the drink from her hand, and handed it to Darian.

Darian and Ridley smiled as they saw what was in my hand, but Kalani looked confused. "What's going on?" she asked.

"I have something for you." I held it up, showing her the front with the Dixie Reapers patch, then turned it so could see the back, where *Property of Tex* was stitched on the leather. She reached out and lightly ran her fingers over it.

"It's like Ridley's and Darian's," she said, looking at the women who were proudly wearing their property cuts.

"Will you wear it?" I asked.

She smiled widely and snatched it out of my hands, slipping it on. It fit her perfectly, but I hadn't had a doubt. It looked damn good on her too. I still had one more surprise for her. I'd been careful the last few days, not removing my shirt when she was around. It had been hell not giving in to her at night when she'd begged me to make love with her, but I'd needed a few days to heal.

I wasn't about to strip right here, though. Giving Ridley and Darian a wink, I grabbed Kalani's hand and led her through the throng of Dixie Reapers and into the back of the clubhouse. Torch knew what I had planned and I'd gotten permission. Pushing open the doors that said Church above them, I ushered her into the room and then locked the doors behind us.

"Tex, what's going on?" she asked, looking around the room.

"I have another surprise for you."

She smiled and moved closer to me. "Oh yeah?"

"And it requires us to get naked. Well, mostly naked. You'd better put that cut back on after you strip out of the rest of your clothes."

She started removing everything, then put the cut back on. Fuck but she looked sexy as hell like that. I removed my shirt and she gasped as she saw what I'd had inked on my chest. She reached for me, her fingers lightly tracing the lines of her name, and the words below it. *Forever Mine.* "Tex..."

I smiled and finished removing my clothes, then pulled her into my arms and kissed her until we were both breathless. Slowly, I turned her to face the table and pushed her down over it. Seeing my name on her back, her pussy wet and waiting for me, made me hard as fuck. I nudged her legs farther apart, then leaned over her, my lips brushing her ear. "Do you want me, wife?"

"Yes. God, yes."

I gripped her hip and ground my cock against her ass. "Are you sure? I'm feeling a little possessive and out of control. Can you handle it? Think you can handle anything I give you today?"

"You'd never hurt me, Tex. I trust you completely."

I leaned back, lined up my cock with her slit, and plunged deep. She cried out as I went balls deep, her wet pussy welcoming me. I didn't think I had it in me to be gentle. I tried to take her slow and easy, but after a few strokes I was slamming into her. Watching her ass jiggle with every thrust just made me burn for her even more. I took her hard and deep, driving into her again and again.

I slipped my hand between her legs and toyed with her clit. It was already hard and begging for attention. It only took a few swipes of that little bud before she was screaming out my name and coating my cock with her cream. I kept pounding into her, not stopping until I'd shot my cum inside her. And still I kept thrusting.

"I love feeling you wrapped around my cock," I said. "I could just stay inside you all damn day, and I'd die a happy man."

I finally withdrew but pressed a hand to her back, holding her in place against the table. My cum trickled down her thighs, and I scooped it up with my fingers, then shoved it back inside her.

Kalani moaned, so I teased her a little. When I pulled my fingers out of her pussy, they were slick with our mingled release. My heart hammered as I thought about what I was going to do next, and hoped it didn't freak her the hell out. I spread her ass cheeks and teased her tight hole with my slick fingers. Her breath caught audibly and every muscle went tight, but soon she was relaxing and making the sweetest sounds.

I worked my finger inside her, trying to take things slow and give her time to adjust. Her body flushed a rosy pink as I added a second finger, stroking them in and out. Her ass wiggled a little, and I could tell she liked what I was doing. I reached into my pocket with my free hand and pulled out the small bottle of lube I'd brought. I squirted some against the tight ring of muscles, working it in with my fingers. As much as I wanted to be inside her, I didn't want to hurt her. I added a third finger, and when I thought she was ready, I withdrew the digits and slicked my cock with the lube.

"Ready, sweetheart?"

She nodded.

I pressed the head of my cock against her tight entrance and slowly pressed inside. "Push out, baby."

She relaxed more and the head of my cock popped through the tight muscles, making me groan at how fucking fantastic she felt. I eased inside her, not stopping until she'd taken every inch. My muscles strained and sweat dripped down my spine at the effort it took to not pound into her ass, taking what I wanted. Slow and steady, I tried to make it just as good for her as it was for me.

"Houston, I want more," she begged in a breathy voice.

With a growl, I gripped her hips tight and started thrusting deeper. Watching my dick disappear into her ass just made me even fucking harder. Seeing that tight little hole stretched around my shaft made my inner caveman want to roar. Soon, I couldn't control myself anymore. I slammed my dick into her ass again and again, not stopping even when I started to come.

"You like that, baby?" I asked. "You like me pounding my cum into your ass?"

She moaned. "God, Houston. I'm so close."

I played with her clit, my cock stroking in and out of her ass, until she screamed out my name. She clenched down on my dick until I nearly saw stars. When her orgasm started to ebb, I pulled free and couldn't help but smile at the sight of my cum leaking out of both her pussy and her ass.

I swatted her ass cheek, leaving a slightly pink handprint on her skin. Then I turned her to face me. "You are something else, sweetheart."

Kalani reached up to kiss me. "I love you," she whispered against my lips.

I thought my heart was going to pound out of my chest. I'd wondered if she felt that way, but neither of us had said the words before. "I love you too, sweetheart. So damn much."

"We should get back to the party," she said. "They might be looking for us."

"Wait here," I said, kissing her quickly. Then I stepped into the adjoining bathroom to wash up. She was still standing where I'd left her when I returned a minute later. I lifted her up and set her down on the table, moving between her spread thighs. "I'm nowhere near done with you yet."

She cried out as I filled her again.

I had everything I'd ever wanted, and what I'd never known I needed. Kalani had my heart, owned me body and soul. I kept her in Church until we were both so satisfied we could hardly walk, then we joined the others, only to find the party all but deserted. Ryker and Laken were talking to Flicker.

I got a chin lift from Ryker on our way past. "Your daughter went home with Torch," he said. "He said he'd bring her by in the morning."

I smiled down at my wife. "Looks like we get the house to ourselves tonight."

"Can't imagine what we'll do to fill the time."

I swatted her ass, then took her home, where I made her scream my name all night long.

Zipper (Dixie Reapers MC 7)

Harley Wylde

Delphine: Six years ago, I did something really bad, and it chased away the guy I've been in lust with ever since my hormones had kicked in. I'd been a stupid teen, and I'd paid the price. But now I need help, and there's nowhere for me to go except straight to the Dixie Reapers, and the one man who probably never wants to see me again. If Zipper won't help me, then I'm as good as dead. I'm willing to pay any price, and I will give him anything he wants. Is it wrong that I hope, at least a little, that all this ends up with me in his bed? I've never stopped wanting him, and I know I never will.

Zipper: The teen girl who had turned my life upside down now wants my help. If nothing else, I owe it to her dad, legendary tattoo artist Hwan Lee, my mentor, the man who gave me a chance when no one else would. He's really the reason I left all those years ago. I couldn't disrespect him by claiming what I wanted. Delphine. Not to mention my ass would have ended up in jail. Now she's here, and she says I can have anything. Naughty girl. Didn't anyone ever tell her not to tempt the devil? Because soon, I'll have her right where I want her -- under me and screaming my name -- and I'm never letting her go. As for the men trying to kill her, it's only a matter of time before they breathe their last. No one hurts my woman.

Chapter One

Delphine

I hadn't seen Mason in so damn long, and I wasn't certain my presence would be welcome even now. I'd had a crush on him for as long as I could remember, even when I'd just been a little girl. My daddy had always taken me to work with him, and I'd gotten to know all the guys at his shop over the years, but it had always been Mason who fascinated me. As I grew, my feelings for him changed from that of a little girl to a young woman. It was my fault he'd left, even though I'd never told anyone, and never would. If my dad had ever found out what I'd done...

I took a steadying breath as I stared at the gates of the Dixie Reapers' compound. No one knew I was here, and I wanted to keep it that way. I was in some serious shit right now, and it wasn't fair to drop it on Mason's doorstep, but I didn't know where else to go. There was no one in my life I trusted right now, not even my own family. No, especially not my own family. Some slut with three kids had convinced my dad to marry her a few years ago, and I'd been pushed to the side. I'd quickly understood how Cinderella must have felt, being given all the crap jobs around the house and shop, and getting nothing in return. At least, as long as I was under the step-monster's roof I wasn't getting anything. Moving out helped a bit.

Things were different now, though, and not in a good way. Before Dad had died, I'd moved out. He'd been helping me pay rent, though, so I could be a nicer area. After his death, that helped came to a screeching halt, and I'd been forced to move into a not-so-great place. I'd found out at the reading of Dad's will that he had apparently left his shop in my care if anything ever happened to him, along with half his life insurance policy. My step-monster only received fifty thousand dollars and the house, which I'd been told had a second mortgage on it. Needless to say, the woman wasn't happy and would stop at nothing to get her hands on my inheritance. It had taken a while for everything to get sorted out and my inheritance actually handed over to me.

I wasn't certain if I wanted to thank my dad for trying to take care of me at the very end, or scream at him for putting me in this position. Legally, there wasn't a damn thing that Tia could do about the shop and money. But then, she'd never been one to follow the rules. I'd noticed some questionable-looking men following me lately, and I wondered if maybe she'd hired someone to do something to me. Especially after a few unexplained accidents happened. According to my dad's lawyer, if anything happened to me, the money and shop would go to Tia. It had been a provision in my dad's will apparently, stating that unless I was married with children, then step-mommy-dearest would inherit if I were to die. And since I wasn't married and didn't have any kids to leave the money to... yeah, I was pretty much screwed. I didn't see how that could possibly be legal in this day and age, but what the hell did I know?

The gates mocked me as I stared at them. I could see the shadow of a man standing just on the other side, likely a guard of some sort. He hadn't called out to me, but then I hadn't exactly gotten any closer either. I took another breath to steady my nerves and approached, putting one foot in front of the other. My fingers wrapped around the iron bars and I stared at the man on the other side. He eyed me up and down, giving me time to look him over too. He seemed to be a few years older than me. "You here to party with the club?" he asked.

"I'm here to see… Zipper." I hated that fucking name. To me, he was Mason, would always be Mason. Or maybe it was *why* he had that name that I hated so much. He'd been part of the Dixie Reapers even when he'd worked for my dad. Then he'd left and opened his own shop. The only times I'd seen him since then were glimpses around town, but I'd always hidden and kept my distance, knowing he probably hated me.

"He expecting you?" the guy asked.

"No. He used to work for my dad. Please, it's important that I see him. I'm not here to cause trouble."

The guy snorted and made a shooing motion. "Sorry, doll, but if you aren't expected, you're not getting in. You're either an old lady, or you're here to suck cock. And since it appears neither applies to you, you can just turn around and walk away."

"But you don't understand…"

He pointed again toward the driveway. There was only one way I was getting inside, but I didn't know if I had the courage to follow through. I rubbed my hands up and down my denim-clad thighs and blew out a breath.

"Then maybe I'm here to party," I said, wishing immediately that I could call back the words.

The man's eyebrows rose, and he opened the gate. I cautiously walked past him, a little worried he might reach out and grab me, maybe force me to suck his cock. I hadn't ever done something like that before, and the thought of sucking off a complete stranger made my stomach bubble and flip. I hurried toward the clubhouse and raced up the wooden steps. When I reached the door, I slowly pushed it open. Music and smoke battered at my senses as I stepped inside.

My eyes went wide when I saw the mostly, and in some cases completely, naked women prancing around. A few couples were openly having sex in front of everyone, and my heart started racing in fear. What the hell had I gotten myself into? And did I really want to see Mason in this setting? I knew he wasn't an angel by any means, but I didn't like the thought of him being with all these women.

I caught sight of him toward the end of the bar, his Dixie Reapers leather cut looking every bit as sexy on him as I'd thought it did six years ago. I felt a tingle working its way through my body, and my nipples hardened as I got closer to him. A few people jostled me along the way, but I forged ahead, hoping like hell I hadn't made a huge mistake.

A tall blond man stepped in my way, blocking me. My gaze landed on his cut and the name Flicker stitched onto it. I lifted my gaze and stared up at him. He slowly reached for me, sliding his fingers down my bare arm, and I shivered. Was he about to force me to do something I didn't want to?

"I don't remember see you around here before," he said. "I'd have remembered a beauty like you."

"I need to see Zipper."

He glanced over his shoulder before looking at me again. "He's busy. Why don't you let me warm you up, and then you can see if he's free afterward?"

My stomach knotted, and I tried to swallow down my panic.

"Please, I really need to see him. I'm not..." I looked around the room. "I'm not like them."

Flicker reached toward him, his hand aiming for my breast, and I took a step back, trying to stay out of his reach. He frowned and looked over at Zipper again.

"Yo, Zipper! Some bitch is here to see you. Thinks she's too good for the rest of us."

Mason looked my way, and I saw anger flare in his eyes when he saw me. I'd changed some over the years, but not enough that he wouldn't recognize me. The nausea that had been building since I'd walked into the clubhouse now doubled as he stood up and came toward me. Flicker got out of the way as Mason came closer.

"What the fuck are you doing here, Delphine? If your daddy knew you were here, that you were seeing all this shit, he'd beat your ass," Zipper said.

My eyes went wide. "No one told you?"

"Told me what?"

"Dad's dead. He died a few months ago from an aneurysm. Just dropped dead in the middle of the shop. I thought his wife had let you know."

His gaze softened. "Hwan's dead?"

I nodded.

He stared at me a moment, but as he looked around and noticed the attention we were receiving, his gaze hardened again, and a light entered his eyes I hadn't seen before.

"Christ," he muttered, then reached for me, gripping my arm tight. "Come on. This is no place for you, and you obviously felt the need to talk to me."

He dragged me out of the clubhouse and outside to the row of bikes. He stopped at the Harley he'd had for as long as I'd known him, and straddled the bike. Then he patted the seat behind him.

"Get on."

"Where are you taking me?" I asked.

"Back home, where you should have stayed."

"No! I can't. Please, I need to stay inside the gates. At least long enough for me to explain why I'm here. If you still want me to leave after that, then I won't ever bother you again."

His eyes narrowed, but eventually he nodded. "Then I'll take you somewhere we can talk."

I swung my leg over the seat of his bike, then wrapped my arms around his waist. I was pressed tight to his back, my thighs cradling his hips. When he started the engine and the bike rumbled between my legs, I had to fight back a moan. It was like one big vibrator. He'd never let me ride on his bike before, and now I understood why. He had to know what it did to a woman.

He pulled out of the parking lot and took off down a road that wound through the compound. A few minutes later, he pulled to a stop in front of a white clapboard home. He got off the bike, then helped me stand. I'd expected him to release me once I was standing on my own, but he began tugging at my jeans. I didn't understand what he was doing at first, and by the time I did, he had them and my panties jerked down to my knees. There was a dangerous look in his eyes that matched the hardness I'd seen at the clubhouse before he'd dragged me out of there.

"What you did was dangerous, Delphine," he said. "Coming to the clubhouse like that? Not smart."

My eyes went wide as he spun me to face his bike and bent me over the seat.

"Mason, what are you…"

His hand cracked across my ass, and I yelped and started to squirm, but his other hand held me tight against the bike's leather seat. He spanked my ass until my cheeks burned, and I wasn't sure I'd ever be able to sit down again. What surprised me the most was the fact I was getting wet with every strike of his hand. He smoothed his rough palm across both cheeks, and I tried not to moan. Zipper dipped his fingers between my legs and rubbed the lips of my pussy.

"So fucking wet, aren't you, baby? You always were a little slut for me."

I whimpered and flushed at the truth in his words. I'd been shameless in my pursuit of him, even though I'd been way too young. He'd realized that even if I hadn't cared at the time.

"You know what I think?" he asked, putting his lips down by my ear, his body pressing over mine. "I think you need to be punished for what you did, and for showing up here, entering the clubhouse like some little fuck toy. What would have you have done if one of my brothers made you drop to your knees or bend over a table?"

"I… I just wanted to see you."

He pulled away and smacked my ass a few more times. "You put yourself in danger, Delphine. Or did you want to be fucked by every guy in there?"

"No," I said, whimpering as his hand struck my battered ass cheeks again.

"Only whores go into the clubhouse at night, unless it's family night. Are you a whore, Delphine? Some biker slut who wants to spread her legs for anyone in a cut?"

"No." I winced as he spanked me again, his hand landing two more blows.

His fingers slipped between my legs again, and he groaned as he rubbed my pussy. He parted the lips and teased my clit, making me cry out in need. Mason rubbed in small, tight circles until I thought I'd lose my mind, then he pinched my clit tight and I came, screaming out my release.

I heard him unfasten his belt and jeans, then he was pressed against me again, his lips teasing the shell of my ear.

"You wanted me six years ago. Teased me, and did bad, bad things no sweet girl should have ever done. You entered that clubhouse tonight like a naughty girl looking for trouble, and now you're going to pay the price."

I felt his cock rub against me, then he pushed deep. I screamed as he drove into me over and over, fucking me hard and deep. Tears pricked my eyes as he ruthlessly claimed my innocence, but I don't think he realized I hadn't done this before. Hell, who would have thought the shameless teen from before would still be a virgin at twenty-two? The pain started to ebb, and soon I wanted to beg him for more. He grunted with every thrust of his cock, and his hand came down on my ass again.

"You were so very bad, Delphine." His hand cracked against my ass again. "Are you going to ever go into the clubhouse uninvited again?"

"N-No."

He spanked me twice more, then played with my clit until I came so hard I saw stars. I felt him come inside me, and my eyes nearly popped out of my head when I realized he hadn't used protection. *Oh, shit!* I wondered if he'd even realized that he'd taken me bare. He'd seemed pretty worked up over me being around his brothers on a night that was clearly all about getting laid, anywhere and anyhow.

Mason pulled free of my body, then cursed.

"What the fuck?"

I slowly stood upright and turned to face him. He was staring in shock at his cock, which was smeared with my blood. His gaze lifted to mine, and I was powerless to look away. Anguish entered his beautiful blue eyes.

"I hurt you. You were a damn virgin, and I took you like..." He ran a hand through his hair. "Fuck!"

"Mason, it's all right. I always wanted it to be you."

I pulled up my panties and reached for my jeans. I got them up under my butt, and the second they touched my poor abused ass, I winced and knew there was no way I could pull them up farther.

Zipper shoved his cock back into his jeans, then knelt at my feet. He pulled off my shoes, then eased my jeans down my legs and took them off me. I felt a little strange standing in the middle of what I assumed was his driveway in nothing but a black tank top and my panties.

"Delphine, I'm so fucking sorry. I saw you there and knew what Flicker had wanted from you, and there were so many of my brothers fucking random women all around the room. I lost my goddamn mind that you'd come anywhere near all that. All I could think was that you needed your ass spanked to teach you a lesson. I never thought it would go that far. Then you got turned on, and I guess I lost control."

My heart constricted at the haunted look in his eyes.

"I took you like some fucking beast and didn't even think about..." He trailed off like it was painful to even continue. My big badass biker, going all soft because he thought he'd hurt me.

I tugged him to his feet and wrapped my arms around his waist. "Mason, did I tell you to stop?"

He shook his head.

"Did I ever once say anything that made you think I wasn't enjoying what you did to me? You said yourself I was wet as hell from you spanking me. Yeah, I may have screamed at first because I'd never had a cock in me before, but the pain didn't last very long, and I loved what we did out here. I've wanted you since the time I was thirteen and figured out boys weren't gross. I wanted you the night you left my dad's shop and never came back. If anyone should apologize for anything, it's me. I ran you off."

He didn't bother fastening his pants, just left them hanging on his hips. With my jeans and shoes lying on his driveway, he scooped me up and carried me into his house. He kicked the door shut behind us and carried me into the living room. When he eased me down onto the couch, I winced and bit my lip. As hard as he'd spanked me, I'd likely be a bit bruised for a few days, but I was glad I hadn't stopped him. I'd always dreamed of what it would be like for Mason to take my virginity, but I'd never thought of him as being so wild and untamed before. Biker, yes, but the kind of man to strip me out in the open, then spank and fuck me? No. That hadn't crossed my mind.

"Jesus, Delphine. I didn't even use fucking protection. I've never fucked a woman without a condom before, and I swear I'm clean. I get tested every month, and I got my last results a week ago. I haven't been with anyone during that time."

"Well, I've never been with anyone before, in any sexy capacity, so I don't think you need to worry about catching something from me."

He ran a hand down his face and paced the room. "Please tell me you're on birth control."

My cheeks warmed and looked away. I couldn't lie to him. "It messes up my hormones, so my doctor said I can't take it."

"I can't decide if I'm upset that you aren't on it because we just fucked without a rubber, or if I'm upset that you wanted to be on it so you could fuck someone else," he muttered as he kept pacing.

"I didn't want anyone else," I said quietly. "But I didn't want to be alone forever either. It was obvious you didn't want me, and I figured you hated me for chasing you off the way I did."

He came to kneel in front of me. His cock peeking through the opening of his jeans made me want him again. My gaze locked on it, still shiny from our mingled release. How the hell could he still be semi-hard after coming? And if he looked that big already, just how much cock had been inside me?

"I left so I wouldn't do something I shouldn't. You were sixteen, Delphine! Do you know how much trouble I'd have been in if I hadn't walked out that night? The last thing I expected when I entered the shop was to find you in my cubicle, naked with your legs spread in invitation. Fuck! You were the most gorgeous girl I'd ever seen, and way too damn young for me. I ran the hell out of there before I did something stupid, because you didn't fucking look sixteen. My cock just saw a pretty, pink pussy and I was hard and ready to go."

"I never wanted to get you into trouble. I just wanted… you," I said.

"I know, baby." He reached up and cupped my cheek. "But I was a thirty-two-year-old man, and you were just a kid. One who looked like a grown-ass woman, but still just a kid. It was beyond wrong. I was so fucking disgusted with myself for reacting to you the way I did I knew I had to leave."

"And now?" I asked. "I'm not a kid anymore, Mason."

"No, you're not," he said with a slight smile. "I'm still too fucking old for you, but damn if this isn't the sweetest, tightest pussy I've ever had."

He reached out and trailed a finger down the center of my panties and my eyes slid shut. He had to feel how wet they were as his cum slipped out of me and coated the material. And why did that make me feel dirty and turned on at the same time?

Mason reached for the waistband of my panties and tugged them down my hips, over my thighs, and let them fall to the floor. He pushed my thighs wide open and just stared.

"You look so pretty covered in my cum," he murmured, and stroked my pussy. "We can talk later. Now that I've had a taste, I want more. You want that, don't you, baby?"

"Yes. Please, Mason."

He stood and stripped off his clothes until he was standing bare in front of me. His body was a work of art, and my fingers itched to trace every muscle, every bit of ink on his gorgeous body. Mason knelt in front of me and pulled my ass to the edge of the couch. His gaze locked on mine.

"I'll get a condom if you want me to, but you felt so fucking good wrapped around me. I know it's like playing Russian roulette, though, and you could end up pregnant."

I looked into those blue eyes that I'd dreamed about for so long. He was right, it was really risky. A risk we shouldn't take, especially while my stepmom was after me, but what if this was my only chance to ever be with him like this? I didn't like the thought of anything separating us. Besides, how likely was it I'd get pregnant the first night I had sex? That only happened in movies, right?

"No condom."

He growled and gripped my hips tight before thrusting deep. "Is that what you want, baby? You want me to fuck you bare and fill you with my cum? You want me to brand you as mine?"

I arched my back and thrust my breasts upward. "Yes! Yes, Mason!"

He practically ripped my shirt over my head, and his lips wrapped around one of my nipples, as he started thrusting into me. He wasn't gentle, and it was almost like he was possessed. Mason pounded into me while he licked and nipped at my breasts. My nails bit into his shoulders as I floated on waves of bliss. I felt his hands inching under me, gripping my poor abused ass, and then he was parting the cheeks. His finger stroked over the tight hole he'd bared, rubbing it in little circles. He applied just enough pressure that I felt naughty, but he didn't press inside. It was enough to set me off. I screamed as I came so damn hard, and still he fucked me.

All of the filthy books I'd read, the porn I'd watched couldn't have ever prepared me for this moment. I knew, though, that if anyone could give me what I craved, that it would be Mason. He bellowed as he came inside me, thrusting his cum deep into my pussy. His chest was heaving as he buried his face in my neck, his cock pulsing inside me. Slowly, he pulled back and looked into my eyes. He stroked my cheek, then kissed me hard and deep. It wasn't a kiss so much as a claiming.

"You're fucking mine now, Delphine. Do you understand?"

I nodded slowly.

"I don't think you do, baby." He ground against my pussy. "No one comes in this pussy but me. You are mine to fuck when I want, how I want. I will take you in every hole you've got and make you scream for more. No barriers. I want my cum all over you, marking you as mine. I walked away before because I had to, but you made the mistake of coming here on my territory. I took this virgin pussy, filled you up, and now you're mine."

"Yours," I said. "I was always yours, Mason."

"Damn right." He kissed me again. "We'll talk later. You can tell me what finally gave you the courage to show up here. Right now, I'm not done fucking my woman. Christ! I'm thirty-fucking-eight years old, and you make me feel like I'm eighteen again."

I bit my lip. "Well, I hope you aren't eighteen because I have a thing for older men."

He growled and narrowed his eyes.

"One older man," I amended. I stroked his strawberry-blond hair, then ran my fingers over his beard. He really was the sexiest man I'd ever seen. And for whatever reason, he wanted me.

"You're going to pay for that slip-up, baby."

The promise in his voice made me shiver, and my nipples hardened even more.

Chapter Two

Zipper

Delphine Lee was in my fucking bed. I stood at the side, staring down at where she lay sprawled across the mattress. I'd fucked her so much that first night and the next two days that I knew she had to be sore, and I may have smirked a little as I looked at the cum dried to her skin. Yeah, I'd been a bastard and marked her the only way I could at the time. Little did she realize when I said I wasn't letting her go that I meant she was never leaving me. This wasn't the type of thing that would fade over time.

If she asked, I wouldn't lie to her. There had been women in the time since I'd left her dad's tattoo parlor. But nothing meaningful. Just a quick fuck here and there, mostly from club pussy, but even those were few and far between. As soon as I came, I was back to feeling empty and like a part of me was fucking missing. I'd never wanted to analyze too closely why that was, but deep down I'd known.

She'd said that first night that Hwan was dead, and I couldn't fucking believe it. The man had seemed indestructible. He'd had Delphine late in life and had been in his fifties when I worked for him. Hwan Lee had found me drunk off my ass in an alley. He'd hauled me into his shop, poured coffee down my throat until I'd sobered up, and we'd done a lot of talking. He'd had room in his shop for another artist, and I had been doing tattoos for about ten years at that point, just not for a fancy shop like Hwan ran.

I remembered little Delphine when she'd been younger, accompanying her dad to work and sitting at one of the drafting tables. She'd had some talent back then, and I wondered if she'd kept up with it. I'd thought about her often over the years. Wondered what she was doing, if she'd met someone her age, maybe even gotten engaged. It wouldn't have surprised me if her dad had decided to play matchmaker and find her some nice Korean boy to marry. From what I remembered, no one in Delphine's family stuck to tradition, but I knew her great-grandparents had come over from Korea, and their children had grown up to marry other Koreans who had either moved to America or been born here. Same for her father. Even if she'd been old enough for me, I didn't think her family would have approved her being with someone like me. I was mostly a mix of German, English, and Irish, but it was the part about me being white that had left me doubting their acceptance. They never turned away a friend or anyone in need, but claiming Delphine? Yeah, that probably wouldn't have gone over too well.

I hoped that Hwan wasn't rolling over in his grave now that Delphine was here with me. Oh, he'd definitely have nailed my ass to the wall if he'd known about all the things I'd done to his baby girl since she'd shown up at the compound. Not that she'd complained. I smiled as my gaze traced over her slender curves.

I'd done my damnedest to not run into her anywhere around town. Not because I hadn't wanted to see her, but because I hadn't trusted myself. Even when she'd grown up, I'd thought it best to keep my distance. She deserved better than me. The few glimpses I caught of her over the years, I'd always turned and walked the other way. I still remembered the conversation I had with Hwan the night I packed my shit and left his shop for good, feeling it was best to sever all ties. Giving him some bullshit excuse of needing to focus on the Reapers had worked at the time, but it hadn't been true. He'd called at first, and I'd answered the first two or three, but I'd ignored the calls after that, and eventually he'd given up. I hated that I'd done that to him, but I'd been thinking of Delphine and what was best for her.

Torch had given me space in the clubhouse to set up a room for tattooing the guys and their old ladies, and I'd only tattooed there for the first six months. Then I'd decided to use some of my money to open my own place. Nothing as big as Hwan's place had been, but I did all right. Now I had two other artists working for me, and I only worked on bigger custom pieces. I left all the flash shit to the underlings.

Delphine shifted on the bed, crooking her knee and spreading her legs open more. I damn near groaned at the sight of her pussy opening, almost as if it were wanting to be fucked again. I'd never had guessed that Delphine could walk on the wild side. She'd not only gotten wet from her spanking, but she'd let me do anything I wanted to do her that first night and the ones since then, and had seemed to love every second of it.

Her eyes slowly opened, and she gave me a sleepy smile. "Morning."

"Morning, beautiful. Are you hungry?"

She nodded and sat up, pushing her hair out of her face. God, I loved those long, brown waves. She'd let her hair grow past the middle of her back, and I'd grabbed a handful of it every time I'd fucked her from behind. I'd ridden her good and hard, those silky locks wrapped around my fist. *Shit.* I was getting hard again just thinking about her, and Delphine more than noticed as her lips curled up in a sinful smile. Hard to miss the ten-inch cock standing upright.

She reached for me, her small hand wrapping around my dick. I hissed in a breath and grabbed her hand, pulling her off me.

"If you do that, we won't leave this bed all day, unless it's for me to fuck you somewhere else around the house. And I think you've had enough of that right now."

She looked out the window at the sunlight streaming into the room. "You know, I've always wondered what it would be like to have sex outside with the sun warming my skin."

"Uh-huh, and I have a ton of brothers running around here who could drive by or walk by at any time and see you. No one gets to enjoy your naked body but me." My brows dipped. "No one has seen you naked, right? Or is there some punk-ass kid out there that needs his ass handed to him?"

"I was a virgin, Mason. A virgin who had never even given a blow job. Do you seriously think I've ever pulled off my clothes for anyone but you?" she asked.

"Didn't mean you hadn't gotten a little frisky without going very far. You're rather adventurous for someone who hasn't done this before."

"I read a lot. And I like porn."

"And just what kind of porn do you like?" I asked, having a hard time picturing her doing something like that. She came across as so sweet and innocent, not someone who'd get off watching people having sex. But then, she had stripped naked when she was sixteen and tried to entice me into claiming her virginity.

Her cheeks warmed, and she dropped her gaze a moment. "I like watching some of the lighter BDSM stuff."

"Like what?"

"Like the guy spanking the woman, tying her up, taking charge. He doesn't ask for anything, just takes what he wants."

"And that gets you off?" I asked. If my dick got any harder right now, I'd be able to pound nails with it. Holy hell. I'd known she'd gotten off on her spanking, but I hadn't realized she'd fantasized about that kind of thing. A trip to Sensual Delights was definitely in order.

She slowly parted her legs, and I could see she was already getting wet again. I groaned and slammed my eyes shut, but it was no good. I'd already seen those pretty pink lips, slick with her arousal, and my cum dried on her skin in various places.

"That was a very bad girl," I said, my voice deeper than usual. "Tempting me when I said we didn't need to have more sex this morning. Do you know what happens to bad girls?"

"What?"

"They get punished. Spread those legs wide, baby. Far as they can go."

She leaned back on her hands and did as I'd said. I braced a hand near her hip, leaning down to get closer to her. Then I toyed with her pussy with my other hand. I rubbed up and down her slit, light strokes that made her nipples hard and gave her goose bumps. I stroked the backs of my fingers against her nipples, then teased them with the hair on my arms. Her clit started to get hard and poke out of her sexy little pussy lips. I brushed my fingers over it, barely touching it but enough to make her want me even more. When she was quivering and ready for more, I stood up.

"Kneel, Delphine," I said, pointing to the floor at my feet.

She slid off the bed and sank to her knees in front of me, her hands folded in her lap. I ran my fingers through her hair, getting a good grip, then pulled her closer to my aching cock.

"Open your mouth. Wide."

She dropped her jaw, then I dragged her lips down my shaft, not stopping until she'd taken all of me. I ground against her lips a moment, and when she choked and her eyes teared up, I pulled out only to thrust back in deep. I set up a slow pace, but fed her every inch of my cock every time. I ground myself against her lips again, and this time when she choked, I ordered her to swallow. I felt her throat close around my cock and it felt so fucking good.

"Gonna fuck your mouth, baby. Be a good girl and take it all. When I come, you swallow it."

She hummed around my shaft, and I started stroking into her mouth faster and harder. Sweat slicked my skin as my balls started to sizzle, and I knew I was close to coming.

"Fuck, yeah. Such a dirty little girl. You like it when I fuck your mouth, don't you?" I asked.

She hummed again, and I made her swallow on my cock once more before I started fucking her mouth even faster. I didn't last but another minute before my cum spurted out of me and filled her mouth. She swallowed it all and when I pulled free, I helped her to her feet.

"Is that pussy hungry for me? Do you ache, baby?" I asked.

She nodded. "Please, Mason. I need you."

I turned her toward the bed, bent her over the mattress, and swatted her ass three times. She still had faint marks from the spankings she'd gotten over the past few days, but she moaned and wriggled, wanting even more.

"No begging. This is your punishment, Delphine. I get to come and you don't. I'm going to keep you on edge for as long as I deem necessary, and if you even think of slipping off somewhere to get yourself off, then I'll be forced to take things to the next level." I stroked her ass cheek, then dipped my fingers into her pussy. So fucking wet. I stroked her a few times, but when I could feel her pussy getting ready to come, I backed off. "No clothes today. You can shower. I'll feed you, but you're going to stay naked so I can play with you when I want."

"Oh, God. Mason, you're going to kill me," she said, her voice muffled from where her face was pressed into the bedding.

"I have a lot of catching up to do, and it seems that you like to be a bad girl."

I helped Delphine stand, then led her into the adjoining bathroom. She fidgeted while I started the shower. When the water was the right temperature, I stepped under the spray and beckoned her inside, then shut the door behind us. I didn't have any girly shit for her to wash with, but I liked the thought of her smelling like me. At least until I could find a more permanent way to warn off any fuckers who might be tempted to sample what was mine. And yeah. She was mine. My woman. My fucking property. Even if I hadn't made it official. Shit. She'd have to meet everyone, especially Torch and Venom. No way she'd be allowed a property patch before then.

"Want to wash me, baby? I'll let you play with my cock again."

She grinned and reached for the shower gel. She took her time soaping me, her little hands roaming my shoulders and chest, scrubbing my back. She reached for my cock, which was already hard again. Delphine wrapped her hand around my shaft and stroked slowly but firmly. Her hands were so damn soft that I groaned as I fucked her fist. Delphine gripped me a little tighter and started stroking faster, and soon I was shooting my cum across her breasts and belly. I hadn't been able to get hard again so fast since I turned thirty, but fuck if I didn't pretty much stay hard around her.

I soaped her, making sure I played with her nipples until they were nice and hard. I stroked my hands down her back, cupped her ass, then teased the tight little hole hidden between those cheeks. I hadn't taken her there yet, but it was on my list. I'd spent a good portion of that first night and the early hours of the next morning getting her used to being touched there. I was barely touching her, just like strokes across that pucker, but when it was time, I wanted her begging for me to fuck her ass. I cupped her pussy and teased her clit with my thumb, getting her all worked up again but not letting her come. I teased her until the water ran cold, then we got out and dried off.

Even though I'd demanded that she remain naked, I pulled on some jeans. No way I was answering the door with my dick out if one of my brothers came by. Flicker had to have seen me haul Delphine out of the clubhouse the night she showed up, so it was only a matter of time before someone got curious. I zipped my pants, then led Delphine into the kitchen. She sat at the small table, but I turned her chair to face the stove so I could watch her while I cooked.

"Spread those thighs for me, baby. Let me see that pretty pussy while I cook something for us."

Her legs parted, and I reached over to tweak her nipples, drawing a moan from her. With a smirk, I turned to get some stuff out of the fridge. I fixed a can of biscuits, some scrambled eggs, and slices of country ham. When I'd plated everything and set it all out on the table with some juice, I sat in the chair at the head of the table. Delphine was to my left, and I still had an excellent view, but I took pity on her.

"Close your legs and eat, Delphine."

Her thighs slammed together, and she turned to face the table, her cheeks flushed and her eyes damn near feverish with need as she kept casting glances my way. I let her eat her meal, and I finished off my plate. After I cleared the table and set everything in the sink, I leaned back against the counter and turned to face her.

"Ready for more of your punishment?" I asked.

"Yes," she said softly.

"Lie on the table with that pussy facing me. Put your heels on the table and spread wide. Show me what belongs to me."

She complied and gave me heated looks. I moved between her spread knees and ran a finger down her pussy. "This does belong to me, doesn't it?"

She nodded.

I reached up and cupped her breasts, squeezing, then playing with her nipples. "And these belong to me?"

"Yes."

My fingers returned to her pussy, then trailed down to her tight ass. "And this?"

She moaned. "Please, Mason. I can't take much more of your teasing."

I circled that tight little hole, then gathered some of her cream on my finger and used it to lubricate her ass, slowly sinking my finger into her, watching her face for any sign that she might be in pain. Some women loved having their ass played with, and for others it was too uncomfortable or painful. And I didn't want to hurt her.

"Does my baby need to come?" I asked.

"Yes. Yes!"

"Do you want to come while I finger fuck your ass?"

"Mason," she moaned.

I fucking loved hearing my name on her lips. To everyone else I was Zipper. And I'd sure as fuck not let another woman call me Mason. Not since I'd gotten my road name. I went slow and easy, giving her time to adjust. Since I didn't have lube handy, I only used the one finger. She was too damn tight for anything else right now, but I *would* take that ass. It was mine and I was going to love driving my cock into that tight hole.

My finger stroked in and out of her, and I dropped to my knees, taking her clit into my mouth. I lashed it with my tongue and nipped at it with my teeth. It didn't take long before she was coming. Her pussy gushed with her release and I lapped up the juices. My cock ached to fuck her, but she was all puffy and pink from being so thoroughly used. The last thing I wanted to do was hurt her for real. Making her ass sore was one thing, but I didn't want to cause her true pain. I still hated that I'd fucked her so ruthlessly and taken her virginity the way I had. I'd wanted to punish her for putting herself in danger, but it hadn't occurred to me that she'd still be an innocent. If I'd known, I would have been gentler, at least until she'd gotten accustomed to having a cock in her pussy. No way I'd have been able to hold back for long from driving my dick balls-deep inside her.

"Come on, baby. I'm going to run some hot water for you. You should soak and ease the aches and pains. And don't even try to tell me you don't hurt at least a little."

"Maybe a bit," she said. "But I wouldn't trade one minute of my time with you. I've loved being in your arms, Mason."

I wrapped an arm around her waist and pulled her tight against my chest. "It's where you're going to stay. You can get dressed when you're done soaking. We still need to discuss what brought you here."

"All right."

We walked back to the master bathroom, and I filled the large, jetted tub with water as hot as Delphine could stand it, then I left her to relax. I cleaned the breakfast dishes, then sprayed the table down with cleanser and wiped it down. Twice. Didn't bother me that she'd come on the table, but other people did occasionally visit and sit there.

I was flipping through channels on the living room TV when the doorbell rang. I'd known it was coming sooner or later. I stretched as I stood and went to answer, finding Flicker on the other side. He still looked pissed as hell about Delphine denying him at the clubhouse, and I couldn't blame him. Delphine was hot as fuck. He'd thought she was a sure thing, then she'd refused to go with him. Good thing too. If she'd slept with him, or blew him, and I found out, brother or not, I'd have beat his ass. Her punishments that first night and the last two days would have seemed mild compared to what I'd have done to her if she'd fucked him.

"What's up with the hot piece of ass from the clubhouse? You know the rules. Pussy in the clubhouse is free to any of us," Flicker said.

"She wasn't there to be club pussy. She's a part of my past and was looking for me," I said, leaning against the wall as he loomed inside the doorway.

"From your past?" he asked, his eyes narrowing. "Is she the reason you hardly ever get your dick wet?"

I shrugged. That was my business and no one else's.

"Her pants and boots are in your driveway," Flicker said.

Shit. I'd forgotten about that. We'd stayed naked ever since I'd brought her home, and we hadn't needed them. Thankfully, it hadn't rained.

"Right next to your bike," he said. "Couldn't even wait to get inside? Just had to fuck her out in the open over your hog?"

"Maybe."

"If I'd have known that, I'd have stopped by for a show. Bet she's loud when she comes."

My hands clenched, and I had to remind myself not to punch the Treasurer of my club. He was an officer and I was just a patched member. If it came down to taking sides, Torch would ride my ass and not Flicker's. Didn't mean I had to like what he had to say about Delphine, though. She was mine. Not some damn club slut on display for him or anyone else.

"Her body is mine to look at, not yours," I said. "She's not up for grabs."

"If she's sticking around for longer than a few days, you need to talk to Torch and Venom. I'll give you until tomorrow. If she's still here then and you haven't spoken to them, I'm making a call. She's not your property, or Dixie Reapers property. Which means she doesn't belong here."

"The fuck she doesn't," I said, my temper rising. "Delphine is mine."

"Then you need to introduce her to the club and put your mark on her." Flicker smirked. "With something other than your dick."

"Smartass," I muttered.

Flicker slapped my arm. "Look, I won't lie. I wanted to go a few rounds with her. She's hot shit, but if you've already laid claim to her, then no harm, no foul. If you want her to have the respect of everyone, though, then you need to do this the right way."

"I know. I still have to find out why she's here. We've been a bit preoccupied. Once I know what's going on, then I'll talk to the Pres and VP. Delphine isn't leaving, though. I told her that her ass was mine, and I'm not letting her walk out of here. If I have to restrain her, then so be it."

"You could always just fuck her until she passes out," Flicker said.

I snorted. "Thanks. I'll take that under advisement, but considering how long she can last, my dick might fall off before that happens."

"Lucky bastard."

"Your woman is out there. Maybe closer than you think."

Flicker stepped outside and I followed him, picking up Delphine's things and carrying them back into the house. I shut the door and carried her pants into the bedroom so she'd have access to them. I could hear her humming in the tub and smiled. It was nice having her here, felt right. She belonged in my bed, in my home. I already had a design in mind for her property ink. I'd known for years what I would give her, even though I wasn't allowed to think about such things back then without being a big perv. Maybe even when she'd been a teen I'd known she was meant to be mine, after she'd done a bit of growing up.

I waited patiently for her to finish soaking and get dressed. It was time for that talk. She'd come to me asking for help, and I had a feeling she needed more than my assistance moving into a new apartment or getting out of a traffic ticket. And now that my dick wasn't ruling my brain, and I wasn't so fucking pissed that I wanted to punish her again and again, I was able to think about things more clearly. She'd come here for a reason, and something told me she was in big trouble. Whatever it was, I'd take care of it. No one was going to hurt my woman. Not now. Not ever.

Chapter Three

Delphine

I knew it was time to tell Mason everything, and I had no idea how he would react. I'd thought the moment he saw me, he'd make me leave. Instead, he'd fucked me until I ached and my ass was tender from being spanked so many times. I didn't regret any of it, and would gladly do it all again. He was everything I'd always wanted, and now that I'd had a taste, I wanted more. He said he wanted to keep me, but I didn't exactly know what that meant. For a week? A month? A year? He'd never been the type to settle down, so I didn't delude myself into thinking he meant forever. It had already been a few days, and that was probably longer than he usually kept a woman around.

Mason had set my jeans in the bedroom at some point and I pulled on my clothes, wrinkling my nose at having to wear dirty panties. But as tight as my jeans were, there was no way I was going commando. If I'd thought ahead, I could have washed my stuff during one of our sex breaks, but my mind had been on Mason and only on Mason. I dressed quickly and went to find him, following the sounds of the TV to the living room. His house wasn't huge by any means, but the place looked like it had a good amount of square footage. I wondered if he planned on filling the extra bedrooms with kids one day.

Pressing a hand to my belly, I wondered if there was one growing inside me already. As often as he'd taken me, we were gambling, big time. I didn't know how he felt about that, or if he'd really thought about it past that first time. We hadn't talked about it past the initial discovery of me not being on the pill and him not using a condom. I'd told him I didn't want him to use one, mostly because I'd wanted to feel all of him, but he had to have worried about me getting pregnant, right? Wasn't that something that freaked guys the hell out? Was he trying to get me pregnant? Or did he just not care?

Butterflies swarmed in my stomach, or maybe it was more like angry hornets, as I stepped into the living room and eased onto the couch next to him. Mason winked at me and reached for my hand.

"Feel better?" he asked.

"A little. I guess we need to talk."

"You didn't come find me in all this time, so it makes me think something big is going on. You need help of some kind. And I know if you'd been looking for another shot at getting into my pants, you wouldn't have waited six years."

My cheeks warmed. He wasn't wrong. Not entirely, anyway. I had thought of coming to see him before now, but I'd been so scared how he would react. Things hadn't ended well between us, with me throwing myself at him, and him walking out and vanishing from my life altogether. If I'd known that I'd get the kind of reception I had that first night, I'd have been here sooner, and maybe my stepmom wouldn't be trying to have me killed. Yeah, I had to admit it. The woman my dad had married, had told me to treat as a mother, wanted me dead all so she could have everything.

"Did you keep up with my dad at all after you left?" I asked.

"He called a few times, and I passed him on the street on occasion. Not like we met for coffee once a week or anything, just a nod as I passed on the opposite side. He tried to keep in touch, but I started ignoring his calls. I never told him the real reason I'd left, but I sometimes wondered if he sensed something else had happened that night."

I nodded. My dad had been rather intuitive, so that didn't surprise me at all. I'd caught a few looks aimed my way the days after Mason had left. At first, I'd been paranoid and scoured every inch of his shop looking for cameras, thinking he'd witnessed my humiliation, but I'd never found any.

"He got remarried a few years ago. Some woman with three kids convinced him she was in love with him. From what I've learned of her over the years, what she loved was his house and the fact he owned his own business. She never did like me, and when Dad died, he left his business and half his life insurance to me. But there was a provision in the will," I said.

"What provision?" Mason asked.

"Since I wasn't married and I don't have any children, if I die, then everything goes to her. Unless I have kids by the time that happens."

"Okay. So, don't die."

I snorted. "That would be easier if she hadn't hired someone to kill me. Even if she hadn't, I could just as easily step off a curb and get hit by a bus, or choke on a piece of chicken. There are no guarantees in life, Mason."

"Wait." His gaze darkened and his lips firmed. "What do you mean she hired someone to kill you?"

"I thought I was just having a lot of accidents at first. Nearly getting hit by a car, having something fall off a building and nearly squish me, a mugging gone wrong. Then I started getting shot at, and I noticed two men are always present when these things happen to me. I tried to tell the police, but I don't have any evidence."

"How did you get through the gate the night you came here?" Mason asked. "I'm glad you're here, don't get me wrong, but the Prospect manning the gate should have never let you in. Did those men try to kill you again? Follow you? Was Ivan worried about your safety?"

"Um. I asked to see you first, and he told me no. Said I could only get in if I was going to suck cock, so... I lied. Told him I wanted to party. He let me through, and I went to find you, and ran into that other guy instead."

Mason tensed from head to toe. "Did Ivan try to..."

"No! He just let me through. I think he might have known I was lying and just wanted me to get a lesson in what happened to women who don't follow the rules. If you hadn't seen that other guy trying to get me to have sex with him, I'm not sure what would have happened. Would he have forced himself on me?" I asked.

"Flicker's a good guy. All of them are. He wouldn't have forced you, but he might have tried really fucking hard to get you to change your mind."

"I don't know what to do, Mason. I doubt those guys can get into your compound, but I can't just stay locked up in here indefinitely. I came crashing into your life and bringing all this trouble to your door."

"Hey." He tipped up my chin and forced me to look him in the eye. "I want you here, got it? Was I pissed to see you standing in the clubhouse? Hell, yeah. That's no place for you. But I'm not throwing you out, Delphine. Did you miss the part where I said you're mine?"

"But your *what*? Your good little whore? Your slut? Are you keeping me for a week, or a month?

You're not the type to settle down, so I know this will end eventually."

He growled and his eyes flashed with anger. "I said you're mine. As in, I'm never letting you the fuck go. I claimed you, Delphine. Told Flicker you're my woman. He's one of the club officers, so I'm being deadly serious, baby."

"What does that mean, I'm your woman?" I asked, feeling a little lost. I'd never once considered this scenario when I'd planned to find Mason. I'd figured I'd be lucky if he'd listen to me at all.

"Babe, it means you're *mine*. My woman. My old lady."

"Old lady?" I looked down at myself. "I'm twenty-two."

Mason choked back his laughter. "Uh, yeah. It's a term in the MC. Kind of like a wife but without the priest. Although, if you want to get married, one of the guys is an ordained minister. You'll be inked as *Property of Zipper* and get a cut with a property patch on it. It's forever, Delphine."

"Forever?" I asked softly looking up at him. "You want me forever?"

He placed a hand on my belly. "Did my best to knock you up the last few days. Yeah, I want you permanently in my life. I'm sorry I walked away and never contacted you again. I was worried I wouldn't be able to say no if you came onto me again. And I really didn't want to go to jail. Your dad might have liked me, but if he'd found out I fucked his sixteen-year-old daughter? I'd have been lucky if he didn't bury me in a shallow grave. I knew back then I wasn't good enough for you, that your family wouldn't approve of us. But I don't give a shit anymore. Even if your dad were still alive, I'd still claim you."

"What do you mean they wouldn't approve?" I asked. "Besides the age difference, why would you think my dad would have had an issue with us being together? He loved you like a son."

"You family has always…" He rubbed the back of his neck. "I'm white, Delphine. I didn't think I had a snowball's chance in hell of getting your dad's approval to be with you. Not as more than a friend."

"Are you calling my dad a racist?" I asked.

"No! Fuck, no! I just… I figured your family was more traditional? Is that the right word? Look, I know your dad and your mom were both Korean, and your grandparents and their parents were Korean. I thought he'd want the same for you."

I tried not to smile. "Mason, my great-grandparents and grandparents had arranged marriages. But my parents? It was just luck they were both Korean. They met and fell in love. Dad's second wife is white. Although, now that I think about it, she's not a stellar example of your race."

"You let me worry about that piece of shit stepmom of yours. You said she has kids? How old?" he asked.

"The eldest is a year younger than me, the other two are still in high school. They're not bad, compared to their mom. I actually get along with them. The only reason she even has custody is because their dad went to prison. Vehicular manslaughter while under the influence. It wasn't his first offense, though, so he got put away for quite a while."

"How the hell did your dad end up with that woman?" Mason asked. "From what I heard, he was going to love your mom forever and never look at another woman, even if he died a lonely old man."

"Guess he got a little too lonely. Or maybe she conned him. She seems the type."

"I'm going to introduce you to the rest of the club, and there's one guy in particular I want you to meet. His name is Wire and he's a hacker. If there's any dirt to be found on your stepmom, he'll find it. But I need to know how far you want me to take this, Delphine. I can bury her six feet under and never think twice about it, but you said she has kids still in high school. I don't know what will happen to them if I make her disappear."

"Disappear?" I asked. "You would kill her? Seriously? As in… murder?"

I could feel my heart racing and my hands began to tremble. I'd known the club wasn't necessarily law-abiding, but I'd never once thought they went around killing people. Did I not really know Mason at all? Had I let a killer take me to bed the past few days?

"Easy, baby. I would never hurt an innocent. Man, woman, or child. Your stepmom isn't innocent. She's trying to kill you. If she has a soul, it's probably pitch-black. I'd be doing the world a favor by getting rid of her. It's not something we do often, but when the need arises? Yeah, we get our hands dirty, and we don't lose sleep over it. Bull's woman was nearly gang-raped. We handled it. Venom's old lady, who happens to be Bull's daughter, was almost sold, and we took down a sex-trafficking ring. We only go after the people who deserve a bullet between their eyes."

"And the rest of the time?" I asked.

"We do a few arms deals, never local. In the past we've dealt some of the lighter drugs, but never to kids. A few of the guys take out the trash for a price on occasion. And sometimes we're just the mules. We run shipments we don't ask too many questions about, from one state to another. We never deal in women or kids, though, and we do our best not to get involved in stuff that will harm innocent people. At least, things we know for sure would harm innocents."

"And you have a tattoo parlor?" I asked.

He nodded. "Slinging Ink opened a few years ago. I still do the club tattoos here, mostly. Well, at the clubhouse. I have a room set up there. I don't charge for property ink or anything club related. The guys want extra shit, they pay for that, though. I have a decent clientele at the shop and do okay, plus I get money from the deals the club handles."

"And this Wire person? He's a hacker? Like the illegal kind?"

Mason bit his lip as his eyes flashed with amusement. "Do you know another kind? He's the best in the world, as far as I know. And he's on our side. I'm going to call my Pres and get him to set up Church in a bit. Women usually don't attend, so I'm going to leave you in the main part of the clubhouse with a drink while we handle business. I'll get them up to speed on your situation, and then you and I will meet with Wire."

"Clubhouse?" I blanched, remembering my first night here.

"Easy, baby. During the day, the place is pretty empty. And the old ladies and kids are in there all the time, unless we're partying. And now that I have an old lady of my own, I won't be doing that very much."

My breath caught. "Very much? But you'll still go? Where all those naked women are…"

"Hey. Calm down, Delphine. I won't touch another woman, not ever. You're mine and you're the only one I want. Fuck, I barely touched them before.

All these years, it's only been you I wanted, as fucked-up as that was."

My heart slowed and I could breathe a little easier.

"I'm going to make my calls. You sit here and relax. After we get things figured out a bit more, I'll send one of the Prospects to clean out your place."

"Clean out… um, why are you cleaning out my apartment?" I asked, briefly wondering if Mason would get angry all over again when he found out where I lived. It wasn't exactly in the best part of town. And what the hell would I do about my dad's shop? If Mason locked me behind these gates, who would oversee the shop?

"Did you miss the part of you're mine forever? I'm having your things moved in here. If you want to keep your furniture, we'll find room for it. Or toss out some of mine and use yours."

"My stuff can be donated," I said. "The furniture and kitchen stuff. I'll want the rest."

He nodded. "Then let me get started on some stuff. The TV is yours to command until it's time for us to head to the clubhouse."

I watched him walk out of the room. Everything felt a little surreal. Had Mason just decided to keep me forever, move me into his home, knock me up with his kid, and arrange my stepmother's demise? What the hell rabbit hole had I fallen down?

By the time he'd finished his calls, I was a nervous wreck about meeting the others. The hours seemed to fly past, and soon I found myself on the back of his bike, my arms around his waist, as he drove us over to the clubhouse. When we walked inside, I wasn't sure what to expect. The place looked nearly deserted except for a guy behind the bar, two more at a nearby table, and some women who didn't look like the skanky ones from my first night here.

Mason led me over to the table of women and I tried to pull back, not sure I was ready to just dive right into meeting his people. But he was relentless and dragged me over to the table. The women looked to be around my age. One held a baby in her arms, a boy if the blue clothes were any indication. The other two were childless, or at least didn't have any with them.

"Delphine, this is Kalani, Isabella, and Darian. Kalani is Tex's old lady and wife, Isabella is Torch's old lady and wife, and Darian…"

"Belongs to Bull," Darian said with a smile. "Sit down and join us."

Mason pulled out an empty chair and I sat. He brushed a kiss on my cheek and whispered in my ear that he'd be back soon. As he walked off, my stomach fluttered with nerves. The other women were smiling, but I'd never been very good at making friends, and I knew these women were important to Mason.

"So, how do you know Zipper?" Darian asked. "I've hardly ever seen him with a woman in the roughly two years I've been here."

Isabella nudged Darian with her arm and gave her a stern look. "What she means to say is that you must be important to Zipper, so we're curious about you. He never talks about having someone special in his life, but he brought you here so…"

I felt like a bug under a microscope. Or maybe one of those butterflies pinned to a board. "Well, he used to work for my dad," I said.

"Who's your dad?" Kalani asked. "Does he work with the club?"

"He was a tattoo artist, owned his own shop. He passed away about six months ago. It's kind of why

I'm here. I needed some help and..." I hated using his club name, but I didn't know if anyone here knew Mason the way I did. "Zipper was the only one I think of."

"Why do you grimace when you say his name?" Darian asked.

"Because of how he got it," I muttered. "His pants unzipped easily when it came to the opposite sex."

Isabella watched me thoughtfully. "That's not the man I've come to know. He seldom hooks up with any of the club sluts, never dates that I know of, and he's always had this haunted look in his eyes. Like there was something in his past he regretted. I'm thinking that might have been you, but you would have had to be a kid back then."

"I threw myself at him," I admitted with my cheeks feeling like they were on fire. "He ran and never came back. I was sixteen and he was in his thirties. I didn't care, but I'd never considered that he might face jail time if we hooked up."

"And now you're here. As what exactly?" Isabella asked.

"Isabella is the Pres's old lady," Darian said. "It's kind of her job to help look out for the club, so what she's asking is whether or not you're trouble."

"I'm not trouble, but it's following me."

Isabella nodded. "Well, I'm sure it's nothing our men can't handle. Won't be the first time they've rescued a damsel in distress."

"Or the last," Kalani said. "Too many of them are still single for this to be the last time. The Dixie Reapers only seem to claim women who need them. Not that I'm complaining. Tex dragging me out of the asylum was the best thing that ever happened to me, and now I have this little guy and an awesome stepdaughter."

"Asylum?" I asked, feeling like there was an interesting story there. Kalani's eyes darkened and she looked away.

"Not good memories," Darian said. "She will probably tell you some of it when she's ready. So, not to sound like an idiot or anything, but are you Chinese?"

"Korean."

Darian nodded. "Didn't mean any offense."

"None taken." And I was being honest. People always guessed wrong so I was used to it.

"So who is after you?" Kalani asked. "My dad wanted me dead, Isabella had the cartel after her, Darian was running from a group of guys, and I've heard the others were in trouble too."

"Well," Isabella said. "Technically, Kayla wasn't in trouble until after Preacher knocked her up. Not from what she's told us anyway. Unless you count Johnny being mad that she was in the clubhouse when she shouldn't have been. But I know he helped her run that same night, so maybe there's some stuff they aren't saying."

"How many, um, old ladies are there?" I asked, still trying to get used to the club terms. It still didn't make any sense to me since none of us were old.

"Well, you haven't met Kayla, and like I said, she's Preacher's woman. Then there's Ridley -- she belongs to Venom. And Mara belongs to Rocky. Of course, there's Laken, but she's not really a Dixie Reapers old lady. Her brother Flicker is a Reaper, but she's the old lady to another club. They have a representative who stays here. I'm sure you'll meet everyone later," Isabella said.

Flicker's sister? As in the guy who tried to get me to have sex with him that first night? I wasn't sure how that meeting would go. For that matter, I wasn't anxious to see Flicker anytime soon. He had to be mad that I'd turned him down.

"Is Zipper in there claiming you as his old lady?" Kalani asked. "I've heard it's supposed to go through a vote, but I don't think they always follow the rules."

"Are you kidding?" Isabella asked. "We were only too happy for Tex to keep you. If Wire hadn't suggested a marriage of convenience, then I'm sure Torch would have pushed him to mark you anyway. And they were right to push Tex in your direction because you're perfect for each other."

Kalani smiled and looked genuinely happy.

"I think he's telling them about the trouble I'm in," I said. "But he did tell me he wants to claim me as his old lady. He offered to marry me if that's what I wanted. I'm still not sure I understand the old lady thing, though. Do you just live with them forever and… what?"

"Some of the guys don't believe in marriage, so they have old ladies and never get married. Then there are guys like Torch who wanted me to have his name. So he married me, and I think he believed it's what would make me happy." Isabella smiled. "I love that man like crazy. I'd have been glad to be his without a ring, but outside this compound, it's hard to explain the old lady concept to others. So women sometimes think the men with old ladies are still up for grabs, just because no one is wearing a ring. It's nuts."

"Why do you think Ridley sends her kids out with Venom as often as she can when he goes into town without her?" Darian asked. "Although, I think that kind of backfires because a lot of women dig the single dad thing, and since he isn't wearing a ring, I've heard he gets hit on a lot. Bull isn't too happy about it because it makes his daughter upset."

My brow furrowed. "So, you're Bull's old lady, and Ridley is his daughter, but she's with Venom?"

Darian nodded.

"So your stepdaughter is close to your age?" I asked, trying to wrap my mind around it.

Isabella snickered. "Darian's younger than Ridley. And Ridley has given Bull hell about it, but she's happy that her dad has someone to love."

Darian reached over and patted my arm. "Don't worry. You'll eventually figure everything out. This place can be a little confusing at first, but you'll have a lot of friends and built-in babysitters when you start having kids. I think you'll like being here, and Zipper's a great guy."

"Yeah." I smiled. "He really is. I've missed him, but it's my fault he left."

A door banged open and booted feet came around the corner. I looked over my shoulder and saw Mason walk into the room with several other guys. Darian got up and ran toward a tall man with long blond hair. He caught her as she went airborne, his wide smile a flash of white in his dark beard. I assumed he was Bull the way she wrapped herself around him.

Mason came closer, an older man standing next to him with a head of silver hair and a full silver beard. Mason helped me stand as the other men gathered around the table. A tall man with a dark beard placed his hand on Kalani's shoulder.

"Delphine, these are my brothers, the Dixie Reapers. This is Torch," he said, motioning to the silver-haired man. "He's the President, which means his word is law."

"It's nice to meet you," I said, then glanced around at the others. "All of you."

"Do you think you have what it takes to be a Dixie Reapers old lady?" one of the men asked.

"Um, I'm still not completely clear on what an old lady is, but I would do anything for Mason." My cheeks warmed. "I mean Zipper."

Isabella sounded like she was choking in an effort not to laugh.

"What's so damn funny, woman?" Torch asked her.

"She hates his road name," Isabella said. "Every time she says it, it looks like she's chewing glass. Then again, I guess any woman who was going to be his woman wouldn't care for it."

Zipper rubbed the back of his neck, his cheeks stained red as he gazed down at me. "I never really thought about how it would make you feel. I haven't been that guy in a long time, Delphine, but it's the name my club gave me."

"It's fine," I assured him. "I don't want to change you, Mas... I mean, Zipper. Might take me some time to adjust to calling you that."

"Wire is waiting to meet you, Delphine," Torch said. "You have the support of this club, and Zipper's request to make you his old lady has been approved. We protect our own, so don't worry about your stepmom. She won't be a problem for long."

"Thank you," I murmured.

"Come on, baby. Let's go talk to Wire," Zipper said, leading me through the crowd of his brothers. I saw Flicker as we passed and he winked at me.

Something inside me loosened a little, since it didn't seem he was as mad at me as I'd thought he would be.

We walked down the hall and stopped at the last room on the right. When the doors were pushed open, I saw a bank of computer monitors, and a ginger-haired man was kicked back in a chair, obviously waiting for us. He smiled and stood, holding his hand out to me.

"Nice to meet you, Delphine. I'm Wire."

"Hi," I said, shaking his hand.

"Why don't you give me some background on your stepmom, and I'll see what dirt I can dig up on her. With some luck, I can make her disappear in a slightly more legal way by letting the police handle her. If not, we'll take care of her," he said.

I glanced at Zipper, but he merely smiled at me.

"Okay. Her name is Tia Lee. It used to be Tia Hopkins before she married my dad. She has three kids, and as far as I know, she hasn't worked since my dad married her. Before that, she was a waitress at some hole in the wall. I really don't know a lot about her. She hated me from the very first, so I tried not to spend much time with her."

Wire nodded. "And your dad left her something when he died?"

"Yeah. Half his life insurance policy and the house."

"And what did you get?" he asked.

"The other half of the policy and his tattoo shop, Lee's World of Ink. My dad set up his will so if I didn't have kids, his wife would get my half if something happened to me. So, I think she's trying to have me killed since I'm currently childless."

"Zipper told us some of the shit you've been through the last few months. I'm sorry you lost your dad, and I'm even sorrier your stepmom is such a bitch."

I nodded, not really knowing what to say to that.

"Let me work some magic and see what I can find," Wire said. "As soon as I have something, I'll let Zipper know. You're one of us now, Delphine. You don't have to fight this on your own."

My eyes teared up a little, and Zipper pulled me into his arms.

"Thanks," I said softly.

Zipper led me back to the main part of the clubhouse and two men with *Prospect* on their black vests were leaning against the bar. Zipper led us straight to them.

"I need the two of you to clean out Delphine's place and bring her stuff here. She said she doesn't want the furniture or kitchen stuff, but everything else should be boxed up and dropped at my place," Zipper said. "Give them your address, baby, and the keys to your place."

I bit my lip. "Twenty-three Forrest Road, apartment B6."

I felt Zipper's laser-focused gaze on me, and I slowly looked up. The fury in his eyes was unmistakable. His jaw clenched, and I would have sworn I heard his teeth grinding.

"You live *where*?" He all but growled the last part.

"Um, I..." I bit my lip again.

"Fuck! Jesus fucking Christ, Delphine! You have could have been raped and murdered in that damn place! What were you thinking?"

"I couldn't afford anything else after Dad was gone, not at first. Even after the will was read, I didn't get the money until the past few weeks. I've not exactly had a chance to move yet. I was a little too busy trying to keep my stepmom from killing me."

Zipper closed his eyes tight and blew out a breath, growling a little more, then he looked at the Prospects. "You heard her."

I pulled the apartment key out of my pocket and handed it over to them, then Zipper practically shoved me out of the clubhouse and over to his bike. I could still feel the anger pulsing off him, and I had no doubt I was about to be punished again. I hoped my poor ass could handle another paddling, and that he didn't have anything more creative in mind.

Chapter Four

Zipper

Furious didn't begin to describe how I was feeling. Knowing that Delphine had been in the absolute worst neighborhood in this town made me want to rip someone apart. I didn't understand how Hwan could have ever let her live in a place like that. He'd adored Delphine, and I wanted to know what had happened between them that he could have ever let her put herself in danger. Just thinking about anything happening to her made me want to kill someone.

I roared into the driveway on the bike, then shut off the engine. Delphine got off and practically ran for the door, but that wasn't going to save her. Oh no. That ass was mine. If things were so dire that she had to live on Forrest Road of all places, then she should have come to talk to me sooner.

I stomped through the front door and slammed it shut, then went in search of my naughty girl. I'd been so fucking pissed that I hadn't been able to ink her the way I'd planned. Another reason to punish her. And if my dick got hard thinking about that, well that was for me to know and her to find out. The hard way. Spanking her, then fucking her over the seat of my bike a few nights ago was mild compared to what I wanted to do to her right now. She'd put herself in danger, and that was unacceptable.

"Delphine! Get your ass in here!"

She peered around the bedroom door at me, then made a squeaking sound and she took off. If I hadn't been so damn mad, I might have found it cute as hell. I slapped my hand against the bedroom door as I stepped through. I must have pushed it harder than I thought since it bounced off the wall. Delphine looked paler than usual, her dark eyes wide. It was enough to make me stop. Was she afraid of me? Like really, truly afraid? I didn't like how that made me feel. Yeah, I was fucking livid, but she had to know that I'd never seriously hurt her. I might make her ass red, or leave her sexually frustrated, or fuck her until neither of us could stand, but I'd never really hurt her.

"Baby, come here," I said, trying to sound calmer.

"Are you going to hit me?" she asked.

Fucking hell! "Del, have I ever hit you? I've spanked your ass, made you sexually frustrated, but have I harmed you? Ever? I mean really harmed you?"

"No," she said softly. Slowly, she came toward me.

I gripped her hair and pulled her head back, making her look me in the eye. "Baby, I will punish you when you've been bad, but I will never cause you any real pain. Understand? I'd sooner cut off my damn arm than do that."

"I'm sorry."

My anger completely deflated at the soft words, and all I wanted to do was hold her close. I lowered my head and kissed her lips. "You have nothing to be sorry for. I'm the one who's sorry. I didn't mean to scare you. I didn't realize you thought I was capable of hurting you like that. But I'm fucking pissed, Delphine. How could your dad have ever let you live there?"

"He didn't know," she said. "He never saw the dump I live in now, and even though the will had been read a few weeks after his death, like I said to Wire, it wasn't until recently that everything was finalized and I received the money and the deed to Dad's shop. There was just so much stuff to do, and then all the accidents started happening. I didn't have time to worry about fixing my situation."

"Do you realize how dangerous it was for you to live there?" I asked. "Do you understand why I got so angry when I heard you say that street name? You could have been raped. Hell, a pretty young woman like you? They likely would have sold you when they were finished playing. If they didn't kill you."

"I know, Mason. I know. I never wanted to move there, and I really was going to get a better place once I got everything figured out. I never intended for it to be a permanent move. I just needed some time."

"You should have come to me when you got into trouble the first time. I'd have helped you cover your rent, or convinced you to move in here. You know I can't let this ride, Del. You did something that could have seriously gotten you hurt or worse."

She nodded. Slowly, she took a breath, then let it out. Delphine pulled out of my arms and approached the bed, then she stripped out of her clothes and laid her torso down across the mattress, her ass in the air. A spanking wasn't exactly what I'd been planning, but I could make this work. I knew how much she loved to be punished, though.

"Put your hands behind your back," I told her, my voice gruffer than usual.

She crossed her wrists at the small of her back, and I reached into the bedside table drawer and pulled out some handcuffs. I clicked them into place and her body tensed, then I smoothed my hand down her spine. Using my booted foot, I nudged her feet farther apart until I had an unencumbered view of her pussy.

I squeezed her ass cheeks with my hands and fought the urge to just shove my cock deep inside her, but that would be even more of a reward. Then again, as much as she liked being punished, I didn't think anything I ever did to her would be a true punishment. She'd gotten off on being spanked, had even enjoyed me sexually teasing her all morning. It seemed my sweet little Delphine was dirtier than I'd ever realized.

My hand cracked against her ass, making her jump. I didn't give her time to prepare and swatted again and again. Blow after blow turned her ass a bright red, my handprints clearly visible on her tender skin. I rubbed my fingers against her slit and felt how wet she was. I gave her pussy a smack, and she yelped and tensed. I smacked it again, and fuck if she didn't get even wetter. I rubbed and pinched her clit, then spanked her ass and pussy again.

"Are you going to do something dangerous again?" I asked.

"Maybe?" she said, making it sound more like a question.

This wasn't working quite the way I'd planned for it to. Reaching back into the drawer, I grabbed the bottle of lube and shoved it into my pocket, then I lifted her into my arms and carried her to the back of the house. She hadn't spent any time on the sun porch, with its wall-to-wall windows on three sides, and not a blind or curtain in sight. It was doubtful anyone would see us since it faced the backyard, and most of my brothers were at the clubhouse, but the possibility was there. I had an idea. The more I was getting to know this older version of Delphine, the more I realized she had a wild streak in her.

I bent her over the arm of the loveseat out there. Her breasts would swing with every stroke of my hand, or my cock, and I'd have easier access to pinch those pretty nipples. It was time to see if Delphine could get off on being punished, come hard enough she screamed.

I fisted her hair and leaned down until my lips brushed her ear. "See all these windows, Delphine? Any one of my brothers could walk by, see you bound and naked, watch me punish you."

She moaned and her eyes slid shut, but her cheeks warmed with arousal. Yeah, that's what I'd thought. I didn't know if she actually wanted someone to watch us, but the thought that someone *could* was enough to excite her. I wasn't too thrilled with any of my brothers actually getting to see her naked like this, but she didn't have to know it wasn't likely anyone would walk past.

"Do you like that, Del? Like the thought of my brothers watching you get punished?" I asked my voice soft and low.

"Y-yes."

"Would it turn you on for them to get hard while you got off?"

She whimpered and I smiled. Yeah, I had a dirty girl on my hands all right.

"Be good and take your punishment, and I'll let you have my cock."

My hand cracked against her ass again. I made that pretty, soft skin nice and red. Hot to the touch. Spanked her pussy too until she was dripping wet. I leaned across her back, my denim-covered cock grinding into her ass, as I pinched and played with her nipples. She was crying and begging, and I knew she was fucking close.

"Please, Mason. Please. I need it."

"What do you need, baby?" I asked, pulling back and swatting her ass again. "Need me to punish this ass? Or maybe your pussy?"

I smacked her clit twice, and she came in a gush. I smirked as I unbuckled my belt and unfastened my pants. I lowered them only enough to pull out my cock, then walked around to the front of the loveseat. Gripping her hair tight, I pulled her head toward me.

"Open."

She licked her lips, then parted them, and I thrust inside. I didn't go slow or easy, I took what I wanted, knowing it was also what she needed.

"That's it, baby. Take all of it. Every fucking inch."

She was squirming again and I knew she wanted to come.

I fucked her mouth hard and deep, not stopping until I came. She swallowed it all like a good girl, then kept sucking. It didn't take long before I was hard as a fucking post again.

I pulled free of her mouth, then stood her up. I left the handcuffs on her as I sat on the loveseat and pulled her down, lowering that sopping wet pussy onto my cock. She was facing the windows, and her thighs were spread, one on either side of mine. I widened my legs even more, opening her up completely. Twisting and pulling at her nipples, I felt her pussy flutter around my cock, then I gripped her hips and helped her ride me, slamming her down with every stroke.

"Fuck yeah, baby. So damn good."

"Mason. I... Oh, God!"

"Take it, Del. Take all ten inches in this tight little pussy. I bet those pretty tits of yours are bouncing, aren't they? You giving everyone a show, baby?"

She moaned and her head tipped back. I couldn't help but smile. I had a view of the entire area and not a soul was around, but it turned her on just thinking people were watching us. My sweet Delphine came twice before I emptied inside her, filling her with my cum. I felt it leak out around my cock, and I had this urge to shove it all back inside her. The more I thought about her belly swollen with my kid, the more I wanted that. So damn much.

I stroked her nipples and played with them, little aftershocks making her pussy ripple around me. I'd come twice and should be worn the fuck out, but my dick hadn't gotten the memo. It wanted more, and I knew exactly what I was doing next. Gripping her hips, I lifted her off me, watching as my seed ran down her thighs. I stood and bent her over the arm again, getting really fucking turned on by my cum smeared all over her pussy and thighs. She was mine, and I'd marked her in the most primal of ways. With my cum, my handprints that were still displayed on her ass. And now I was going to make her mine in another way.

Pulling the bottle of lube out of my pocket, I spread her ass cheeks and let some drip onto her tight hole. She gasped and went completely still as I worked it into her. I took my time, getting her get used to having one finger in her ass, then two. I eventually worked my way up to three, stroking them in and out of her, scissoring them to loosen her up some more. Then I lubed my cock and placed the head against her.

"You ready for this, Del? Ready to be mine completely?" I asked.

"God, yes, Mason. I've dreamed of you doing this."

I closed my eyes a moment, trying to get control. "You dreamed of me fucking your ass?"

"Yeah."

She was always surprising me, and in the best of ways. I had a feeling that there would never be a dull moment with Delphine in my life. I held her open and slowly pushed into her. My teeth ground together as the head popped through, and then I sank deep. She was so fucking tight! I worried a little she'd make me come before I'd even gotten started, and that would be a travesty. As long as I'd waited to fuck this ass? I wanted to enjoy every second of it. She squeezed my cock several times, and I damn near detonated.

"Baby, I can't hold on. I wanted to do this nice and slow, but fucking hell, Delphine. You keep squeezing my cock, and it's all I can do not to fuck the hell out of you."

"Do it," she said, sounding breathless. "Fuck me, Mason. Make me feel like the dirty girl I am."

Oh, shit. It was like lava poured through my veins and my balls started to sizzle. Hearing those naughty words out of such a sweet mouth was my undoing. I pulled back until just the head was inside her, then slammed deep. She cried out and squeezed me again, and the dam broke. I fucked her hard, deep, every stroke driving my dick into her ass as far as I could go, and even then I wanted in deeper. I rode her, taking what I wanted, and not stopping until I shot load after load of cum into her tight little ass.

"Fuck yeah, Del." Kept thrusting into her, even after the last drop had been wrung from me. Feeling how hot and wet she was, my cum easing the way even more, it was really damn hard to make myself stop. I think I could have fucked her ass for hours if my cock had stayed hard long enough.

Slowly, I pulled out of her, watching as my cum leaked out. I held her ass cheeks open, that tight little hole all pink and swollen now. I'd used her hard, but she hadn't uttered a word of complaint. She also hadn't come. Dammit.

I smoothed my hands over her ass cheeks, up and down her spine, then teased her clit. "Such a good girl. Are you ready for a reward? Does my baby want to come?"

"Mason, I..." She hesitated and I wanted to know what she'd been about to say.

"No secrets between us."

"Could you..." She looked over her shoulder at me and her cheeks were blazing. This time it looked more like it was from embarrassment. "Could you hold me up in front of the windows when you make me come?"

"Jesus, Del. I have quite the exhibitionist on my hands. Do I need to worry about you stripping naked in the middle of the clubhouse?"

"No," she said indignantly.

I helped her stand and walked over to the window I knew definitely wouldn't have anyone walk past. I teased her breasts and pulled her on nipples while I nibbled the side of her neck.

"Do you like that?" I asked.

"Yes. More, Mason. Please."

I slid one of my hands down her soft belly and stroked her pussy. Parting the lips, I rubbed her clit until she was riding my hand and crying out for more. My cock was getting hard again, just listening to her, but I ignored it. This was about her, what Delphine needed. I made her come twice before I picked her up and carried her to the bedroom. I unlocked the cuffs and rubbed her wrists.

"Why don't you lie down and take a nap?" I suggested. "After all that, you have to be worn out. I didn't exactly go easy on you."

She spread out on the bed and bent her legs, parting them. "You got me all messy."

"You like it when I get you messy." Hell, so did I. And I loved the view she was giving me.

She nodded. "I like it when you spank me too. And I really liked what we just did on the sun porch. Maybe we can do it again sometime. Or maybe… when it's dark out, you could take me into the backyard and fuck me."

"You do realize I'd have never done that if I'd thought for a second someone would actually see you, right? Your body is mine to enjoy and no one else's."

"I know. But I like the thrill that someone *might* see what you're doing to me."

"How did someone so sweet and innocent end up with such a dirty mind?" I asked in amusement.

"Remember, I said I liked porn," she said matter-of-factly. "Lots of porn. That and some super sexy books."

I snorted and then laughed. "We'll watch it together sometime, and you can show me your favorites. Then I'll show you mine."

"Deal."

"Rest, baby, then take a hot bath. I need to run to town in a bit, but I'll post a Prospect outside in case you need anything. Don't answer the fucking door naked, Del. I swear you won't like the punishment you get if you do. Don't test me."

"All right." She smiled sleepily. "You know you're the only one I really want looking at me anyway. It's always been you."

I leaned down and kissed her, then I headed into the bathroom to get cleaned up. I hadn't lied. I really did need to go into town. When I realized that Delphine had made a mess of my clothes, I stripped out of them and decided to take a quick shower. After pulling on clean clothes, I checked on my sleeping beauty, then headed to the clubhouse. I wanted to check in with Wire before I left. Depending on what he found out, I might need to make an extra stop along the way.

When I got to the clubhouse, there were only a few bikes out front. I'd expected most of the single Reapers to be here, the party just getting started. The place was rather subdued compared to normal. I went up the steps and pushed the door open. A few Prospects were hanging around and two patched members.

I gave them a nod as I went in the back to find Wire. His door was shut, but I knocked anyway, hoping he was there. I knew he had a house inside the compound and only used this room for work.

The door swung open and he motioned for me to step inside. I shut the door and leaned against the wall, my arms folded over my chest. Wire ran a hand through his hair and waved a hand at the monitors.

"Tia Lee is into some serious shit, and none of it good. From what I can tell, before she met Hwan Lee, she was hanging with the dregs of society. And not just hanging out. She's helped with drug deals, and even set up some young ladies to fall into a certain pimp's hands. All so she could line her own pockets."

"And now she's after my Delphine?" I asked.

"From what I've been able to figure out, she expected to inherit everything. While the life insurance policy wasn't all that large, Hwan's business is worth a decent amount. Even if she had gotten everything, it wouldn't have lasted her very long. Not with the way she spends money."

"So what are we going to do? Is this a Reapers situation or a law kind of thing?"

"I don't have proof that she's after Delphine, but I did find evidence of her receiving large sums of money from known drug dealers and the pimp I mentioned. I'm not sure if it's enough for the police to arrest her, but they will definitely bring her in for questioning and will likely keep a close eye on her for a while."

"Delphine said she thought her stepmom had hired someone."

Wire nodded. "There was about five grand transferred to two known thugs right after the will was read. They're likely the ones who are after Delphine. As long as she remains behind these gates, she's fine, but you can't keep her caged forever," Wire said. "We could always take out those men and send Tia Lee a message."

"Make the arrangements. Get those men here, and I'll take care of it. Right now, I need to run a few errands in town. Text me when it's time."

Wire nodded. "I'll let Torch know what's going on, and Venom. You know you have their support. Delphine is one of us now, and we protect our own."

I slapped Wire on the back. "Thanks, brother." I left the clubhouse and rode my bike into town. I checked on my shop and decided to stop by Hwan's. With Delphine stuck at the compound, I figured someone should see how things were going. Then made a special stop at the Sensual Delights adult store.

I grabbed a few toys I thought Delphine might enjoy, stocked up on batteries, and then headed back to the compound.

Even though I knew she was safe behind the gates, I didn't like leaving her. The thought of her stepmom getting her hands on Delphine made my blood run cold.

Whether my woman liked it or not, she was under house arrest until all this was sorted out.

Chapter Five

Delphine

The intensity of what happened between me and Mason on the sun porch must have drained me more than I'd realized. I'd slept through the rest of the day and into the next. Even though I'd been up and moving in the days since then, I was still feeling a little lethargic. Guess really great sex could take it out of you. Not that I'd had anything to go by except for what I'd read in books or watched on TV.

I'd fallen asleep during the day, again, and it was already dark outside. I could hear Mason banging around in the kitchen. I groaned as I pulled myself out of the bed, and I used the bathroom while the large tub filled with steamy, hot water. There was a small box on the bathroom counter with the things from my apartment that I had yet to put away, even though Mason insisted this was my home now. I dug around until I found the bath minerals I used whenever I was hurting after a long day at work at the diner, a job I'd hung on to even after I inherited Dad's place. Or tried to. My hours had been drastically cut already.

Shit. I hadn't called my work since I'd been here, which meant I now didn't have a job. And I hadn't called the tattoo shop to let them know I couldn't be around until this was sorted. I wanted to bang my head on the wall in frustration, but knew that would only give me a headache. Instead, I added the minerals to the water, then turned off the taps and dimmed the bathroom lights. I tied my hair up in a knot on top of my head and got into the tub. I winced as my skin stung from the heat and started to turn red, but I knew I would adjust in a minute or two. Anytime I tried to fill the tub with less than burning hot water, within five minutes I was cold.

I tipped my head back and sank up to my neck in the water. The soothing scents of eucalyptus, lemon grass, and mint teased my nose. I breathed in deep, then exhaled slowly, already feeling more relaxed than I had in days. Who would have guessed that having lots of sex could make your muscles sore? Well, probably everyone who had ever had sex, but I was still new to all this.

When my fingers started to prune, I drained the water and got out. With a towel wrapped around me, I went in search of my clothes and had to dig through more boxes in the corner of the bedroom. I really needed to settle in, but I think some part of me worried that Mason would get tired of me and ask me to leave. I tried not to think that way, but after the way he'd left when I was sixteen and how broken I'd felt when I realized he was never coming back, it was hard to believe he wanted me for the long haul. Yeah, I was an adult now, but I guess I was still insecure when it came to him.

Since it was night already, I pulled out my favorite pair of panties and my comfy pajamas. As I looked down at myself, my lips twisted and I wondered how Mason felt about kittens, since my pink pajamas were covered in the balls of fluff. Sexy was not the word I'd ever use to describe my everyday sleepwear, but then I'd never had anyone to impress. I did own a few skimpier tanks and short sets, but I never wore them. So far, I'd just slept naked with Zipper, but I refused to wander the house without clothes, unless he'd ordered me to.

I found him in the kitchen setting the table with two plates heaped with spaghetti and large meatballs.

It smelled divine, and my stomach rumbled in anticipation. He looked me over, but it wasn't laughter I saw in his eyes, like I'd expected.

"You look like some sweet, innocent little girl. I suddenly feel like a dirty old man because even that outfit doesn't diminish how much I want you. If I didn't know you had to be starving by now, I'd bend you over the table and pull those kitten pajamas down to your knees."

I snorted as I fought back a laugh. "Maybe you are a dirty old man if these pajamas turned you on."

He winked. "Or it's just the goddess wearing them. Believe me, baby, you're sexy in anything. Although, I definitely prefer you in nothing at all."

My stomach growled again and he sighed, then patted a chair. Looked like sexy time was put on hold long enough to feed whatever monster had taken up residence in my stomach. I reached for a bowl in the center that looked like it had freshly grated cheese, and spooned some over my pasta. The sauce was still hot enough that the cheese started to melt before I'd had a chance to take my first bite.

"There's more if you're still hungry after that," he said. "I was going to make garlic bread, but I didn't have enough garlic for the sauce and the toast."

I'd just taken a bite and my eyes went wide as the flavors burst on my tongue. "You made this? Like from scratch?"

He'd mostly ordered pizza and Chinese since I'd been here, or requested food from the clubhouse and had a Prospect deliver it. This was the first time I'd seen him really cook in the kitchen, other than throwing together a simple breakfast or making sandwiches for lunch. It was also the first time either of our culinary skills had come up in conversation. Guess we'd been focused on other things, like how many times we could make each other come.

He nodded. "I got tired of eating shitty food or having to eat out, so I picked up some cookbooks and taught myself how to make a few decent meals. This is one of them. I can also make shepherd's pie, chili, and chicken n' dumplings."

"I thought you couldn't cook."

"I suck at breakfast stuff. I can make those few dinners, and I can grill. That's the extent of my culinary expertise. It beats going out for greasy food every night. I tried making biscuits from scratch, tried omelets, and tried waffles. I screwed them all up."

I ate another bite, savoring just how damn good it was. "I can make breakfast. And Dad taught me to make a few Korean meals. Mine aren't as good as his were, but they're all right."

"I'm sorry about your dad," he said softly. "Hwan was a great guy, and he died too young. Not too sure he'd have liked to know you were here with me, though. I'm probably not the kind of guy he pictured with his only daughter."

"Smart? Good-looking? Hard-working? Artistic?" I asked. "Dad saw the man behind the Dixie Reapers cut, and you know it. I know he missed you after you left, and I felt like shit because I'd known it was my fault you were gone."

"You don't know what an old lady is, but you remember what a cut is?" he asked, a slight smile on his lips.

"Well, you never really talked about having an old lady, but I remember calling your cut a vest the first time I saw it and you corrected me. I always remembered the stuff you said."

"Wire found out some stuff about your stepmom. I should have told you sooner, but I was hoping he'd found out something new, like maybe she'd gotten arrested or hit by a bus. I wish I knew how she'd gotten to Hwan. She's in some serious shit, Delphine, and I don't think she's going to stop coming for you until we make her. Wire thinks he has enough to have the cops bring her in for questioning, but there's no guarantee she'll get locked up, or that she'll stop the hit she put on you."

"So, what are you going to do?" I asked.

"First, I'm going to take care of the two men she hired to kill you. And I'm going to use them to send her a message. We'll see how she reacts, and then I'll plan my next move."

"Just don't do anything to get locked up, okay?"

He nodded. "There's one other matter. Your ink."

"Ink?" I asked, my brow furrowed. "I don't have any."

"I know." His eyes gleamed. "I get to be the first to ink that virgin skin. You need a property stamp. Most of the women have them on their arms, but some prefer them elsewhere. I already have one designed for you."

"What's a property stamp? Is that the tattoo you mentioned before?" I asked.

"Yes, it's a tattoo that will say *Property of Zipper* so everyone knows you're mine, even if you're not wearing a cut."

"I forgot you said I'd get a cut," I said, sitting up a little straighter. "Is it like yours?"

"Yeah. With a property patch on it."

"So how big is the tattoo you want to give me?" I asked.

"It needs to be at least the size of your fist to look right, but bigger wouldn't bother me."

"And it needs to be somewhere visible?" I asked. "Like visible all the time?"

"Most of the women have them somewhere it can be easily seen, but it's not a requirement. What did you have in mind?" he asked as he finished off his spaghetti.

"My left shoulder blade. You can make it as big as you want back there, and if I wear a tank top, it should be visible. I know I can't wear one all the time, but at least some of the time people could see it."

"That would work. Are you up for it tonight?" he asked.

"I think I am. I…"

His phone rang, and he held up a finger as he answered. He got up, speaking in hushed tones as he left the room, that made me think it was likely a Dixie Reapers issue and none of my business. I'd like to think if it had something to do with me that he'd keep me in the loop, but knowing Mason, he'd call himself protecting me.

He came back as I was clearing the table, and the tense lines around his mouth said it wasn't good news.

"I have to go deal with a few things. I need you to promise that you won't leave the house until I get back. There will be a Prospect outside the door in case you need something. It's not likely anyone is getting into the compound, but I don't want to take any chances with your safety."

"I'll be fine, Mason. Go do whatever it is you need to do. I'll just clean up the kitchen, then watch a movie while I wait for you. Do you think you'll be long?"

"Maybe an hour or two. Depends on how things go."

I nodded. "I'll be fine. Promise."

He came toward me, sliding his hand around my waist, then pulled me tight against his body. His lips claimed mine in a kiss that was both possessive and full of promises. With a heated look, he left me in the kitchen and I heard the front door open and shut a few minutes later, then his bike engine revved in the driveway. I knew this would be different. This would be the first time I'd really been alone since I got here. In some ways, Mason's house was starting to feel like home, but I was still worried about settling in too much. I didn't understand how he could want me to stay permanently, even if he did say he was claiming me.

I finished cleaning up the kitchen, then settled on the couch to watch a movie until he got back. I heard a strange noise on the front porch, but remembered that Mason had said a Prospect would be out there. Part of me wanted to go investigate, then I reminded myself of all the horror movies where the woman goes to check out a noise and ends up dead. When your deranged step-monster was after you, you didn't go check out weird noises. Nope, you kept your ass planted on the couch behind a locked door. Except…

My nape prickled as I realized that I had no idea whether or not Mason had locked the door. I got up to check and found the front knob locked, but I clicked the deadbolt into place too, just to be safe. Then I decided to check the back of the house. I hadn't remembered seeing a door on the sun porch that led outside, but there had to be backyard access from somewhere. Despite the fact I'd been living here about a week, I still hadn't had time to check out all of the rooms. Well, I'd been in just about every room, but Mason was usually between my legs. When I found the door, everything started to spin. It was not only unlocked, but it was standing wide open. There was no way Mason had left that door open.

My palms grew damp as I edged toward the door. Booted feet were attached to a prone body. I moved in closer and saw the Prospect patch on the guy's back, and I realized my bodyguard was out cold. My heart was beating so hard my chest ached. Slowly, I retreated into the house and closed the door, although I had a feeling it was way too late. I tried to move as quietly as possible as I searched for my phone, then cursed when I realized I didn't have Mason's number, or anyone else's for that matter. Not anyone who could help at any rate. Sure, I could call the police, but what were the chances they would help me while I was inside the Dixie Reapers' compound? Not to mention, that Mason and his brothers probably wouldn't like me getting the law onto the property.

With my phone clutched in my hand, I crept toward the front door, unlocked it and opened it. No one was out front, not even the guy who was supposed to be guarding me, which meant that had likely been him in the backyard. Barefoot and still in my pajamas, I eased out the front door, scanning the darkness for some sign that I wasn't alone. I knew there were other houses, could even see them. I just didn't know if anyone was home at any of those places.

I bolted across the lawn, racing toward what I hoped was an occupied house. I'd nearly made it when a sharp pain pierced my upper back, and the world went a little fuzzy. Stumbling and staggering, I eventually fell face-first onto the grass, a good three yards from the house I was running toward. A woman's crazy laugh filled my ears as my stepmother's face loomed in front of me.

"Never send a man to do a woman's job. Flash a little boob, lift my skirt, and it was easy to get access to you. Stupid kid at the gate would have done anything to have his cock sucked. I've done worse things in my life. Did you really think you could hide forever, Delphine?" she asked. "My men have been watching this place, but they couldn't get to you here."

"Wh-what are y-you going to d-do to me?" I asked, my tongue feeling thick and heavy, like it didn't belong in my mouth.

"Right now? Nothing. That poison should do the trick. Don't worry. You'll be asleep by the time you asphyxiate." She smiled. "I'm not a complete monster after all."

That was debatable. The world started to grow dim, and I heard her walking away. All I could think was that I'd never told Mason I love him, and I wished I'd come to find him sooner. We'd lost so much time together, and it was all my fault. I hoped finding my body wouldn't send him over the edge.

That was the last thought I had before darkness closed in on me completely.

* * *

Zipper

My knuckles were busted and covered in blood, but the two men who had tried to kill my woman didn't even resemble humans anymore. I'd had to remove my cut and my shirt so they wouldn't run red. Even stripped off my jeans when things started to get messy. I'd shattered every bone in their faces, broken their fingers, hands, knees. I was sure a few ribs had been busted too, not that it mattered. I wanted them to suffer, and then I was going to end them. Once they were dead, I'd send a message to Delphine's stepmother. A rather graphic one that I was certain would get the point across.

A phone rang and I heard Torch talking in low tones, but I was still focused on my prey. One of them had passed out from the pain, and I wanted him awake. I picked up a bucket of cold water and threw it on both of them, making sure I had their attention. I grabbed the knife off a nearby table and plunged it into the thigh of one of the men before doing the same to the other. They screamed like the little bitches they were and begged for their lives, from what I could tell anyway. With broken jaws, they weren't making much sense anymore.

"Zipper," Torch said softly, coming up to my side. "You need to hand this off to someone else."

"Why? I'm not done yet."

"Yeah, you are." He sighed. "It's Delphine. Coyote is at the ER with her. He found her unresponsive in the grass between your house and his, and the Prospect you left to guard her was knocked out."

"What do you mean unresponsive?" I asked, my gut clenching. "What the fuck happened to her?"

"New guy at the gate hadn't been briefed on what was going on. Tommy? Tony? Fuck if I remember. He's only been here three days. We think he let Delphine's stepmother into the compound. He said a woman in her late thirties stopped by, offered to suck him off if he'd let her in. Guess he was thinking with his dick and not his brain, but it won't be an issue. Tank is going to make sure the little shit pays for his crimes, then his ass is out of here," Torch said.

I went to the sink on the far wall and washed the blood from my hands and body, then pulled my clothes back on and ran for my bike. I didn't know why Delphine was still alive, but I was fucking thankful. If her stepmother had gotten to her, she should have been dead. Right now, I needed to get my ass to the hospital, and then I could figure out what the fuck was going on. And after my woman was settled and taken care of, then I'd make sure that bitch who'd married Hwan Lee never saw the light of day again. I didn't give a shit if she did have kids. As far as I could tell, they'd be better off without her. A fucking rabid dog would be a better parent.

My bike roared through the compound and out the front gate. I broke every speed limit between the compound and the hospital, but no one pulled me over. At the hospital, I parked in the ER parking area, then hauled ass inside. I saw Coyote slumped in a chair in the waiting area, and I went to him first to see if he'd heard anything. He looked up when he saw me and got to his feet.

"I did what I could to keep her breathing. I was going to call an ambulance, but I didn't know if they'd get there in time. There was a dart sticking out of her back, and with her passed out, I figured it was likely she'd been poisoned. I had Ivan drive the truck and I sat in back with her, helping her breathe when it looked like she was struggling," Coyote said.

"Any news?" I asked.

He shook his head. "Ivan went to get us some coffee. I'll send him a text to get a third cup."

I prowled the waiting area and then went up to the triage desk.

"I wanted to check on my fiancée," I said. "She was brought in recently. Delphine Lee."

The woman clicked on her computer. "It looks like a doctor is with her now. You said you're her fiancé?"

I nodded.

"I'll let them know you're here. I'm sure someone will come to speak to you as soon as they know something." She smiled and I had to hold back the urge to growl and demand that she let me back there with Delphine. I didn't want to do anything that would slow her getting help, though.

I sprawled in the chair next to Coyote, and Ivan returned a minute later with three steaming cups of coffee in his hands. He handed mine to me, and I immediately took a gulp. I would have preferred something stronger right now, but I wanted to stay clear-minded. I knew that Tank and Torch would figure out what had happened, and that helped a little, but knowing Delphine was helpless right now and that I wasn't by her side was killing me. I wanted to hold her hand and let her know she wasn't alone.

It felt like we waited forever before a doctor came toward us.

"Delphine Lee's family," he said.

"That's us," I said, standing.

"She's stable. We had to do some lab work to find out what she'd been poisoned with it. It had strychnine in it, but it shouldn't harm the baby. She'll need to be monitored closely during the pregnancy in case there are any complications, but I don't foresee any."

I swayed a moment as his words sank in. "Baby?"

"She hasn't been awake long enough to tell us much, but we ran a blood test for pregnancy before treating her just to be safe. It came back positive. The baby is too small to show on an ultrasound, so it's likely still very early."

Coyote slapped me on the back. "Congratulations, Daddy."

"After the stress her body has been through, it's possible she could lose the baby. I'm not saying it will definitely happen, but there's a chance. If she makes it through the first trimester, then she should make it full term."

"What happens now?" I asked. "Can I see her?"

"Of course. She's not very coherent, but maybe hearing your voice will be comforting to her," the doctor said. "You can follow me, but your friends will have to stay out here."

I gave Coyote and Ivan a nod, then followed the doctor through the double doors into the heart of the ER. He ushered me into the room where Delphine lay on a bed, wired to machines. I claimed the chair next to the bed and reached for her hand. She seemed so small and fragile right now, almost lifeless.

"Del, baby, I'm right here," I said, holding tight to her hand. "I'm not going anywhere, okay? I'll be here when you're ready to wake up."

"We're going to move her to a room when one's available," the doctor said. "She needs to stay overnight for observation, and if she's doing well tomorrow, we'll release her."

"Thank you, doc."

"If you need more coffee or anything else, just let a nurse know. There's a call button on the side of Miss Lee's bed. Someone will check on her shortly."

I nodded as he stepped out of the room and shut the door behind him.

"It's just you and me, baby," I told her softly. "Can you open those pretty eyes for me?"

She didn't move and didn't open her eyes. My chest ached and I gently laid my other hand over her belly, hoping our baby made it. I didn't know how Delphine would feel when she found out she was pregnant, but I liked that she was the one carrying my kid. I couldn't think of anyone who would be a better mother for my son or daughter, or anyone else I'd want to spend the rest of my life with.

"Come back to me, Delphine. I've gone too long without you already."

I kissed her hand, then leaned over and softly kissed her cheek. I'd do whatever it took to make sure she was safe. I'd never killed a woman before, but I was going to make an exception for Tia Lee. As far as I was concerned, she wasn't a woman. She was a monster. And I wouldn't allow a monster to live, especially one after my family.

Chapter Six

Zipper

The hospital had found a room for Delphine, but she'd only opened her eyes once and promptly gone back to sleep. I was scared shitless that I might lose her, but the nurses seemed to think she was doing okay. I still couldn't believe that fucking bitch had poisoned her. If she'd killed Delphine, if she'd made her lose the baby, I might have literally ripped her apart one piece at a time with my bare hands. As it was, I still wanted to make her suffer. A lot.

There was a knock on the door, then one of the local police officers stepped into the room. I hadn't thought about the hospital getting the law involved, but since Del had been poisoned that made sense. It was probably procedure or some shit. The man slowly approached the bed, his gaze on Del, but I had no doubt he'd already cataloged me from head to toe, paying attention to my cut.

"I'm Officer Daniels. I wanted to ask Miss Lee a few questions about what happened tonight."

"As you can see, my fiancée isn't awake. She's barely opened her eyes. She'll look around, and then she goes right back to sleep. I guess it's her body's way of healing after the poison that was in her system."

"And what do you know about that?" he asked, pinning me with his stare.

There was a gold band on his finger, so he was either currently married or had been. I wondered if that was the way to get him to back the hell down. The last thing I wanted to deal with were accusations, like I'd ever hurt Delphine.

"Officer Daniels, I wasn't with Delphine when this happened, or I sure as fuck would have stopped the person who hurt her. I love her, and I want to marry her."

"Stopped them? I know the Reapers reputation. Is that stopped them as in detained them or murdered them?" the officer asked.

"What would you have done if someone injected your wife with poison?"

His lips firmed. "Off the record? I'd have nailed their ass to the wall and beat the shit out of them. But as an officer of the law and an upstanding citizen of this town, I'd have let my blue family take care of them."

"Blue family? What are you, a fucking smurf?"

The officer's eyes darkened with anger. "As in the Thin Blue Line. But as an outlaw, you wouldn't know anything about that, now would you?"

Nope, I didn't know shit about law enforcement, except how to stay out of jail. I'd done a pretty good job of that so far. I didn't want to piss off Officer Daniels, not while Delphine needed me. Maybe trying another tactic would work better. When I was little, my grandmother had always told me to kill them with kindness. It hadn't ever worked out, but her heart had been in the right place. Maybe just a few decades too far in the past.

"Look, Officer. I don't want to cause any trouble. You want the truth? I was off with my brothers when I got the call that Del had been found unconscious in the grass between my house and another Reaper's home. She was already at the ER by the time someone called to tell me. It scared the shit out of me, and then I found out she's pregnant, so you'll have to pardon me if I'm a little shaken right now." I looked at Del. "She means everything to me. The thought of losing her, of losing our baby, scares the fuck out of me because without them, I'm lost."

"People don't end up poisoned out of the blue, especially young pregnant women. Does your club have enemies who would strike out at Miss Lee, maybe to get to you?" Officer Daniels asked.

"No, this isn't about the Reapers. This is about Delphine and the inheritance her father left her when he died earlier this year. She thinks her stepmother is trying to kill her. If Delphine dies before she has any children, then Hwan Lee's tattoo shop and the half of the life insurance money he left to Del will revert to the stepmom," I said.

As much as I wanted to fuck that bitch over, I didn't have time for that right now. Delphine needed me, and now that the police had been called, taking out Tia Lee on my own, or with the Reapers, would be suicide. Even if I hadn't volunteered information, they would have eventually put things together and gone looking for the woman. Delphine had given them enough ammunition to lock the bitch up. We didn't need a bloody trail leading to our gates.

"Do you know her stepmother's name?" Officer Daniels asked.

"Tia Lee. I can't remember what Del said the woman's name was before she married Hwan Lee. I'd be willing to bet everything I have that Tia was behind this. There's no one else who could possibly want to harm Delphine." I wasn't about to tell him Wire had been investigating the woman and probably knew every damn thing about her by now, including any allergies and her high school locker combination.

"I'll look into it. If she wakes up and stays awake, I'd like to talk to her about what happened. Since it happened inside your compound, that means it had to be someone your brothers let through the gate. Are you sure this isn't a Reapers issue?" the officer asked.

"I'm sure. Random women are let in all the time. It wouldn't have been all that hard for Tia Lee to gain access to Delphine. I had a man watching over her, and I heard he was found knocked out cold. Whoever did this wasn't just trying to scare her. They wanted Delphine dead."

Officer Daniels nodded. "If you think of anything else, or she can talk to me, give me a call."

He handed me his card and I slid it into my pocket. With another glance at Delphine, the officer left, closing the door behind him. Part of me was relieved that more people were going to look into it, and the other half wanted to exact revenge on the woman responsible for nearly killing Delphine. I hadn't lied to the officer. She was the most important thing in the world to me, her and the baby I now knew grew inside her.

Now that Delphine was in a room and not stuck in the ER, my brothers and their families were able to stop by. There was a never-ending line of visitors throughout the next several hours, not that Del noticed since she slept through it all. It was nice to know that people cared, though, not just about me but about her too. Ridley, Venom's old lady, had stopped by my house and gathered some clothes for Delphine so she'd have something to wear when we were able to leave. I hadn't even thought that far ahead, but I was grateful that someone had.

Torch stepped into the room, hands in his pockets, and he looked Del over before his gaze settled on me.

"The job you started was finished. Thought you'd want to know," Torch said. "How's she doing?"

"She wakes up here and there, but not for very long. They're keeping her overnight, and then they want to assess her tomorrow to see if she's okay to go home. They said since she was poisoned they'll need to monitor her pregnancy closely to make sure the baby wasn't harmed."

"Yeah, I'd heard she was pregnant. Coyote filled us in when he got back to the compound. Do we know for sure it was her stepmom who did this?" Torch asked. "Want me to have her picked up?"

"A police officer came by asking questions. I guess the hospital notified him that Del had been poisoned. He's going to look into Tia Lee, so we should probably keep our distance. I don't want any of this shit to blow back on the club."

Torch nodded. "Maybe it's for the best they got involved. I know you wanted to settle the matter yourself, but this way you can focus on your woman and baby, and not figure out how you're going to make that woman pay for her crimes. We'll let the law handle this one, and if they fumble it, we'll go from there."

"It will be hard to make her disappear after the police have been watching her. Since I'm the one who gave them the woman's name, they'll come to us first if something happens to her," I pointed out. "As much as I want that woman six feet under, I don't want any of us going to prison over it, or having the local law sniffing around and looking into other club matters."

Torch smiled. "I'm glad to see that even with all this shit piled on your doorstep that you can still think about the well-being of the club and your brothers.

Some men would get tunnel vision and only be thinking of revenge."

"Revenge has its time and place. When I look back on the day I found out I was going to be a dad, I don't want to think about murder and the blood that stains my hands. My kid deserves better than that."

Torch patted my shoulder. "You're a good man, Zipper. Always thought so. Even when you told me why you were hiding out at the clubhouse and no longer working for Hwan Lee, I didn't think any less of you. Hell, even when my woman wasn't quite legal yet, I couldn't deny she was beautiful. I think you reacted to Delphine the way you did because even back then you knew she was supposed to be yours."

"Maybe. It's what helps me sleep at night anyway." I smiled faintly. "I don't know what her dad would think of all this. He was a good man, an honorable man. I'm not sure he'd think I was good enough for his little girl."

Torch rubbed his beard. "I don't think any father ever thinks a man is good enough for his daughter. You probably could have performed miracles and walked on water, and the man still would have had his reservations. But you've proven that she means a lot to you and that you'll put her first. I'm pretty sure that's all any man wants for his daughter. Someone to love her, protect her, and treat her like a goddess."

"And if Lyssa grows up and wants to marry… Johnny for instance? How would you feel?" I asked. The Prospect was a good kid, and I knew he'd be patched in. But I wanted to make a point. "He's honorable, loyal, and he protects your woman and daughter like they're his family. What if he wants Lyssa when she's eighteen? There would be twenty years between them."

Torch looked pained for a moment. "I don't want to think about my baby being old enough to be someone's old lady. I don't think the age difference would really bother me so much, as knowing for sure whether or not he would take care of her. If it were Johnny? Yeah, I'd probably give my blessing unless he fucks up in the next sixteen years."

"I'll remind you of that when it's time for Lyssa to start dating," I said. "Of course, Bull's son is only a year younger than Lyssa. She'd probably be more likely to fall for him."

"God help us if he's anything like his dad," Torch muttered.

Delphine moaned and I focused on her, practically holding my breath while I waited to see if she'd wake up this time and stay awake. Her eyes fluttered and she slowly took in her surroundings. When her gaze locked with mine, she gave me a slight smile.

"Hey, beautiful," I said. "You going to stay with me this time?"

"I think so." Her voice was a little scratchy, but it was the most wonderful sound I'd ever heard, because it meant she was here with me, awake, and she seemed to be okay.

"Good to see you awake, Delphine," Torch said. "How do you feel?"

"Like I was hit by a bus," she said. Her eyes went wide. "It was Tia. She darted me with poison, said it would kill me."

"Coyote found you in time, and he had Ivan drive you to the ER. Coyote helped keep you breathing until they got here, and the doctors were able to counteract whatever you were given. They said it had strychnine in it, so they want to monitor..." I trailed off, not knowing if she was aware she was pregnant.

"On that note, I'm heading out," Torch said. "Call if you need anything."

"Thank you," Delphine said.

After I heard the door shut, I focused on Del. "Baby, there's something you need to know. When they were trying to save your life, they ran a blood test. The doctor said you're pregnant."

She blinked a few times and didn't say anything, and I was starting to get worried. "Pregnant?" she asked. "Isn't it too soon to tell?"

"They said they couldn't find the baby yet with an ultrasound, but the test was positive. If you want, in another week or two we can make an appointment and you can have another test done just to be sure. But I think we need to move forward as if you're pregnant and accept the test results for now."

Her hand went to her stomach.

"Baby, are you all right? I know you probably hadn't planned on us starting a family right away."

She smiled and reached for me. "I hope the test is right. I think you're going to be an amazing father."

"There's something else you need to know. A police officer came by asking questions. I gave him your stepmom's name as a possible suspect. Which means the Reapers can't touch her, but maybe she'll be locked up. He wanted you to call when you were ready to talk. If you know for sure it was Tia, then I'm sure he'll arrest her."

Delphine nodded. "Can you call him but ask him to wait a little before stopping by? My head still feels a little fuzzy, and I'd like to drink something, maybe wake up a little better before I try to talk to him."

"Anything you want, sweetheart." I leaned over and kissed her. "You scared the shit out of me, Del. When I heard Coyote had found you unconscious, I thought my heart was going to stop."

"She said the poison she gave me would asphyxiate me after I passed out. She made it sound almost like it was humane that I wouldn't be awake when it happened, but all I could think about before I passed out was you."

"Me?" I asked.

She nodded. "I never got to tell you…"

"Tell me what, Delphine?"

"That I love you," she said softly. "I always have, Mason. Even when I was a stupid teenager who chased you away, I loved you."

"I love you too. Think I always have."

"What do we do now?" she asked.

"Well, you're going to tell Officer Daniels about your murderous stepmom, then we're going to work on getting you out of this hospital. One day at a time, okay?"

"You asked me before if I wanted to just be your old lady or if I wanted to get married." She licked her lips. "Would you really not mind marrying me?"

I smiled a little and reached over to stroke her cheek. "Sweetheart, I can't think of anything I'd like more. We'll wait a little bit for your tattoo, maybe even wait until after the baby is born. But you can wear the property cut, and I'll make sure to put a ring on your finger so everyone knows you're mine."

"I'd like that." Her eyes started to close again, but she slowly opened them. "I think I need to rest a little more. Maybe we can call the officer tomorrow."

"Rest, baby. You should sleep while you can. The nurses will likely be in and out all night, trying to keep an eye on you. The hospital isn't exactly the best place to go if you want to get some sleep."

She smiled a little and reached for my hand. I wrapped my fingers around hers and held on even after she'd fallen back to sleep. Using my free hand, I sent Wire a message, letting him know I needed a marriage license as fast as possible. Yeah, I could do things the completely legal way, but I wanted to make her mine and I didn't want to wait to apply for a marriage license. If that meant bending the law a bit, then so be it. What was the point of having a hacker in the club if we didn't use his services?

Wire: You do know there's a chapel at the hospital. I can get the license to you by morning.

He wanted me to marry Del at the hospital? That wasn't the most romantic thing I could think of, but it would legally make her mine, and I wouldn't have to worry about scheduling with a church or having the clubhouse scrubbed and decorated. I had a feeling she'd want a dress, though, and I didn't have a ring to give her.

Wire: Let the club handle the details. Just be prepared to marry your girl tomorrow in the hospital chapel. If she wants a bigger wedding later, I'm sure Isabella and Ridley will help her plan one.

I sighed, knowing he was right. It might not be the wedding Del had always dreamed of, if she'd dreamed of one at all, but at least it would make her mine. That was the important thing, right? There was a gift shop and a florist inside the hospital. Maybe I could arrange for a bouquet at the very least, maybe find some ribbons or something to use for decoration. Or maybe I needed to get my ass down to the chapel to check the space out. I hated to leave her, though.

Her room door swung open, and Bull came in with his old lady, Darian, and his father-in-law. I didn't know why Scratch was here, but where there was one Devil's Boneyard brother, there was usually another.

"We wanted to come check on her," Darian said. "I told Dad what was going on with Delphine, and he arrived tonight with a few others."

Scratch held out his hand to me. The VP for the Devil's Boneyard looked tired, but I knew he was a strong, capable guy. And if he was here to help, I'd take it.

"Torch said the police are involved, but it never hurts to have a little extra security for right now," Scratch said. "I brought Jackal, Shade, and Phantom with me. We'll help make sure your woman has a security detail until all this blows over."

"Thanks. I was actually hoping to go downstairs for a bit, but I didn't want to leave her alone," I said.

"We'll stay," Bull said. "With three of us here, no one will get to her. We won't leave even if they try to force us out."

I nearly snorted at the thought of the nursing staff trying to move Bull. He was fucking huge and just as stubborn as his namesake.

"Thanks," I said. "I'll be back in a bit. I need to check on a few things and maybe grab some food from the cafeteria, if it's still open." I paused at the door. "Wait, you said you brought Jackal with you?"

Scratch nodded.

Well, fuck. That wasn't going to go over very well once Tank found out. The Devil's Boneyard member had run off with Tank's sister a while back, and there was a discussion that Tank wanted to have with the man. "Does, uh, Tank know that Jackal is here?" I asked.

Scratch's gaze sharpened. "Not yet. Why?"

I ran a hand down my face and Bull started laughing softly. Yeah, he knew what was up and hadn't let his father-in-law in on it. I only hoped that war didn't erupt at the compound once everything came to light. It seemed we just went from one shit storm to another with no break in sight.

"No reason," I muttered and made a run for it. If Scratch was still curious, I'd let Bull explain things. At least he was family and not likely to end up shot for his trouble. I had a feeling Darian would be upset with her daddy if her husband ended up wounded or dead.

The rest of us weren't quite so safe, though.

Chapter Seven

Delphine

It took two days before the hospital was ready to release me, and Mason was on edge. I could tell he was hiding something, but I didn't know what it was. While we waited for my discharge paperwork, Isabella came in with a garment bag draped over her arm and another small sack hanging off her fingers. She smiled brightly and nodded to the door. Mason ducked out, giving me a wink before the door shut.

Well, that wasn't the least bit odd.

"Isabella, what's going on? Mason's been all weird yesterday and today, and now you're here with... what is that?" I asked. "Am I secretly dying and you've brought clothes so I'll look decent for an open casket service?"

"Your wedding dress and shoes," she said, laying the garment bag on the bed and unzipping it as she rolled her eyes at me. "I got your sizes from the things at your house. Ridley and Darian helped me pick these out. And trust me, if you were dying, Mason would be losing his shit right now, not ducking out with a smile on his face."

She pulled out a blush-colored dress with beadwork on the bodice. It was sleeveless, and the skirt was long and flowing. My eyes misted with tears as I looked at it. Then she pulled out a matching pair of satin shoes. They were beautiful, and they made my heart ache. I'd always thought when I picked out my wedding dress that my dad would go with me, since Mom had been gone a while. But now I didn't have either of them. "You got me a wedding dress?" I asked. "But why?"

"Mason wanted to make it a surprise. Let's just say you need to put this on and get downstairs after you're discharged. Ridley is right behind me with some shower stuff. We thought you'd want to wash and dry your hair."

Ridley barreled into the room, out of breath, with an overloaded tote bag slung over her arm. They practically shoved me into the bathroom with a bottle of shampoo, shower gel, and a razor that looked like the ones I had at Mason's house. My house. I'd need to get used to thinking of it as mine. I tried to wash quickly, not knowing when the hospital would tell me to vacate the room. I doubted they would shove me out the door wet and naked, but I wasn't going to chance it.

When I was finished, I put on one of the nicer bra and panty sets I owned, which Ridley had also shoved into the bag she'd brought. It felt a little awkward that she'd been digging through my underwear, but maybe that was because I'd been alone for so long. I hadn't really had friends. When I was a teen, everyone thought my dad was the coolest, and I quickly learned they didn't want to hang out with me for me. So I distanced myself, and I never really let anyone get close after that. Not anyone my age anyway. As I glanced at Isabella and Ridley, I had to admit that having friends might be nice.

Isabella worked on drying and styling my hair while Ridley added a touch of makeup to my face. I never wore much, but she focused on my eyes, added a hint of color to my cheeks, and a sheer lip gloss. I had to admit, when Isabella and Ridley were finished I didn't look like a woman who had just been nearly killed and spent a few days in the hospital. I didn't look much like me either, though. The dress fit me perfectly, and so did the shoes. I felt like a princess. The finishing touch was a small tiara that Isabella placed on top of my head and someone clipped into my hair so it wouldn't fall off.

A nurse came in and made me sign a bunch of forms, then I was given my freedom. Isabella and Ridley carried all of my things and ushered me downstairs. We stopped outside two wooden doors labeled *Chapel*.

"Wait. I'm getting married *right now? Here*?" I asked, my eyes going wide. I'd kind of figured something big was going to happen, and since I was wearing a wedding dress the odds were Mason wanted to make things official. But I had never even thought of getting married at the hospital.

"Yep. Wire procured you a marriage license, and Preacher offered to do the honors. Zipper arranged to use the chapel for the occasion," Ridley said. "That man is crazy about you."

Isabella pushed the doors open and I nearly cried at how beautiful everything looked. There was a stained-glass window at the front of the chapel and colored light danced across the floor. Mason was waiting up front, in dark wash jeans, a black tee, and his cut. I should have known the man wouldn't wear a tux even to his own wedding. It made me laugh a little as I walked toward him. I noticed he'd trimmed his beard so that it was tighter against his jawline, and his hair was brushed and looked like it had some sort of product in it. It warmed my heart that he'd tried to look his best for our special day, while still remaining true to himself.

I scanned the chapel, which was nearly packed. It looked like almost all of the Dixie Reapers were present, and their old ladies. There were a few cuts I didn't recognize that said Devil's Boneyard, and one of the men was sporting a black eye. I had a feeling there was a story there, but right now, I was focused on the man up front waiting for me. Another Reaper was holding a Bible and smiling as I approached. I hadn't had a chance to meet Preacher yet, but I figured that's who he was, and his cut said as much as I got close enough to read it.

"I hope this is okay," Mason said. "I know it's not very romantic to get married at the hospital."

"Are you kidding?" I asked. "This is the most romantic thing anyone has ever done for me. You planned a wedding for us, and made sure I had a beautiful dress. I love you."

"Love you too." He leaned closer and kissed me.

Preacher cleared his throat. "We haven't gotten to that part yet."

I laughed and pulled away. I barely heard the words spoken but somehow managed to get through my part, and soon we were kissing again. This time as husband and wife. I could hardly believe that the man I'd loved for so long was actually mine, that I was his wife, and we were going to have a baby. My life seemed pretty much perfect right now. Well, except for the problem known as Tia Lee.

"I wanted to take you on a honeymoon," Mason said. "But I'm not taking any chances with your safety until your stepmom is found and locked away. Or dead. Dead works for me."

"I still can't believe she just vanished and left her kids like that," I said, recalling Officer Daniels' words when he'd stopped by yesterday. I'd met with him after I'd woken up again, and when he'd gone to question my stepmother, no one could find her. She'd been missing at least two days, maybe even as early as when she darted me. I had to admit I was a bit apprehensive, waiting to see when she'd strike next.

"We're going to honeymoon at home until she's caught. Wire's trying to track her, waiting to see if she uses a credit card somewhere or withdraws money from the bank. Until then, between the Devil's Boneyard and the Reapers, there will be two or three men watching our house at all times," Mason said.

"And Hades Abyss," Ryker said as he came toward us.

I'd only met Ryker briefly, and it touched me that he was worried about my safety, even though I was still a stranger. I was a little confused still about why he was with the Dixie Reapers. Even though his woman was related to Flicker, I didn't understand how a non-Dixie Reaper was living at the compound. I tried not to stick my nose in, though, figuring if it was my business someone would explain it to me. The way everyone came together wasn't something I'd ever witnessed before, and I was more than happy to be a part of the Dixie Reapers, in whatever capacity they would allow. I knew as Mason's old lady, and now his wife, that meant I was family in some way, but I still hadn't wrapped my head around the MC thing and I was learning as I went along.

"I talked to my dad this morning. He's sending a few guys down to help out. He wanted them to talk to Tank anyway, so the timing worked out," Ryker said.

Mason and Ryker shared a look and I knew whatever reason Hades Abyss was really coming had to do with a job of some sort, and it was probably one I didn't want to know about. I knew that the Reapers weren't exactly law-abiding, but they also tried not to hurt innocent people. Mason would never be an angel, unless it was a fallen one, and I was okay with that. I loved him just the way he was, imperfections and all. Although, I sometimes wondered if those imperfections were what made him so perfect for me.

"I had someone bring a truck here," Mason said, addressing me again. "I didn't want you on the back of my bike while you're recovering. Hell, I'm not sure you should ride on it while you're pregnant."

"What about your bike? Did you ride it here?" I asked.

"It's already back at the compound. Come on, my beautiful wife. Time to get you home," he said, smiling at me.

I kissed him once more and let him lead me out to the parking lot. There were a lot of bikes in the lot, and I saw a few of the trucks I recognized as Reapers' property. Mason led me over to one, then helped me into the passenger seat. Isabella and Ridley placed my things in the backseat, then gave me a wave as they went to find their men. The ride back to the compound was relatively uneventful, unless you counted Mason getting a speeding ticket. He was so happy about being married to me, he didn't even seem to mind getting pulled over.

Officer Daniels gave him an assessing look as he handed the ticket over. "Try to go the speed limit the rest of the way home. You don't want that woman of yours getting injured because of reckless driving."

I bit my lip, wondering if five over the speed limit could really be considered reckless. The officer stared at me a moment, his gaze taking in my wedding dress, then he shook his head.

"Are you sure you want to tie yourself to this one?" he asked. "You seem like a nice girl. Too nice for the likes of him."

I saw Mason's eye twitch, and I hoped he didn't explode and go off on the police officer. The last thing I wanted was for him to be locked up on our wedding day. I could just see my grandkids asking one day about my special day, and me having to tell them that their grandpa had been locked up for assaulting an officer on the way home.

"I love him," I told Officer Daniels. "And despite his rough exterior, he treats me like a princess. I know Mason will never hurt me. He'd lay down his life for me."

The officer nodded. "You two be careful. I have officers patrolling the area around the compound in case Tia Lee comes back to finish the job. Wouldn't hurt to be extra vigilant until she's brought in."

"We have it covered, Officer Daniels," Mason said. "Some other clubs are even going to help with security until this is over."

The officer's jaw firmed, but he nodded then went back to his cruiser.

"Are you going to pay that?" I asked, as I looked at the ticket on the seat between us.

"Nope. I'll have Wire make it disappear."

I rolled my eyes. Of course he would.

"Was it smart to tell him other clubs were coming here? Or are already here?" I asked.

"If he thinks they're only here to help protect you, then he won't look too closely when he sees them around town. This time anyway."

I worried at my lower lip as Mason pulled back into traffic and headed for home. "Mason, I know the club isn't completely legal, but you aren't doing anything that will get you taken away from me, are you? I just found you and…"

He pulled over again, then wrapped his hand around the back of my neck, pulling my lips to his as he kissed me long and hard. "I'm fine. The club is fine. Some of the guys are ex-military, including Torch, and those skills come in handy. Plus, we have Wire. I don't want you to worry, okay? We're not in a war with other clubs, and we're not dealing in women or kids."

"All right," I said softly.

"I'm not going to do something stupid, Del. I want to be there for you and our kid. But I'm not going to turn my back on my club either. If Torch needs me to handle a job, I'm going to do it. I'm always careful, and I'll be more so now that I have a family to come home to."

"I just love you so much. It would kill me if you were taken from me," I said.

"Not going anywhere, baby. They'd have to put me six feet under, and even then I'd still watch over you."

I smiled faintly, even though that wasn't exactly encouraging. When we got to the compound, I saw that not only was a Prospect at the gate, but someone wearing a Devil's Boneyard cut was standing there too. It was the guy with the black eye, and I wondered how he'd beaten us back to the compound. We pulled through, and Mason went straight to our house. Three more men were outside when he came to a stop in the driveway. One was another Prospect and the other two were Dixie Reapers I hadn't met yet.

Mason helped me out of the truck, then stopped long enough for introductions.

"You've met Ivan before," he said, motioning to the Prospect. "These are two of my other brothers. Rocky and Tempest."

"Tempest?" I asked.

Tempest winked. "When I get finished with someone, it looks like they've been tossed by a fierce storm."

Mason snorted. "He has anger issues. Rocky got his name because he's as big as a fucking mountain."

Rocky just grinned at the description, and Tempest gave Mason the finger.

"How many others have I not met yet?" I asked.

"A few. You'll likely meet Wraith at some point. He tends to be ghost-like and is only seen when he wants to be. Keeps to himself, but he's a badass you want on your side. Then there's Gears, Bats, and Sarge."

"And Devil's Boneyard is related to all of this how? I know Ryker's club is Hades Abyss, even though I'm still a little confused about how he's living here and not a Reaper," I said.

"Darian's daddy is the VP for the Devil's Boneyard, but Scratch also helped Ridley get here when she was in trouble. They've helped us out from time to time. Kind of like an extension of our family," Mason said. "You'll see them here off and on... mostly Scratch because he likes to come visit his daughter and grandkid."

"Jackal," Rocky said behind a cough.

Mason frowned. "Yeah, I'm not sure how that's going to play out yet."

"Who's Jackal?" I asked.

"A member of Devil's Boneyard, but he kind of hooked up with Tank's sister a while back. Needless to say, Tank isn't happy with the way things turned out," Mason said.

I wondered if that was the guy with the black eye.

"I haven't met Tank's sister, have I?" I asked.

"Not yet."

They shared a look, and I knew there was a lot more to that tale, but for whatever reason, they weren't sharing. I'd have to ask Ridley or Isabella about it later. I sometimes felt so lost. If I was going to make the Dixie Reapers my family and make my home here at the compound, I needed to get to know everyone better, and find out the secrets that didn't pertain to jobs they were doing. It felt a little like being dropped into a soap opera. Or maybe more like high school, but with motorcycles and illegal dealings. Then again, that sounded a lot like the high school I'd attended.

"Any other clubs I need to know about?" I asked.

"There are others around, but we don't really deal with them much. We sometimes deal with the Reckless Barbarians, but it's not often. They're pretty decent guys, just a little wild," Mason said. "They live in Louisiana in the New Orleans area, so they don't make the trip more than once or twice a year. I think they have a chapter in Texas too, and one somewhere in the northwest."

"I sometimes feel like I've been dropped down a rabbit hole," I muttered.

Mason smiled and led me up to the front door. "Come on, baby. Time to celebrate our wedding. These guys will make sure no one bothers us, right?"

All three nodded and began to spread out, probably to cover the perimeter of the house. Part of me was glad that we had extra security, especially after what happened with my stepmom, and the other part... well, things were about to get very loud inside the house, and I had no doubt they'd be able to hear everything. My cheeks warmed at the thought. I also knew for certain Mason would avoid the sun porch while they were out there. While I'd enjoyed the thrill of possibly being seen that day, I didn't really have a desire for anyone to watch Mason punish me or fuck me. I wasn't quite that adventurous. But I'd enjoyed that day so much I'd hoped we could do it again. Looked like that would have to wait until my stepmonster was brought to justice.

He swept me up into his arms and carried me over the threshold, which I thought was sweet. Then he kicked the door shut and went straight back to the bedroom. My heart was racing when I realized that while we'd been sleeping together for about a week or more, this was our first time as husband and wife. I knew it wasn't really different, but for me it was a big moment. A memory I knew I would cherish all my life, and that made me both excited and nervous. I wanted today to be perfect in every way.

Mason let me slide down his body; then he slowly began to undress me. He set the tiara on the dresser, then knelt to remove my shoes, carefully setting them aside. Moving around behind me, he slid down the zipper on my dress and I stepped out of it as it pooled around my feet. He picked it up and draped it across a chair in the corner. My eyes misted with tears, knowing he was trying his best to move slow and not ruin my wedding finery. I'd see about having the dress preserved later, and I was grateful that he was being so thoughtful.

I stood before him in nothing more than my bra and panties, but the way he looked at me made me feel like I was wearing the sexiest lingerie he'd ever seen. But then, Mason always made me feel beautiful and cherished. I could probably wear a burlap bag and he'd like what he saw. Being with him was everything I'd ever dreamed it would be, and so much more.

"I love you," I said softly.

"Love you too." He smiled, then kissed me.

My toes curled as I gripped his biceps and held on. It amazed me that something as simple as his lips against mine could make the room spin. No matter how many times we kissed, it just seemed to get better every time.

Chapter Eight

Zipper

I'd stripped off my clothes as quick as I could, letting them fall to the floor and tossing my cut across the top of the dresser. It still seemed a little surreal that I was holding my wife as her curves pressed against me. I'd never thought I'd get married, hadn't been interested in keeping a woman. Except for Delphine. Even when she'd been too damn young, I'd wanted her. I'd known it was wrong, and I'd been disgusted with myself, but I couldn't deny that I'd felt a pull to her. Not that she'd been a typical sixteen-year-old. She'd been wise beyond her years, could hold a conversation with an adult without any problem, and didn't seem to care for hanging out with kids her age. If I hadn't been worried I'd give in to temptation, I'd have stayed and maybe we'd have been together a lot sooner.

But she was here now, in my arms, and she was mine in every way possible. I had a property cut for her in the closet, and I'd give it to her in the morning. After the baby got here, and I knew she was one hundred percent healthy again, then I'd ink her. For now, the gold band on her finger was enough for me. The way she looked up at me, her eyes soft, with a sweet smile curving her lips, made me feel like I was the most important person in the world. At least, in her world, and that's the one that mattered most to me.

"Are you going to fuck your wife, Mason?" she asked, her voice low and sultry.

My cock got even harder, but no, I wasn't going to *fuck* my wife. Today was special, a day that we would hopefully remember forever. A new beginning for both of us. When I looked back on this day in twenty years, I wanted to remember loving my new wife slowly, wringing every drop of pleasure from her that I could, making her toes curl, and hearing her scream my name. I wanted her claw marks down my back, and I wanted to make sure she knew that she was it for me.

"No. I'm going to make love to my wife," I said softly.

I kissed her slowly, deeply, letting my hands roam over her curves, then settling on her hips and pulling her tighter against me. I took my time, tasting her and exploring her soft skin. Dragging down the straps of her bra, I pulled the cups down, then lowered my head to tease first one nipple, then the other. I sucked on them hard, drawing them to a point, before stroking them with my thumbs. She shivered as she gripped my shoulders tight. I wanted to give her the night she deserved, the kind of loving that I'd never had with another woman. Something that was just ours.

"So beautiful," I murmured before taking a nipple into my mouth again. I grazed it with my teeth, then bit lightly before smoothing the ache with my tongue.

"Mason, I appreciate that you want tonight to be special, but… what makes it special is that I'm with you. I'm yours, and you're mine. And I love how things are between us in the bedroom, and every other room in the house. You don't have to change for so much as one night because I love it when you're all rough and demanding."

"What are you saying, Del?"

"This softer side of you is nice, and maybe when I'm the size of a whale I'll appreciate it more, but right now? Right now, I want my husband to make me his. I want your mark on my body. When I get up tomorrow, I want your handprint on my ass, I want whisker burn on every inch of me, I want the marks of your fingers on my hips from where you held me tight and pounded into me."

"In other words…"

"I want you off this leash you've put yourself on. I want you wild and reckless. I want the Mason I fell in love with, the Mason I married. Not some watered-down version because you think that's what I want or need tonight."

I smiled, then walked her toward the bed and pushed her down onto the mattress. "Stay right there."

I walked over to the closet and pulled the bag off the top shelf, where I'd stored it after my little trip to Sensual Delights. I'd been waiting for the right moment to pull out the things I'd purchased for Del, and it seemed that today was it. Setting the bag on the floor beside the bed, I reached inside and pulled out some bejeweled nipple clamps, giving her a wicked smile as I showed them to her.

She caught her lower lip between her teeth and leaned back on her arms, giving me room to work. I attached first one clamp, then the other, giving them a little tug that made her moan and squirm. Her legs parted enough for me to see that her panties were soaked. I rubbed against the wet material and couldn't wait to be inside her. I tugged on the nipple clamps again and she shivered.

"Lie in the middle of the bed and put your hands up by the headboard," I said.

She reached for her bra, but I stopped her. "No, that stays exactly as it is."

Her eyes darkened as she hurried to obey. When she was in position, I reached into the bag and pulled out some fuzzy handcuffs, then locked her hands to the headboard. After the last time I'd used cuffs on her, I'd wanted something that wouldn't leave a mark on her wrists. I trailed my hands down her body, toying with the clamps again before moving my palms down her sides to her hips. I gripped her panties and peeled them down her legs, tossing them aside.

"Open for me," I said.

She bent her legs and spread them wide, giving me a nice view of that pretty pussy of hers. Before I did anything else, there was one more thing I needed. I pulled out a blindfold. Her eyes went wide when she saw it, and I paused.

"Trust me?" I asked. If the thought of being blindfolded freaked her out, then I wouldn't do it.

"I trust you," she said.

I moved closer and slipped it over her eyes, making sure the elastic band didn't get caught in her hair. Waving my hands in front of her face, I made sure she couldn't see anything. It was my hope that by making her rely on her other senses she'd have an even bigger orgasm than usual.

I rummaged in the bag again and pulled out a vibrator that was maybe half the size of my cock, and some warming lube. With a smirk, I reached back inside and grabbed the ribbed anal vibe I'd picked out. Now that I knew how much she liked having my cock in her ass, I could think of other ways to have fun with her. I'd already put batteries in everything, so I'd be prepared when the time came to use it.

Her pussy was wet enough she didn't need lube for the first part. I clicked the vibrator on, putting it on a low setting, then slid it up and down the lips of her pussy. She gasped and her thighs trembled. I touched the tip of the vibrator to the nipple clamps and she cried out, the bedding growing damp as she got even wetter. I traced her slit again, all the way down as far as I could go. She whimpered and lifted her hips, and I smiled, knowing what she wanted, what she needed.

I teased her some more before parting her lips and rubbing the vibe against her clit. Delphine cried out, her back arching as I circled the hard little nub. It only took a few seconds before she was coming, but I refused to back down. I kept tormenting her until she'd come a second time, then I plunged the vibrator into her pussy. I thrust it in and out several times before rubbing her clit with it again.

Her body was straining, and I knew she would come again with little effort. I set the vibrator aside and lubed the anal vibe, then lubed her ass too. I worked my fingers into her until she was nice and slick, then I eased the toy into her tight little ass. When it was fully seated, I turned on the vibration and Delphine went wild, pulling at the cuffs, screaming out her pleasure as her body bucked and twisted.

I gripped her hips and held her still as I plunged into her pussy, shivering as I felt the vibrations from the anal plug along my shaft. I reached for the other toy again and held it against her clit, turning up the vibrations to the highest setting. Delphine detonated, coming loud and hard. I took her hard, fast, and deep, letting the toys work their magic. Her orgasm seemed never-ending as one rolled into another. She twisted in my grasp as if she were trying to get away and get closer all at the same time.

I pounded into her, her cream coating my cock with every stroke, until I came inside her. I didn't slow down, not even after every last drop of cum had been wrung from me. Delphine was nearly sobbing as she came again and I fucked her through it. When I knew she couldn't handle any more, at least not at the moment, I pulled the vibrator away from her clit and shut it off. But the one in her ass felt too fucking good. I ground against her, my dick still rock hard.

"Fuck, Del. I want you again, but I don't think you can handle it."

"Don't stop," she begged. "Please. I want more."

I drove into her again, riding her hard as my hands gripped her hips. With every stroke, I felt the plug in her ass, and it amplified my arousal by ten. I'd never share her with another guy, but I liked feeling her stuffed full of me and the toy. I barely touched her clit with my fingers and she was coming again, taking me with her. When I pulled out, I reached down and eased the anal vibe from her ass, then shut it off and tossed it aside.

I collapsed onto the bed next to her, and slipped the blindfold off so she could see again. She gave me a soft smile, her eyes still glazed.

"That was amazing," she said.

"Let me catch my breath and I'll uncuff you. Then I'll get one of the Prospects at the clubhouse to go pick up something for us to eat. Do you want to try that Mexican place near the hospital? I've heard they have good quesadillas."

"Sounds good. Make sure to order salsa and sour cream with mine. Chicken."

I kissed her, then released her from the cuffs. I stood and stretched before I got my phone out and called the clubhouse. Gabe answered and took the order down and promised to leave it at the front door.

While Delphine rested, I cleaned the toys before placing them on the bedside table. As much as she'd enjoyed that, and as much as I'd enjoyed the vibe in her ass while I fucked her, I knew we'd be using them again today. I pulled on some boxer briefs so I wouldn't have to retrieve our food naked, and lounged in the bed with my wife while we waited.

"I wasn't too rough?" I asked. "I probably should have gone easy on you since you've been in the hospital. Hell, you nearly died."

"Honestly?" she asked.

It made me tense, but I nodded. If it had been too much, I needed to know so I could reel myself back in. When it came to Delphine, I had a tendency to lose control.

"I think I'd like it a little rougher," she said. "Maybe after we have dinner."

Damn. Was she ever going to stop surprising me? I winked at her, then gathered her in my arms. She traced hearts on my chest until the doorbell rang a little while later. I reluctantly left her so I could get our food and make sure she had something to eat. The hospital food had looked disgusting and she'd barely touched it.

I carried everything into the bedroom, stopping on the way to grab two sodas from the fridge. We propped up in bed and enjoyed our dinner, stealing glances at each other, and sharing bites here and there. When we were finished, I carried our trash to the kitchen, then returned to the bedroom. I pulled off my underwear and crawled back into the bed with my sweet, tempting wife.

I kissed her lips, then trailed kisses between her breasts, which still had the nipple clamps in place, across her belly, then parted her thighs. Our mingled release had coated her pussy and thighs, and all I could think about was marking her again. I drew away from her, then flipped her onto her stomach. She let out a startled squeak, then got onto her hands and knees.

"Do you want me to handcuff you again?" I asked. I leaned over her, pressing my chest to her back and nipping her ear with my teeth. "Do you want to be helpless, Delphine? Completely at my mercy?"

"Yes, please, Mason."

I chuckled and retrieved the cuffs. I locked her to the bottom part of the headboard and pressed her chest closer to the bed.

"I want those nipple clamps to brush the bed with every stroke of my cock. They'll tug and feel so damn good, baby."

I kissed my way down her spine, then gave her ass a playful smack. I took the anal vibe off the bedside table along with the warming lube. Once I had the toy inside her and turned on, I smoothed my hands over her hips and admired how fucking sexy she looked. Legs spread with her pussy slightly parted. Toy in her ass.

She moaned and rocked her hips, then I heard her gasp and knew those pretty nipples of hers had dragged across the bedding. I cracked my hand against her ass, leaving a handprint on her cheek. Delphine cried out, but her pussy got wetter. I spanked her again, then drove my cock into her . I toyed with her clit as I thrust into her again and again. She was close, but I couldn't seem to tip her over the edge. While I pounded her sweet pussy, I smacked her ass again and it sent her flying. I fucked her hard and fast and alternated between spanking her and playing with her clit. Delphine came three more times before I filled her up with my cum.

I stayed buried inside her, the toy buzzing against my shaft. My cock twitched and flexed, but I was still hard. Reaching for the other vibrator, I switched it on and pressed it to her clit. I didn't move, just let the toys do their job, and soon she was screaming through another orgasm, this one even stronger than the others. Every muscle in my body tightened and I ground my teeth to keep from coming.

"Give me another one, baby," I said, teasing her clit with the toy.

It didn't take her long to come again, and the way her pussy gripped my cock made me fill her up with more cum. I thrust a few times before I pulled out of her, watching my cum slide down her thighs. I switched off the vibrator and set it aside, but I wasn't quite done with her. The anal vibe was still on. I eased it out a little ways, then pushed it back in. Delphine gasped and her body tensed. I did it again twice more before she was rocking back against me.

"What do you want, Delphine?" I asked.

"Your cock in my ass."

I eased the toy out of her, shut it off, then set it aside. She was still slick from the warming lube I'd used with the toy, and she was a lot looser now. I pushed into her ass, gripping her hips tight. I didn't stop until she'd taken all of me. "Ready, baby? It's going to be a fast, hard ride."

"Fuck me, Mason. I want it rough."

Holy hell. My wife was going to kill me. I held her tight as I drove into her, every thrust harder than the first. I sank into her balls-deep every time. I claimed her, branded her as mine. There was nothing gentle as I pounded my cock into her ass. She cried out and twisted in my grasp as I pulled off the nipple clamps. I growled and my grip tightened even more. I knew she'd have marks on her in the morning, but she didn't seem to care. Had even begged for it. When I came, I roared out my release, driving every bit of my cum into her tight little hole. My cock twitched as I caught my breath, then I pulled out of her. I smoothed my hand down her back, then spanked her ass hard.

"My naughty wife. You liked that, didn't you?"

"You know I did. I love it when you get all rough and demanding with me."

I fisted her hair and pulled her head back, my body covering hers. "You get off on being used like a fuck toy, don't you?"

She smiled at me. "Only when it's you doing the using."

"I think I unleashed a monster. A cock-hungry monster."

Delphine giggled and I kissed the side of her neck. I unlocked the cuffs and set her free before I cleaned up the toys again, as well as myself. She joined me in the bathroom and I started the shower. We would no doubt end up in bed again, or fucking somewhere else in the house, but we might as well have a fresh start. Even if I did like seeing my cum on her.

"Come on, baby. We'll get cleaned up and find some other way to enjoy ourselves for a little while. If I fuck you all day and all night, you won't be able to sit tomorrow. Especially since I definitely will be fucking that ass again."

She bit her lip and smiled at me. I didn't know what I'd ever done to have earned the sex-crazed temptress I'd married, a woman who seemed to like her pleasure with a spike of pain, but I was going to thank every star in the heavens for bringing her back to me. And I was going to do whatever it took to keep her happy and in my arms. If that meant letting Officer Fuckface catch Tia Lee, then so be it. But I was only going to wait for so long. He either caught her ass soon, or I'd make sure she stayed gone for good. I knew Wire was working on tracking her, and once he found her, I'd have a decision to make. Either find a way to get the info to the police and let them handle it, or take justice into my hands and do things the Dixie Reapers' way.

Whatever happened, as long as Tia Lee was gone and couldn't harm my wife and kid, then I was fine with it. If the police arrested her, she'd eventually get out. Might take a while, but she'd walk free. Or I could have someone take care of her on the inside. Wouldn't be the first time we'd arranged something like that. We never killed innocents, but Tia Lee was far from innocent. One way or another, that woman was going to have an accident. Might not be quite as violent if she let the cops catch her first. If I had her in my grasp, I couldn't guarantee I wouldn't make her suffer for a while before I ended it. Ended her.

For now, I was going to enjoy my wedding day with my new wife. I'd take her as often as I could in every room of the house, then make her a nice dinner. And we'd collapse into bed later, exhausted, and ready for some sleep. Unless it looked like it was too much for her to handle. She said she was fine, but I couldn't help being worried. She'd damn near died and acted like it was no big deal. I figured she had to be worried, maybe even falling apart a bit on the inside, but I wasn't going to push her to talk if she didn't want to. Maybe she'd come to grips with her stepmom wanting her dead a while ago. If she needed to fall apart, if she needed to vent or cry, then I would be here for her. Until then, I'd act like everything was fine, because that seemed to be what she needed right now.

"Love you, Del," I said as the shower soaked us both.

"Love you too. Husband." She smiled, and I couldn't help but kiss her. God, but I was crazy about this woman. Loved her more than anything on earth. And I was the luckiest of bastards because she loved me too.

Chapter Nine

Delphine

The days passed slowly, and before I knew it, another week had gone by. Mason was doing his best to keep me occupied, and trying to keep my mind of Tia as much as possible. He didn't just distract me with sex, though, even though there had been plenty of that too. My ass and hips bore marks from Mason's hands, and I loved it. Some women might get freaked out over bruises or not being able to sit down comfortably, but those things just made me remember the wild nights and days we had together.

My stepmom was still missing, even though she had three clubs and the police looking for her. It was almost like she'd just disappeared into thin air. The strange part was that her kids didn't know where she was either, and her car was in the garage at the house. The police had said the kids would have to go into foster care, the two who weren't eighteen yet. I hadn't wanted that, so Torch had offered to get the club lawyer to look into things. I was technically old enough to be their guardian, at least until another relative was found. It wasn't their fault that their mother was the spawn of Satan.

Wire had given Mason a report. My stepmom wasn't using her credit cards, and hadn't stopped at an ATM to get cash. I had no idea how she was surviving, or where she was, but I knew she'd strike again when she had the opportunity. Assuming she was still alive. Part of me wondered if something had happened to her. With the unsavory types she dealt with, it was possible she'd landed on someone's list. If she was alive, though, she wanted me dead so she could have it all. She wasn't the type to cower or change course just because the police were looking for her. Tia was probably delusional enough to think she'd get away with it all.

Even with my life in utter chaos, I'd still been watching the calendar on my phone. My monthly alarm had gone off two days ago to let me know it was shark week, except I hadn't started my period yet. I was pretty sure the hospital had been correct and I was pregnant. Two days wasn't much, but I hadn't been late before. If anything, I was usually a few days early. Mason wanted me to see a doctor and have another blood test done, but at the same time, he didn't want me to leave the compound while Tia was still out there. I couldn't blame him. He was in protective mode, and I loved it. Some people might feel suffocated, but I knew he was worried about losing me. He nearly had when Tia poisoned me.

I was cutting bell peppers for whatever concoction he'd decided to make for lunch when the doorbell rang. I heard Mason's booted steps head in that direction, so I kept cutting up vegetables and let him handle it. People came and went frequently, though he seldom let any of them into the house. Of course, that might have more to do with me practically living in my pajamas since our wedding. I didn't see a point in getting dressed up if we weren't leaving the house. Even now, I was in shorts that showed the bottom of my ass cheeks and a tank that didn't cover much of the rest of me. It was comfortable, and it wasn't like Mason hadn't seen, or licked, every inch of me.

The voices at the front of the house were getting louder, but unless I crept closer I wouldn't be able to make out what they were saying. I set the knife down and snuck across the kitchen and closer to the front door. Mason was blocking it with his body, but I recognized the voice of Officer Daniels. I just didn't know why he was here, or how he'd gotten through the gate. I walked up behind Mason and placed my hands on his lower back, tucking my fingers into his belt. He tensed and glanced at me over his shoulder, and the look he gave me said my ass would be hurting later. And not in a fun way.

"Del, go back to the kitchen," he said, his voice deep and gruff.

"I need to talk to your wife. If you don't let me in, or let her come out, then I'll get a court order. It should be enough that your President let me through the gates," Officer Daniels said.

"Mason, just let me talk to him and see what he wants," I said.

"Del, I said go to the kitchen."

I sighed and pressed my forehead against his broad back. "Mason. Honey. Husband. Love of my life. I'm not three years old. I appreciate that you want to protect me, but do you really think Office Daniels is going to hurt me? He's supposed to uphold the law, not break it."

I heard the officer cough to hide his laughter, but he didn't succeed very well, which just made Mason angrier. I pushed at my husband, but it was like trying to move a two-ton boulder. He wasn't budging unless he wanted to. I smacked him between the shoulder blades and turned to head back to the kitchen. Then I paused, a delightfully evil thought entering my mind.

"Mason," I called out.

"What?" he asked, or more like barked.

"You know, it really upsets me that you won't let me speak to Officer Daniels. What if I'm upset enough that while I'm working on lunch the knife slips and I cut myself?"

He cursed, slammed the door in the officer's face, and stormed toward me. He dipped down, grabbed me around the waist, then hauled me over his shoulder and stomped back to the bedroom. While it hadn't been the outcome I was after, I had to admit the view was rather nice. I grabbed his ass with both hands and gave it a squeeze.

His hand cracked against my ass. "Behave."

"Sir, yes, sir," I snapped, and stifled a giggle.

Mason froze mid-step, then started moving forward again. I had a feeling I'd pay for being a smartass later, but it was fun throwing him off his game, even if just for a moment. Besides, I liked it when he punished me. He always made sure there was pleasure with the pain, and really, a smack on the ass only stung for a bit. And the sexual frustration he sometimes let build up inside me only meant that I exploded even harder when I did get to come.

He dropped me onto the bed and I bounced as my ass hit the mattress. Mason placed his hands on his hips and stared down at me. I could see the indecision in his eyes and wondered what exactly he was debating. Was it possible he was thinking of letting me talk to the police? It only made sense. Maybe they had news about Tia.

Mason reached for his belt and slowly unfastened it, then pulled it free of his pants. He reached for my hands and looped the belt around my wrists several times. I didn't move, barely breathed, waiting to see what he would do next.

"You disobeyed me, Del."

"Yes, I did."

He started to unfasten his pants. "You know that I want to take care of you, that when I tell you to go do something it's for your own good. It's my way of protecting you. What if that officer wanted to come in here and arrest you?"

I licked my lips. "Why would he do that?"

"What if your stepmom framed you somehow in her disappearance?" he asked.

"Mason, I…"

He reached out and grabbed a handful of my hair while his other hand pulled his cock free of his pants. He pulled me closer, dragging my lips toward his cock. My heart raced in my chest and I squeezed my thighs together.

"Open," he demanded.

My lips parted and he thrust inside. He wasn't gentle, and he took what he wanted. Mason fucked my mouth with hard, deep strokes, making tears blur my vision as I fought to breathe and not choke. Before he came, he pulled free, then flipped me over. He jerked my shorts down my thighs and before I could say or do anything, he thrust inside me. My pussy stretched and welcomed him, my nerve endings zinging from the pleasure of being filled by him.

There was banging on the front door again, and Mason hesitated a moment before he began taking me harder.

"Yes, Mason." I moaned. "Please don't stop."

He took me hard and fast, and he came within a dozen strokes. Leaving me aching and needy. I cursed him, knowing this was his way of punishing me. Getting me all wound up and ready for him, then leave me hanging.

He smacked my ass, and when I started to get up, he pushed me back down. "You're going to stay there, just like that, until I get back."

I heard him zip up his pants, and then he walked out. The front door opened and a moment later slammed shut again. He must have turned the lock really damn hard because I heard the click all the way in the back of the house. When Mason returned, I tried to look at him over my shoulder. He flattened his hand in the center of my back, holding me still. I heard his pants being unzipped again, then he slammed inside me. Mason growled as he fucked me hard, stopping every few minutes to keep himself from coming, then he'd start again.

"I love you, Delphine. I'm not going to let some police officer into our home unless I know what the fuck he wants. I'm not taking a chance on your safety."

He drove into me again and again, pushing me close to the edge, then backing off. My nipples were hard and the friction against the bed as he fucked me just made the fire inside me burn brighter. I needed to come in the worst way, and I started to worry that he wouldn't let me. Not for a while anyway.

He still pressed a hand in the center of my back, holding me down, pinning me in place as he took what he wanted, and what I would freely give to him anytime he wanted. Then I felt his hand slide around my hip, and as he thrust deep, he pinched my clit hard. Stars burst across my vision and I screamed as I came so damn hard I was sure I'd squirted. He released my clit but didn't stop, just kept powering into me. Mason growled and I knew he was about to come. He pinched my clit again, harder this time, and I came just as hard as before. He grunted as he filled me up with his cum, then ground himself against me.

When he pulled out, he rolled me over and released my hands, rubbing at the red marks from the leather. Gently, he kissed my wrists, and gave me a tender look. He might have been upset that I'd put myself in what he considered to be harm's way, but I knew he loved me. And truthfully, I got off on his punishments, so I didn't mind them in the least. I'd actually be rather sad if he stopped.

"Did I hurt you?" he asked, his voice soft and calm.

"No. I was a little worried you weren't going to let me come."

He smiled and kissed my lips. "I'll always make sure you get off. Might not be right away, might not even be within the first hour, but I'll eventually let you scream my name."

"Mason, I need to know what Officer Daniels wants. If he has information on Tia, or on my stepsiblings, then I need to hear it. I know you're worried, but you can be right there with me the entire time. Invite some of the other Reapers if you want, but I need to hear what the police have discovered."

He sighed and ran a hand down his face. "Fine. I'll see if he's still around. I slammed the door in the man's face, and I'm sure he didn't like that too much. Then I'll ask Torch to come sit in on whatever that asshole has to say. But you're not wearing that if people are coming into this house."

He helped me stand and I stepped out of my shorts, then pulled my tank over my head. He stared at my breasts, then sighed as if he were a child being denied his favorite toy, and turned to walk away. I smiled as I heard him muttering under his breath, then I quickly cleaned up in the bathroom and pulled on clothes that would be appropriate for company coming over.

I went back to the kitchen and finished chopping the vegetables Mason had said he needed for our lunch. By the time I was finished, Officer Daniels and Torch were coming into the kitchen with Mason right behind them. I wiped my hands off on a towel and sat down, waiting for everyone else to do the same. Mason decided to stand, and kept his hand on my shoulder, probably as a way to show Officer Daniels that I was not only claimed, but I wasn't going anywhere.

"I wanted to let you know that we tracked down some family to take in your stepsiblings. They had an aunt they've never met who lives a few states over. She's arriving tomorrow to get the kids and sign all the proper paperwork," Officer Daniels said.

"So my stepmom still hasn't surfaced?" I asked.

He glanced at Torch, and I watched as the silver-haired man gave a nod. What the hell was going on? I reached up and grabbed Mason's hand where it still rested on my shoulder, trying to prepare myself for whatever was about to be said.

"Parts of your stepmother have been found," Officer Daniels said.

"What do you mean parts of her?" I asked.

"A finger was sent to the station with a note to stop searching for her. Then in a burned-down building outside town, two more fingers were found. The fingerprints matched your stepmother. So if she's alive, she's missing three fingers right now," Officer Daniels said. "What I think is that the people she does business with decided she was expendable and got rid of her."

I wanted to say that I was saddened to hear that she was dead, but I wasn't. I only wished that she'd died before my dad. More than once, I'd wondered if being married to a woman like that had been what killed him. He'd still been young when he died, only in his early sixties. I felt like I'd been cheated out of a future with my dad all because he'd fallen for that lying bitch's stream of bullshit.

"I guess they won't be admitting that they killed her," I said. "Is it possible that we'll never know?"

"Honestly, I think her remains will be found sooner or later," Officer Daniels said. "Until then, it wouldn't hurt to maintain your extra security. I don't think you need to remain locked away inside the compound, though."

"If she's dead, what happens to the house and money she inherited from Delphine's dad?" Mason asked.

"I don't know if Tia Lee had a will or not. As much as I hate to say it, everything will likely be split between her kids," Officer Daniels said. "But you'd need to talk to a lawyer about all that."

"It's fine, Zipper," I said, patting his hand. "I don't need the house when I live here with you, and I've barely touched the money he left me. I do need to figure out what I'm doing with Dad's shop, though. I have no idea how to run a tattoo parlor. I've been paying them and paying the bills, but I have no idea if they're doing good work or if the scheduling is handled properly. I'm totally lost."

He grinned at me. "Good thing you're married to someone who does. Don't worry about your dad's business. We'll keep it open, and one day, maybe one of our kids will want to run it."

"If there are any new developments, we'll be in touch," Officer Daniels said as he stood. He glanced at Torch. "If that hacker of yours runs across anything, it would be nice if you gave us a heads-up so we can close out this case."

Torch smiled and nodded. "We'll be in touch."

Officer Daniels showed himself out, but Torch didn't get up. He looked at me and Mason, then focused on me again.

"I know you feel like a prisoner in your own home, and for that I'm sorry. If you'd like to go out somewhere, I think it would be safest if you had at least three men with you. Once we know for certain that Tia is dead, and that no one else is coming for you, then things can go back to normal," Torch said.

I snorted. "What the hell is normal?"

"Fair enough. If the two of you need anything, the club is at your disposal, and the Hades Abyss and Devil's Boneyard both still have members at the compound. I'll ask them to stay until everything is resolved. Never hurts to have more manpower, even if it means we have to return the favor later on," Torch said.

"Thanks, Pres," Mason said.

"Anytime, Zipper. You take care of our girl, okay? She's carrying precious cargo. It's nice to have so many families inside the Reapers now. Before long we'll have more family picnics and a lot less club pussy. Although, I guess the new guys will always need ways to blow off steam." He stood. "I'll see myself out."

Mason squeezed my shoulder, then went to the sink to wash his hands. "Want to help make lunch?"

"What exactly are we having?" I asked as I stood.

"I'm going to sauté the vegetables in olive oil with a little salt, pepper, and minced garlic. Then I'm going to stir-fry some cubed chicken and add a pinch of Kickin' Chicken seasoning to it, and we'll mix the veggies and cooked chicken and serve it over pasta."

"And where did you learn to make this?" I asked.

He shrugged. "I'm making it up as I go."

I snickered and hoped we didn't end up with food poisoning. It wasn't that he was a bad cook most of the time, but it amused me whenever he decided to experiment in the kitchen. Like the time he decided to make cabbage soup, which consisted of cabbage, water, salt, and a few hunks of ham. I'd made him order pizza that night.

"So, what's the plan today?" I asked.

"Lunch. Movie. Then I think we should cuddle in bed and take a nap because I've been wearing you out. You have shadows under your eyes, you nearly died, and you're pregnant. I'm not being a very good husband," he said.

"Mason, you're the best husband. I love you, and I love being with you. I know if I pushed you away and said I was too tired or too sore that you'd stop."

"A nap wouldn't hurt us. Then, if you'd like to get out of the house, I'll ask some of the guys to go with us and I'll take you out to dinner. They can sit at another table so we'll have our privacy, but you'll be protected."

"We can really leave the compound?" I asked.

"Yeah, baby. I'm sorry I've kept you under lock and key this past week, but I didn't want to take a chance on something happening to you. If Officer Daniels thinks the threat is likely over, then we can venture out, as long as we have several Reapers with us, or some of the guys from Hades Abyss or Devil's Boneyard."

"Can I ask you something?" I asked.

"Sure."

"What's the deal with Jackal?" I asked. "Did Tank give him the black eye he was sporting at our wedding?"

He glanced at me before watching the food on the stove. "Yeah, Tank gave him that black eye, and it was well-deserved."

I waited, but he didn't say anything else. "And?"

"Not my story to tell, Delphine. You haven't even met Josephine. When the time is right, everyone will know what's going on. For now, stay out of it."

I sighed. "Fine. You're no fun."

He winked at me. "You weren't saying that when I was balls-deep inside you. In fact, I think they heard your screams of pleasure and delight all the way up at the clubhouse."

I flicked the end of the kitchen towel at him, but I was smiling. We finished cooking, then ate our lunch at the table. After the dishes were washed and put away, we curled up on the couch and watched a comedy that had me laughing so hard tears ran down my cheeks. I'd only been married a week, but I'd never been happier. Being with Mason was everything I'd ever dreamed it would be, and so much more. And I couldn't wait to see what our future would bring.

Epilogue

Zipper
Two Months Later

Delphine still wasn't showing, but our kid was making himself, or herself, known. My poor wife was puking her guts up morning, noon, and night, which meant we hadn't had as much sexy time as I would have liked. I probably spent more time rubbing her back and running to the store for every possible cookie, herb, or cracker that might possibly get rid of her nausea.

Right now, she was curled into the arm of the couch, moaning softly and looking paler than usual. Her pajama pants were covered in teddy bears, and she'd paired them with a pink tee. She was fucking adorable. And miserable. I was happy to see the cutesy shit, though. After the first few nights, she'd started wearing skimpy things to bed, taunting me with short shorts and barely-there tanks that drove me mad with all the skin they showed. We had company drop in all the damn time, though, and she hated having to go change, so the bears, bunnies, kitties, and other innocent-looking things had made a reappearance.

I eased onto the couch next to her and handed her a cup of chamomile tea with a touch of honey because she said it was too gross without it. I wrapped my arm around her waist and helped her sit up. Steam rose from the mug and she blew across it before taking a sip. She drank half the cup before she handed it back to me and I set it on the coffee table.

Delphine curled against me and I hugged her tight. "What do you need, baby? Do you feel up to eating something?"

She groaned and shook her head. "Don't talk about food."

I let her go and went down to my knees in front of her. Lifting her pajama top, I pressed my lips to her stomach. "Little one, this is your daddy. Could you please stop giving your mom such a hard time? We love you, but she needs to be able to eat."

Delphine ran her fingers through my hair. "Maybe she'll listen to you."

"Or he." I grinned. "I'll love our kid either way. It's just that with a boy, I won't have to increase my gun collection by a few dozen handguns and rifles by the time the teen years get here. And if it's a daughter and she's anything like her mother, then holy hell! We're in for a wild ride."

Delphine giggled. "Maybe she'll find a hunky, tattooed, artistic biker to chase after."

"Over my dead body," I said, growling.

Del sighed. "I think my stomach is settling. Maybe she really did listen to you. Do we have any more of that chicken noodle soup from last night?"

"Yep. I saved a container of it for you, just in case. I'll go warm it up and bring it to you. Just sit here and relax."

"Love you," she murmured.

"Love you more," I said, giving her a wink, then I went to fix her some soup.

The doorbell rang, but I heard Del answer it so I stayed in the kitchen. Tia Lee's body had been found last month, and with it, the threat to Del had gone away. She'd apparently stolen some drugs from very bad people, and had been tortured and killed. They'd tried to weight her body before dumping it into the lake a few towns over, but she'd eventually surfaced. Wire had done some digging, just to make sure no one else was after her, and we'd gotten the all clear. Just in time for her to be stuck in the house with all-day sickness.

Torch and Wire entered the kitchen and set a large envelope on the table.

"What's that?" I asked as I stirred the soup in the pot. No way I was going to microwave my wife's food.

"That would be your kid's inheritance," Torch said.

"Um, what?" Del asked as she took a seat at the table. "What inheritance?"

"Well, the provision your dad put into his will also had a clause in there to protect you," Wire said. "In the event of Tia's death, the house was to be given to you. The money she got from the life insurance gets split between her kids. Guess your dad wanted to make sure they were taken care of."

"Wow," Del said, staring at the envelope. "So, my childhood home is mine?"

"Yes," Torch said. "And while it's not common for a Dixie Reaper to live outside the compound, if the two of you want to move into your childhood home, then you have my blessing."

I stopped stirring the soup and turned to face him. "Live outside the compound?"

Torch nodded. "We'll keep this house empty for you. If something goes down and trouble comes knocking, you'll have to move your family back into the compound. But if the two of you would like to live in Delphine's childhood home, then I don't have a problem with it."

Delphine chewed on her lower lip. "What if… What if I turned it into a rental property? Just until the baby graduates high school? Then we could give the house to him or her."

"If you want to set it up as a rental, I'll take care of it," Wire said. "I can make sure all of the money goes straight into your account."

"Let her think it over," I said. "We don't have to make a decision right now."

Torch leaned down and kissed Del's cheek, then patted her shoulder. Wire smiled at her as he walked past, but Torch lingered a moment.

"You two need anything?" Torch asked.

"A baby that lets me consume food and not throw it back up?" Del asked.

He smiled and patted her shoulder again. "I'll ask Dr. Myron to pay you a visit tomorrow. There's a flu strain making its way around town, so it's probably best if you don't go to his office right now. Don't want you getting sick."

"Thanks, Torch," she said softly, then laid her head down on the table. "I'm tired of being miserable and feeling weak."

Torch looked at me, not with the soft look he'd given my wife, but one of steel and determination. "Come by the clubhouse in the morning. I have a job we need to discuss. Nothing that will take you away from Delphine for longer than a day."

"I'll be there," I said.

"I'll make sure someone comes to sit with Delphine, in case she needs anything while you're gone," he said, then he walked out, and I heard the front door shut a minute later.

"Soup," my wife croaked at me.

I smiled and poured her soup into a bowl, then handed it to her. She slurped at it, and slowly some color came back into her cheeks. I sat next to her and just watched. Being with Delphine left me with mixed emotions. Some days, I worried that I'd fuck everything up and she'd leave me. But most of the time, I was just in awe of her. This beautiful, sweet, adorable woman was mine. Mine to love. Mine to punish. Although, I'd had to back off on the punishments as sickly as she'd been with the pregnancy.

"I love you, you know that, right?" I asked.

She smiled weakly. "I know. I love you too."

"You're my entire world, Del. You and our kid."

She set her spoon down and focused on me. "Mason, I've loved you since I was a teen and you were forbidden fruit. You're my everything, and I'm only sorry it took me so long to come find you."

I clasped her hand and lifted it to kiss her fingers. "We're together now. And I'm not letting you go anytime soon."

"Good." She smiled. "Because I'd just come right back if you pushed me away. Now let me eat while this kid of yours isn't making me puke."

I chuckled and watched her eat. My heart was full, and I was happier than I'd ever been before. The night Delphine walked back into my life was the moment my life changed forever. I'd thought I'd lost her, that she'd never be mine. Now she wore my ring, my property patch, and was carrying my kid. Even though I'd marked her in every way I could, and would ink my name onto her skin after our kid was born, she'd written her name onto my heart with every smile, every touch, every time she screamed my name.

Del might have been mine, but I was most definitely hers. Always.

Harley Wylde

When Harley is writing, her motto is the hotter the better. Off the charts sex, commanding men, and the women who can't deny them. If you want men who talk dirty, are sexy as hell, and take what they want, then you've come to the right place!

An international bestselling author, Harley is the "wilder" side of award-winning scifi/fantasy romance author Jessica Coulter Smith, and writes gay fantasy romance as Dulce Dennison.

Harley Wylde at Changeling: changelingpress.com/harley-wylde-a-196

Jessica Coulter Smith at Changeling: changelingpress.com/jessica-coulter-smith-a-144

Dulce Dennison at Changeling: changelingpress.com/dulce-dennison-a-205

Changeling Press E-Books

More Sci-Fi, Fantasy, Paranormal, and BDSM adventures available in E-Book format for immediate download at ChangelingPress.com -- Werewolves, Vampires, Dragons, Shapeshifters and more -- Erotic Tales from the edge of your imagination.

What are E-Books?

E-Books, or Electronic Books, are books designed to be read in digital format -- on your desktop or laptop computer, notebook, tablet, Smart Phone, or any electronic ebook reader.

Where can I get Changeling Press e-Books?

Changeling Press ebooks are available at ChangelingPress.com, Amazon, Barnes and Nobel, Kobo, and iTunes.

ChangelingPress.com

Printed in Great Britain
by Amazon